EYE OF THE
DRACO
DARKFALL

KADIN SETON

Book cover design by atrtinkcovers.com. Formatting services by BookCoverCafé.com

First edition 2013
ISBN: 978-0-9897184-0-0 (pbk) 978-0-9897184-1-7 (e-bk)

For Dad

"I often think that the night is more alive and more richly colored than the day."

~Vincent Van Gogh

A NOTE FROM THE AUTHOR

Thank you so much for choosing to read *Eye of the Draco: Darkfall.* I hope you have as much enjoyment reading the following pages as I had writing them. I grew up in the town of Pittsford and fondly recall roaming the streets with my friends. We had a strong sense of adventure and spent many hours dreaming up imaginative stories. I've tried to capture that spirit in this book. While some of the locations and structures within the story actually exist, I have taken fictional liberties with historical events, distances, and anything underground, including basements, caverns, sewers and other facilities. Any resemblance to actual events, locales or persons, living or dead, is entirely coincidental.

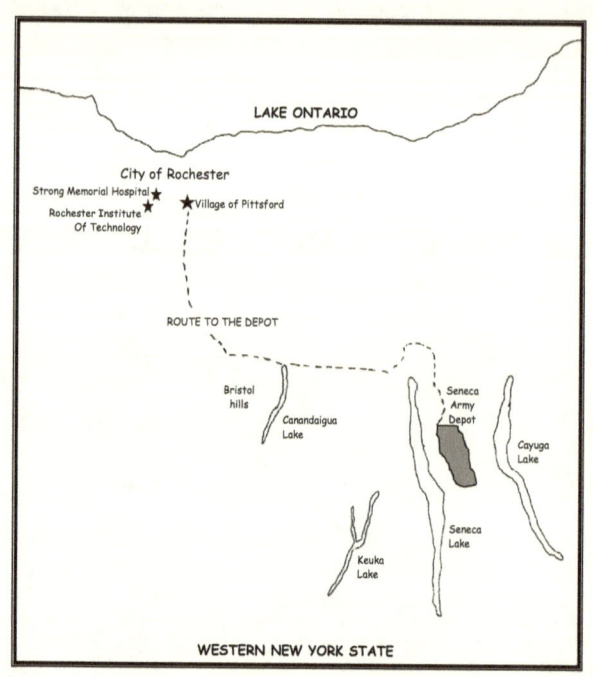

WESTERN NEW YORK STATE

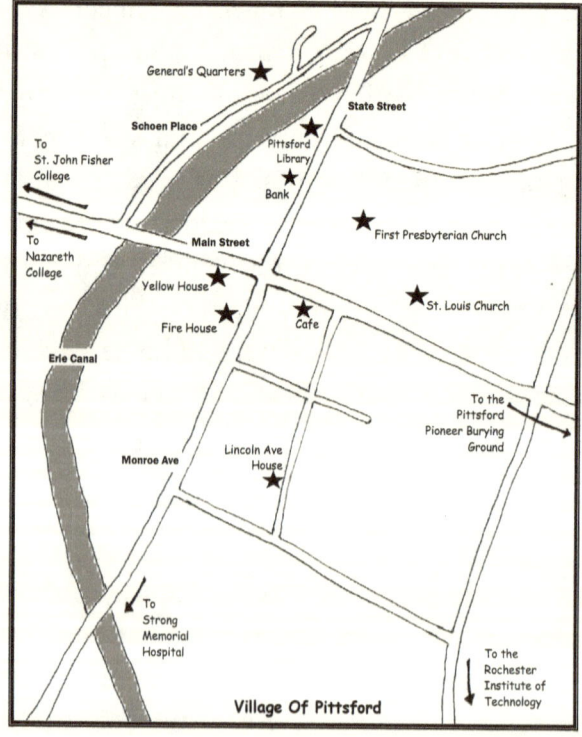

Village Of Pittsford

PROLOGUE

The end came on a Sunday afternoon in early January. Thinking back, the most vivid memory I have from those first few days is the persistent smell of death.

Most of our friends and family were gone and there was nothing the remaining few could do about it. It's hard to understand that you have lost just about everyone you know and love within such a short space of time. Afterwards you're not the same; you're more like a fraction of yourself, with a tangle of terrible emotions to deal with.

Through the use of incomprehensible weaponry and power from their ships, our executioners were able to wipe out the masses over a few short hours. The extermination was completed so effectively that most people didn't know what was going on until it was too late.

Then the soldiers arrived. They went to work on foot, eliminating the survivors with a stick-like device that discharged a beam of lethal orange light. Once hit by the beam, the victim's flesh would burn painfully, while a rapid short-circuiting process shut down the electrical current in the major organs. Death took about two seconds.

Smoldering corpses were then thrown onto transport vehicles and hauled off like garbage. Young children, however, were typically captured alive and whisked away. Once they disappeared we never saw them again, and truth be told, we became more terrified of the unknown horrors of imprisonment than we were of death.

Earth's merciless new inhabitants had successfully erased billions of people without causing any harm to the surrounding environment. What remained was our vast infrastructure, which would only require a few minor adjustments before it was ready to support a new global population.

These new inhabitants became known to us on Earth as the Draco. This name was chosen because NASA had first detected unknown objects moving at inconceivable speeds as they were passing the eye of the dragon in the constellation Draco. Hours later, the ships descended in the northern sky and our planet was forever changed.

The few who didn't perish in the early days had managed to hide in obscure places that somehow defied detection. I had been on a nature walk in the park with a group from my church. Ivy Monahan, our group leader, reacted quickly and took us into a storm sewer, where we hid for three days. Not far from us, other kids had been playing pond hockey and a few of them managed to disappear deep into the woods. My best friend, Nathan McCaffrey, had been at the village library and had hidden in a metal dumpster. Beating the survival odds had boiled down to quick reactions and a lot of plain old dumb luck.

During the first week, while the smell of death still hung in the air, survivors found each other in the darkness, and natural leaders began to emerge. When our group grew too large to remain safe, the leaders divided us into five separate sectors. We kept our new groups small and agile, and did our best to remain hidden from the enemy. Food and medical resources were in short supply, and given that the temperatures were well below freezing in western New York, we struggled to make it from day to day. It didn't take long to learn that if you didn't stay alert, fast and healthy, you'd be dead faster than you could blink.

I was assigned to Sector Three, located within the village of Pittsford. The leader of our sector was a former marine named Colonel Twist. The moment the Draco arrived, the colonel had ducked into his homemade bomb shelter, which he had long ago stocked with weapons, supplies, and ammunition. He claimed to have been expecting something like this for years, and he was well-prepared and ready for combat. It didn't seem to matter to him that our weapons were ineffective against the enemy.

My friend Nathan claimed that the colonel was a nutcase, yet despite his mental state, his vast military knowledge helped us gain a new understanding of our situation. He shared countless military stories and often quoted from a small book called *The Art of War*.

A month after the invasion we had lost five of our sector

members. As the numbers decreased, Colonel Twist found himself leading a team comprised solely of young people, ages six to nineteen. Regardless of our years, he set up a strict military hierarchy, teaching us how to use a wide range of weapons, and assigning formal job responsibilities to each and every member. In this way the colonel kept control of the situation; he often told us that structure and discipline would be the difference between life and death. We listened and learned fast.

Our leader may have been a walking encyclopedia when it came to military operations, but he had his weaknesses. He drank too much whiskey, talked too much, and almost never slept. Due to his lifestyle, no one was surprised when the colonel caught a bad cold during the damp month of April. We tried to take care of him, but he continued to drink heavily and forego sleep, causing the infection to settle deep within his chest. A few short days later his lungs could no longer clear out the build-up of fluids.

Several members of Sector Three stood guard near the road while we dug a shallow grave in the Pittsford Pioneer Burying Ground. We paid our respects and placed Colonel Twist among soldiers of past wars.

At the gravesite we stood by our new leader, General Henry Reynolds, as he said a prayer. Now that the colonel was gone, Henry was the eldest in our group. At nineteen, he had inherited the unwanted responsibility of safeguarding thirty-five fragile young lives.

The other four sectors had a handful of adults between them, but it was all each group could do to take care of their own. Thanks to the colonel, we were prepared to fend for ourselves, but when we heard rumors that the other sectors expected us to be wiped out within the week we made a pact to follow the colonel's lessons strictly and to work as a tight team.

From the outside, Sector Three may have seemed like a bunch of kids who were facing an inevitable death sentence, but sometimes, when you look closely enough, things aren't always what they seem.

CHAPTER 1

I froze when a stray mutt barked on the far side of the road. The sound carried through the shattered window and echoed eerily off the high ceiling of the library. The few dogs that remained often gave us early-warning signals; many of us owed our lives to those orphaned neighborhood pets.

Nathan spun around and looked at me, his brow wrinkled as it always was when he was worried. He took a step closer to the window and strained to listen past the sounds of the uneasy dog and the rustle of fallen leaves. I tightened my grip on a box of damaged books we'd been trying to salvage as a vibration crept up through the ground and tickled the soles of my sneakers. A second later, the vibration grew into a loud electronic hum. Things had just gone from bad to horrible.

"Land vehicle. Hurry, Allie!" Nathan gestured for me to follow as he darted behind the library's checkout counter and into a dark hiding spot.

I ran in Nathan's direction, but the library floor was an obstacle course covered with torn books and debris. In the dark, I misjudged the distance to a broken chair on my left and tripped over the jagged wooden leg. A messy cloud of dust puffed out around me as I smacked the floor on all fours. My eyes stung and I blinked hard to wash away the dirt.

Crap. I'd just made a deadly slip-up. The few seconds it took me to fall were exactly what I'd needed to make it safely to Nathan's side.

The electronic hum shut down and bright lights zapped through the broken window. I was out of time, so I threw myself against a wall just a few feet from the lights. Within seconds I heard heavy footsteps crunch bits of glass and rubble. The mutt outside growled long and deep, sending a clear warning to the soldiers.

My instinct was to run, but Nathan had lectured me on this topic a thousand times: *Stay put and don't move.* He had told me this so many times that it was forever burned into my brain. I took a deep breath and concentrated on calming my shaking legs.

Snarling, the stray mutt followed the soldiers. A moment later an agonized yelp was followed by sickening silence. The smell of death drifted into the library, carried by a gentle fall breeze. My stomach felt queasy and I fought the urge to gag. Seconds ago the dog was fighting for its life, much like my teammates and me. Now, for no good reason, it was dead and smoldering.

At fourteen years old I wasn't ready to die. Not tonight, anyway.

As the Draco soldiers moved closer to the window, I counted two sets of footsteps and immediately noticed that the telltale scuffle of the stinkbugs was absent. We knew that leaving the hunting bugs behind made their rounds much easier and faster. This was often the case with the night crew, as they were lazier than their daytime comrades and constantly looking for shortcuts. But regardless of day or night duty, the soldiers were single-minded in their mission: their directive was to track down the remainder of the indigenous population and eliminate them.

Beads of sweat started to form on my forehead despite the chilly night air. Spotlights crisscrossed the interior of the library, revealing broken shelves and highlighting the dust particles hanging in the air. My dark clothing blended in with the smoke-damaged walls, and with the exception of one unruly strand of strawberry-blond hair sticking out from under my baseball cap, I was almost invisible.

I stayed perfectly still and held my breath. The simple act of heavy breathing could be enough to set off their motion detectors and I wasn't taking any more chances.

I said a silent prayer for the soldiers to lose interest and leave, but I wasn't so sure God listened anymore. Since the Draco had arrived ten months before, most of my prayers had been ignored and I couldn't begin to understand why.

Before the invasion I'd had a happy family life and my days were carefree. Back then, I was certain that God saw everything and heard everyone's prayers. I used to take for granted something as simple as waking up each morning, but now my former life and my family were both gone, and the presence that I once believed ruled the universe was nowhere to be found.

The two soldiers spoke to each other in their strange guttural language. The Draco made sounds from deep in their throats, using their curiously placed vocal cords. This gave their tone a strange quality, making them sound almost like croaking reptiles, only with a much deeper voice. Their hair was long and silvery, and beautiful in its own way as it flowed over their shoulders. With their helmets on they almost looked like us, but on closer inspection you immediately knew they came from somewhere else. Their faces lacked noses, which gave them an odd, aristocratic look, and their jet-black eyes, which lacked the white area around the iris, seemed to pierce the very objects they looked at.

I thought they looked like something that had crawled up from hell, but Nathan was always quick to remind me that they hadn't come from below; instead they came from above— *far* above.

One of the soldiers at the window croaked a few words to his comrade. He was a good foot and a half taller than me, but that was short compared to the typical seven-foot Draco. Still, I felt insignificant and small so close to him. I was skinny and had always had a body like a boy. I was definitely no match for the Draco's superior strength. My mother once told me that I was a late bloomer and that one day I would become tall and strong, like all the women in our family.

Right now I felt like a weakling. The soldier was so close that I could easily have touched his long muscular arm. I didn't allow myself to breathe or even blink.

A shrill alarm blasted from the land vehicle, causing my body to jump involuntarily.

Shit! My eyes filled with tears as I thought about how I had just done something stupid that could cause my death. I knew better than to move. Every muscle in my body urged me to bolt and get the hell out of there, but in my mind I heard Nathan's stern words: *Runners always die.* Stay put.

As my brain fought with my muscles, the shrill alarm blasted a second time. I was barely able to contain another involuntary muscle jerk when the Draco soldiers promptly spun around and returned to their vehicle.

After waiting for what felt like an eternity, the vehicle powered away. When the hum had faded into the distance, I let out a ragged breath and fell to my knees. Double alarms were something new to us and we had no idea what they meant, but at that moment I didn't care. The soldiers had left and I was still alive.

I was fully aware that my stupid mistakes would someday get me killed, but the fact that I had put Nathan in danger was unacceptable. He was smart in a way that the rest of us couldn't begin to understand, and he had special gifts that needed to be protected.

Nathan's uncanny way of figuring things out had proved invaluable when our recon team captured a lone, unarmed Draco civilian.

Nathan spent countless hours with the prisoner, learning how to communicate and getting answers to our endless questions. He was able to get the Draco to explain that the soldier's helmets allowed them to track their prey through motion detection and electromagnetic waves. The motion detector picked up on short-range gross motor movement, yet could easily be beaten by not moving.

The electromagnetic tracker was a bigger problem, as it had a range of miles and picked up on all forms of technology—everything from electricity to telephone, radio and TV waves. This form of tracking left us with only one solution: either stop using all forms of modern equipment, or risk being executed on the spot. Once we understood how to deal with Draco tracking technology, the deaths on our side came to an abrupt stop.

But before long, the soldiers had taken a new approach and we were in trouble again. Outsmarting the technology inside the soldiers' helmets was one thing, but within a few months the Draco had bioengineered a living bug-like creature that used its sense of smell to track us down. The soldiers used their new tool in the same way that our police had once used bloodhounds to track down missing fugitives.

Unlike dogs, the bug creatures had a tough gray shell, forty-two legs, stood about sixteen inches tall, and were almost two feet long. They also left behind a trail of green-and-yellow goo, which smelled like a cross between rotting meat and the worst diarrhea. For that reason we began calling the creatures stinkbugs.

"Allie, are you okay?" Nathan asked as he ran over to me.

I nodded and wiped away a tear in frustration. "I'm sorry, Nathan, this was all my fault."

If we had followed orders, we would have been long gone before the soldiers arrived, but I had insisted on staying in the library longer than we should have to pick up some extra children's books for the younger kids. As usual, Nathan had let me have my way.

"It's okay. Come on, let's go before they come back." Nathan's blue eyes were sympathetic as he brushed his shaggy brown hair to the side. He never got angry with me, despite my shortcomings.

We picked up our boxes and moved carefully, sidestepping broken furniture and piles of damaged books. A beam of moonlight streaked through the glass in the rear door, guiding our way out of the library and into the back parking lot. About a dozen cars remained parked, some with flat tires. Along the perimeter of the lot, large trees still held onto orange-and-red leaves, creating a dark passage for our travel. We had become children of the night out of necessity and our eyes had become accustomed to the darkest places.

According to our prisoner, the Draco's sight was acclimated to a binary star system, which had allowed their pupils to evolve to withstand round-the-clock sunlight. This made the soldiers nearly blind at night, and we soon learned that they cut back their operations after sundown, preferring the bright openness of day. We took full advantage of their weakness and lived our lives after darkness had descended upon the village each evening.

As Nathan and I ran silently through the back lots, we carefully stayed within the deep shadows of trees and buildings.

CHAPTER 2

We cautiously crossed the road and darted over to the historic yellow house at 21 North Main Street. Glancing at my self-winding watch, I realized it was ten minutes past midnight. We were late. We circled to the back of the house.

Ivy Monahan met us on the cellar steps with a concerned look in her eyes. "What took you guys so long? I was getting worried," she whispered.

"The soldiers paid us a visit. We had to freeze for a few minutes," Nathan said casually.

Ivy nodded and opened the door for us. A cold breeze blew her straight black hair across her face. Ivy's mom was a Seneca Indian and her dad had been an environmental lawyer. She was a combination of the best of both parents: good-looking and smart.

She pointed toward the basement. "I made a pot of coffee, it's still hot."

"Thanks, I sure could use some," I replied.

We all drank a lot of coffee and I liked mine with two scoops of sugar. A steady stream of caffeine had become like lifeblood to us. It made me jittery sometimes, but it also kept me awake and alert, and that's all I cared about. And thanks to the local coffee shops and almost every household in the village, we had an entire closet full of aromatic grinds and beans.

We carted our boxes downstairs and into the basement living area. Forty years ago the yellow house had served as the village library, but when the number of books outgrew the space it was moved around the corner to State Street. Eventually the old yellow house had been converted into the Pittsford Village Hall, but the bookcases in the basement remained intact. When our prisoner told us that the library was slated for demolition to make room for a food-processing plant, we began collecting books and bringing them back to the old house. Somehow it seemed fitting that we were repopulating the shelves again.

For the last ten months, the basement of 21 North Main Street had also been my home. Living in the cellar had its challenges, yet it was the safest area in the house. We had found that the soldiers were predictable in their routines, consistently inspecting a building by entering on the main floor, then checking the upper floors, and lastly the basement. This left us with a few precious seconds each time to make our getaway by using well-mapped escape routes.

I lived with Nathan, Ivy, Martin and Squirt; we were a team. In our sector, a maximum of five people were allowed to live in each home, and at least one member was required to be an officer.

Martin Connor was the commanding officer of our team and had the rank of colonel; he had just turned eighteen. He was also street smart and tough, and he didn't take any crap from anyone.

Ivy, our captain, was seventeen and was expected to advance to major at the next promotion. She had natural leadership skills and would most likely be transferred to another home when an officer was needed.

Nathan was a gunnery sergeant, and when he turned sixteen, which was the minimum age for officer status, everyone expected him to jump several ranks and immediately be promoted to a senior officer.

Nathan and I had grown up together and I was thankful to still have him in my life. At fifteen, Nathan may have been brilliant, but he had endured a difficult childhood. After the death of his mother when he was five, his father became an abusive alcoholic. My mom always left our back door unlocked and told Nathan to come over any time, so in the middle of the night it wasn't unusual to find him sleeping on our couch.

Despite the ongoing bloody noses and bruises, Nathan had an incredible hunger for knowledge and had attended private schools on full scholarships. When he had entered college at the age of thirteen, his professors called him a prodigy. Nowadays, our sector general relied heavily on Nathan for intelligence, strategic planning, and communication.

Squirt was the final and youngest member of our household. He hadn't spoken a word since he joined us. The general had informed us that a group of officers had found him hiding in a metal garbage can, starving and severely dehydrated. We were able to nurse him back to physical health, but mental health was another story. No one knew for sure how long Squirt had been hiding or what he saw, but it was an easy guess that he witnessed the slaughter of his family. We never learned his name, but Martin had nicknamed him Private Squirt and it stuck.

My name is Allison Spencer but my friends just called me Allie. I was a mere corporal. Other than being good at gun maintenance, I lacked any real talents.

Martin met us downstairs with his arms folded, wearing his usual scowl. The basement was lit with candles, and a roaring fire in the woodstove took the night chill out of the air.

"What took you guys so long?" he asked, cocking an eyebrow.

"It was my fault," I answered, trying not to sound as irresponsible as I felt. "I wanted to pick up some extra books for the kids. Then the night patrol came by."

"Goddamn it, Allie. You had orders to come straight back. That was a rookie mistake, you should know better." Martin's eyes narrowed as he glared at me. "We lost the first and second sectors because of stupid errors like that. You know it only takes one small mistake for a whole sector to go down."

Nathan stepped forward. "There was nothing to worry about. We froze and they left in a hurry when a double alarm went off. No big deal."

Martin considered the situation for a moment. "After you unpack, we need to report this to the general."

I began unpacking right away and glanced over at Nathan nervously. I didn't want the general to know I'd caused a delay.

Small mistakes were as deadly as big ones and I wasn't in the mood for a reprimand.

Nathan winked and smiled at me. This was his way of reassuring me that everything was okay and not to worry, but I usually worried anyhow.

As we crammed books onto the old warped shelving, a freckled-faced, redheaded little boy peeked around the corner of the bunkroom doorway and spied on us.

"Hey, Squirt," I said, "I found some Dr. Seuss books for you."

I picked up the short stack of books we had just risked our lives for and set them on the wooden table where we ate our meals. Squirt gripped his worn teddy bear, otherwise known as Big Bear, and cautiously made his way over to the colorful books, eyeing them carefully. He picked up the stack and darted back into the bunkroom.

We took extra special care of Squirt, yet we all worried about him. When something went mentally wrong with a person, they got labeled as "snapped." Sometimes we could fix physical injuries, but we hadn't had much luck helping the snapped minds. Since the invasion, several of our sector members had committed suicide, a few had curled up and refused to eat, and some had overdosed on drugs or alcohol. When someone chooses to leave this life, it's not too hard to find the means.

Nathan once told me that anyone who wanted to survive would have to stay as tough as nails and have a strong will to live. If there was one thing I was sure about, I knew I wanted to live.

CHAPTER 3

We had been scampering around the village since we were little kids and knew it like the back of our hands. Prior to the invasion, this had been a happy thriving community, just southeast of the city of Rochester, NY. Many of the buildings were old, but they had been beautifully preserved, and the streets were lined with sidewalks and mature trees.

My mother had been a history professor at the University of Rochester. She told me that the village of Pittsford was first settled in 1789 and had sprung up because of its location along the Erie Canal, back when horses towed boats loaded with trade cargo from city to city.

Now, post invasion, the neglected canal served as our primary water source, and collecting and sterilizing the murky brown liquid had become a daily—and dangerous—chore.

At 0100 hours, Martin led us to the general's headquarters. The moon was high and bright in the night sky, so we stayed tightly in the shadows. Martin took us down Main Street, across the canal bridge, and onto Schoen Place.

Nathan, Squirt and I followed directly behind him. Squirt gripped my hand, with Big Bear securely wedged under his arm. Going anywhere without the threadbare animal wasn't an option.

Ivy trailed several yards back, using her keen senses to guard the rear of our group. She had a sixth sense and could pinpoint an approaching soldier long before any of us had a clue he was there.

Squirt squeezed my hand and pulled himself close to my side. He looked tired and worried. Staying up all night and sleeping during the day wasn't the best lifestyle for a little kid who was afraid of the dark and plagued by bad dreams. Lately Squirt's sleep patterns had improved, but the demons that haunted him sometimes returned, leaving him red-eyed and exhausted.

As we walked along the edge of the street, I recalled the day Colonel Twist had passed away. Before he died he made a last request to have Henry Reynolds advanced to the level of general to take his place.

Henry was uneasy with his promotion, yet he dived into his new role and set up his headquarters in the basement of an old canal-side warehouse. From that day on, we stopped calling Henry by his first name and always referred to him as "the general."

The general's assigned resident staff consisted of two senior officers and two guards, all trained in the use of guns, knives and explosives. We knew all too well that our weapons were ineffective against the Draco military, yet they had proven effective when our recon team had captured the Draco civilian, so the general continued with the colonel's teachings and kept Sector Three heavily armed.

As we approached the warehouse, Martin motioned for us to stop. "Wait here," he said.

Martin continued down the narrow path along the side of the building. Stopping at a blackened ground-level window, he bent down, knocked twice and paused, then knocked three times and paused, then knocked five times. After a few moments, the window opened and a panting yellow dog stuck his head out.

Martin waved us over. "Max, get out of the way," he said, giving the dog a gentle push.

We helped Squirt through the opening and into the arms of Jackson, the general's most senior officer and right-hand man. I went through next, then Nathan, then Ivy, and lastly Martin. We stepped onto the cracked concrete floor.

The general's guards, Jon and Josh, were standing on either side of the window. The twin brothers were each armed with a Colt .45 semi-automatic pistol, and their belts were fully loaded with knives, spare ammunition clips, and grenades. This was standard protocol for entrance into the general's quarters. The brothers made an imposing picture.

"Hey, Allie," Josh said. "Thanks for repairing my rifle yesterday. Works great."

"No problem, that's my job," I responded with a smile.

As the sector's official armorer, I knew my way around weapons. I could disassemble, clean, repair, and reassemble a gun faster than anyone. This job also allowed me to spend a lot of time hanging around headquarters picking up pieces of information that a corporal normally wouldn't hear. I was good at my job—and good at eavesdropping.

Max, the general's Labrador retriever, was wagging his tail and making Squirt laugh by jumping up and licking his face. A camping lantern lit the room and the smell of an endless pot of coffee filled the air.

I noticed strangers, two boys and two girls, sitting together on the green couch along the far wall. They looked over at us, their faces exhausted and dirty. The two boys looked to be in their late teens and the two girls seemed somewhat younger. Alex, one of the general's senior officers, brought them over some boxed cookies, but the strangers showed little interest. I saw the numb look of heartbreak in their eyes. I'd seen that look dozens of times before.

"Come on," Jackson said, urging us to move quickly down the hall and into the general's office.

Max trotted behind us with his tail waving in the air.

General Henry Reynolds sat behind a wooden desk covered with stacks of handwritten papers and maps. Off to the side was the large round table with five chairs used for important, officer-level meetings only.

As we entered, the general looked up, surprised to see us. "What's up, Martin?"

"Nathan and Allie ran into the night patrol at the library. They heard a double alarm," Martin replied matter-of-factly.

The general leaned back and looked at Nathan. "Tell me exactly what happened, and give me the events in the exact order they occurred."

"There's not much to tell," Nathan said. "We were gathering books when I heard the soldiers approaching. Allie and I froze. It sounded like there were two of them, and fortunately there were no stinkbugs. Then the double alarm sounded and they left in a hurry. Allie was the closest."

The general looked over at me. "Did you notice anything else, Allie? Any changes in procedure or equipment?"

I shook my head. "Nothing out of the ordinary."

I hoped that was the end of the questioning, because I really didn't want him to find out it was me who had caused the dangerous delay.

The general rubbed his eyes. Dark circles were permanently etched beneath his brown eyes. "I'm thankful you're both safe," he said, "but I'm worried because that's the third double alarm we've heard in two days. Things are heating up too fast."

"We need to find out what's triggering the alarms," Nathan pointed out.

The general stared at a wrinkled piece of paper on his desk and closed his eyes as if he was in pain. "I think I know," he replied in a low voice.

Abruptly, the general stood up. "I'm sending out another reconnaissance mission. Martin, Nathan and Jackson, suit up. You're out of here in ten minutes."

My stomach churned as Martin and Nathan nodded obediently and followed Jackson to another room to suit up for the mission.

I hated the recon missions. They were high risk, and we had lost two officers since they started. But I also understood that they provided important information and insight into

Draco activity. I reminded myself that Martin and the team had achieved a huge victory by capturing our Draco prisoner on one of these missions.

CHAPTER 4

I thought back to the night Martin brought back our Draco prisoner, who had been in far more danger than our recon team was tonight. I had just finished cleaning and oiling the last of three revolvers when I heard banging and thrashing coming from the main room.

I ran out of the armory to see what had caused the commotion and was shocked to find Martin holding onto a Draco soldier; only he didn't exactly look like a soldier. The silver-haired giant wasn't wearing the usual body armor or helmet, but instead wore a dark blue, one-piece suit. He didn't seem as muscular as a Draco soldier either. His hands were zip-tied behind his back and he had a bloody gash on the side of his pale face.

Martin shoved him down onto the floor, hard. The Draco made an *oof* sound as the air rushed out of his lungs. Josh and Jon stood near Martin with their pistols ready to fire. Nathan and the general watched quietly from the sidelines as Martin gave his captive a good swift kick in the side and another in the mouth. The Draco groaned and spat out some thick blood.

The general frowned. "That's enough, Martin. Throw him in the back room and cuff him to the bed. And don't forget to lock the door."

"Yes, sir."

Martin grabbed the enemy by the arm and dragged him down the hall and into a small room with no windows. I watched as Martin ignored the wooden chair and rusty wrought-iron bed and threw the prisoner onto the floor. The door slammed shut and after a moment we heard a number of grunts, crashes and *oofs*. Several minutes later, Martin emerged from the small room with scraped knuckles, sweat on his forehead, and a satisfied smile on his face.

The Draco had created an ideal military post about two miles north of our village in the old St. John Fisher College. From there they could keep an eye on multiple surrounding towns.

Our prisoner confirmed that the soldiers had positioned themselves similarly in every city and town on the planet. The posts were protected by some sort of force field, but these fields protected the buildings only. As long as our recon teams didn't touch the actual college structure the guys were safe to move around the grounds.

Over time, our teams had become expert at snooping around the local military base without getting caught. Still, I made myself sick with worry every time a recon operation went out.

Squirt grabbed my arm with both hands and squeezed. His

uneasy expression seemed to magnify the butterflies already flapping about in my stomach.

"It's okay, Squirt. The recon missions are the best way for us to stay one step ahead of the bad guys." I smiled and gently ruffled his red hair, trying to appear calm.

The general stood up and handed Ivy the wrinkled piece of paper that had been on his desk. "This came about two hours ago," he said, his voice barely above a whisper.

I could see that it was a handwritten letter. As Ivy straightened the paper and read the words, her eyes widened and the color drained from her face. My butterflies were starting to feel more like a nest of angry hornets.

A moment later, Martin, Nathan and Jackson returned to the office wearing their black recon outfits and loaded toolbelts. As a finishing touch they had smeared black muck on their faces to help them blend with the night. I reminded myself that they were three of our best, and if anyone could pull of a successful mission, they could.

"Now that we're all here," the general said, "Ivy, would you please read the letter out loud."

"Yes, sir." She swallowed hard and began to read. "'The Draco discovered Sector Four on Thursday October twenty-fourth, at twelve hundred hours. They brought in multiple teams from other outposts to search the buildings simultaneously. Most of the younger children have been taken. Those over sixteen were fried and their bodies left in the streets as an example. I am sending this letter with as many survivors as I can find. I have chosen to remain behind in hopes of locating others. Tom.'"

We were silent for several seconds. Tom was the leader of the Bushnell's Basin sector, and sadly, we all knew it was doubtful he would survive. Losing the neighboring sector was bad enough, but we knew it was going to get worse. Considering how close Bushnell's Basin was to us geographically, it probably wouldn't be long before the Draco used the same search method in our sector.

"How many survivors?" Ivy asked the general, her voice barely a whisper.

"Only four." He took a long, uneven breath. "You saw them when you arrived. I've already sent a warning alert to Sector Five in Brighton."

Worry lines were permanently etched across the general's forehead, and gray hair peppered the temples of his dark brown head, making him look older than his nineteen years. In the old life, the general had been a star hockey player with a 4.0 grade average at a good college. In this life, he had been handed a no-win situation by being put charge of Sector Three.

The general looked over his recon team. "I need you guys back here before six hundred hours to attend a meeting. Can you do that?"

Jackson, the senior member, nodded. "Yes, sir."

"Good. Gather what intelligence you can and return immediately. Don't stay near the Draco outpost for more than three hours, and do not—I repeat, do *not*—do anything heroic. You know the rules."

The general looked toward Ivy. "Take Allie and notify all sector personnel of the oh-six-hundred meeting. We'll use the usual location. And Allie, take your weapon."

I opened my coat and showed the general my pistol already strapped to my belt. "What about Squirt?" I asked.

"Leave him here with me." The general walked over to Squirt and gave him a pat on the back. "He can help me prepare for the meeting and play with Max. Now go quickly, stay alert, and return immediately after you've completed your assignments."

Ivy and I crawled out the window and headed down the path alongside the warehouse, where we watched the recon team depart. They rode off on old-fashioned bicycles, which were quiet, fast, and couldn't be picked up by the electromagnetic detectors. They would be able to arrive on the outskirts of the post within ten minutes and could spend their time finding the right spot to spy from.

After the guys left, we walked toward the main road.

Ivy stopped suddenly and held up her hand. This was her signal for 'Be quiet and don't move'.

I froze as she looked around carefully and put her hand back down.

"I thought I heard something. Must have been the wind," she said calmly, yet I noticed that the expression on her face was anything but calm.

I took a deep breath. "Are you sure?"

Ivy nodded and began walking again.

Since we had only five other houses to notify, not including our house or the general's quarters, our assignment wouldn't take long. The procedure for distributing communication from the general required us to speak with the lead officer of each house and ensure that the message flowed down the chain to all personnel. Most of the residences were located in or near the heart of the village and had been chosen specifically for their easy access to escape routes and availability of a heat source in the basement.

We ran from house to house, delivering the communication methodically. We were fortunate to find everyone at home at the first four houses.

On our way to the final residence, Ivy stopped suddenly and again held up her hand.

I froze, my heart rapidly picking up its pace. "What is it?" I whispered.

"Shhh." Ivy looked around with a worried expression. "Wait, do you hear that?"

A cold chill ran down my back as I strained to listen, but all I heard was a soft breeze rustling leaves in the distance. "No, I don't hear anything."

Ivy put her hand back down. "I think it's stopped."

"What was it?"

"I don't know." Ivy scowled. "It sounded almost like a stinkbug … minus the hissing noise."

I didn't like the possibility of stinkbugs being nearby. "I thought hissing was the only sound they made."

"So did I, but something sounded familiar." Ivy started walking again. "Let's go notify the last house and wrap this up."

Within minutes we arrived at an old masonry Victorian home, which was partially covered in thick brown vines. We sprinted around to the back and rapped out the secret code on a thick glass window.

Serena Anderson, a nine-year-old girl with dark skin, answered our knock. Her eyes were round with fear. "Have you seen Laurie and Zack?" she asked tensely.

Laurie Banks was the lead officer at this location; she was eighteen and had the rank of major. Zack Smith, a member of Laurie's team, was fifteen and had the rank of sergeant. They were both strong and competent, and it was strange that they would have left the younger kids alone.

"No, we haven't," Ivy said. "When did you last see them?"

"About an hour ago. I heard something outside, so Laurie and Zack went to investigate." Serena pointed toward Main Street. "They went that way."

Two more sets of eyes peered out from behind Serena. They belonged to seven-year-old Michael and six-year-old Sam. They looked uneasy, so I gave them a friendly wave and a wink.

"What did you hear exactly?" Ivy asked Serena.

"I don't know what it was, but it sounded like ... like something clicking."

Ivy shot me a concerned glance. "Serena, you stay here with the boys. Allie and I will look for Laurie and Zack. If we're not back in exactly thirty minutes, I want you to take the kids straight to the general's quarters," she instructed in a controlled calm voice. "Do you understand?"

"Yes." Serena nodded as the boys clung to her side. "But please come back soon."

"Don't worry, we'll be back before you know it," I added, sounding far more confident than I felt.

CHAPTER 5

Ivy led the way through the deep weeds of once-manicured lawns. The crisp October air nipped at our cheeks and turned our breath into puffs of white smoke. As we passed the fourth house she stopped abruptly and held up her hand again. I stood rock still and didn't say a word.

A full minute went by as she looked around and listened intently before lowering her hand. She shook her head and we resumed our pace. I tried to calm my nerves and keep a brave face. We rounded the corner onto Main Street, where the businesses were once located.

I heard the strange noise myself and grabbed Ivy's arm. "There it is. I hear it. It's coming from behind the old Hicks and McCarthy's Café." It sounded exactly as Serena had described—like clicking.

As we looked toward the café, a piercing scream ripped through the quiet night and made both of us jump. We exchanged worried glances, knowing the sound had most likely come from one of our friends.

"Come on," Ivy whispered, grabbing my hand and pulling me along. "At least we know it's not the soldiers at work."

She was right. When the Draco killed there were no screams, just the quiet smell of death.

In a crouched position we slowly made our way toward the back parking lot. The clicking noise grew louder and more terrifying with every step we took. As we neared the back of the building, we spotted what appeared to be blood smeared low down along the white siding. This was strange, because the Draco killed in a very efficient manner—they didn't smear blood on buildings.

Ivy motioned for me to wait as she cautiously looked around the back of the café and into the parking lot. She jerked back and took a ragged breath. "Holy shit! Take a look."

She stepped back around me so I could get a clear view. My hands were shaking as I focused on the scene not ten yards away. A huge stinkbug had Laurie pinned against a six-foot-high wooden fence. Laurie was trying to fight the bug with a long stick while pushing Zack up and over the fence at the same time. Her jeans were ripped and her lower leg was bleeding heavily from a deep gash. I watched helplessly as the angry bug clicked its feet wildly against the pavement, grabbed her stick with its mouth and snapped it in two.

We had never seen a stinkbug act like that. Normally they didn't attack. They just sniffed around until they picked up the scent of a human. Once the bugs had tracked down their prey, they hissed victoriously at their find, but the actual slaughter was always left to their masters. Under the control of the Draco, the bugs were docile, but for some unknown reason this particular creature wanted to rip Laurie to shreds.

Instinctively, I glanced around for signs of the soldiers and saw nothing. "What should we do?" I asked Ivy.

She took a deep breath. "We need to get the bug away from Laurie and Zack. Look for anything you can use as a weapon, but *not* your gun. And stay alert for soldiers. Let's go."

As we ran toward Laurie, she spotted us immediately.

"Help us!" she screamed, just as the bug latched onto her leg again.

I found a good-sized rock and heaved it, and Ivy pulled a knife from her belt and expertly threw it, but it was like trying to fight a giant cockroach with toothpicks and pebbles. The creature was intent on chewing through Laurie's leg and it wasn't going to be easily distracted.

I pulled out my handgun and looked toward Ivy for the okay to shoot. Firing a gun in the open would be a big risk, potentially alerting soldiers to our position, but I didn't know what else to do.

"Wait," Ivy said, and pointed to a large metal garbage can alongside the neighboring building.

I put my gun away and we ran to the container. We each grabbed a handle and dragged it toward the bug.

Ivy looked at me. "Okay, let's do this on three. Ready?"

I nodded.

"One, two, *three.*"

We flipped the can over and slammed it down on top of the bug, yanking it away from Laurie's leg. Trapped inside the can, the creature hissed viciously and threw its body repeatedly against the metal walls. As the trashcan began to take on a life of its own, we pressed all of our body weight on top of it. The bug was more powerful than any of us could have imagined.

Ivy shook her head. "Wow, that thing is pissed off. I just don't get it."

"We can't stand here and hold this can down forever," I pointed out. "We need to secure it with some kind of lid."

Laurie limped over to us, holding her leg.

Zack jumped down from the fence. "I saw a piece of plywood in the back of the lot," he said.

Ivy nodded. "That'll do. Go get it."

Zack returned quickly, carrying the thin piece of old wood. It was nearly square and slightly bigger than what we needed. He slid the board between the pavement and the can, agitating the creature further and causing another bout of angry noises. Working as a team, we turned the can over, keeping the board in place. The bug fell to the bottom of the can, hissing and clicking wildly as its forty-two legs scraped against the metal, unable to find footing.

The four of us stood silently, staring at the container as it pulsated. It was like catching a poisonous snake. Once you had it, you didn't know what to do with it.

Laurie fell to the ground, holding her leg. "That fucking thing took some of my skin."

Ivy quickly took off her jacket and tied it tightly around Laurie's wound to slow the flow of blood. "The bug stays here for now," she said. "We need to take care of Laurie's injury first."

Zack and I wedged the can securely against the fence so the bug couldn't get out and helped Laurie limp back to the house. Once again Ivy led the way, stopping every few minutes to listen to the night sounds. Each time she turned her ear to the wind, she would shake her head and move on.

I admired Ivy, because she was always strong and in control, the complete opposite of me. Months ago Nathan made me memorize a quote by Franklin P. Jones, and at times like this, I tried to remember it: *Bravery is being the only one who knows you're afraid.*

We brought Laurie into the basement and settled her onto a comfortable sofa. Serena and I attempted to clean and bandage her wound, but despite our efforts the blood continued to ooze from the deep gash.

"I'm fine. Stop fussing over me," Laurie said with a scowl.

I looked up at Ivy and shook my head. She nodded and quietly left to retrieve Doc Hiro.

Better known as Akihiro Tokushima, Doc Hiro was the eighteen-year-old son of two successful surgeons. His father was well known for having developed a successful new procedure for treating pancreatic cancer. Like Nathan, Hiro had graduated from high school at a young age, completed his undergraduate degree in three years, and had just entered medical school when the invasion came. Although he never achieved his dream of becoming an actual doctor, for us he was the next best thing. Over the last ten months, Doc Hiro had saved more lives and tended to more injuries than we could count.

Within minutes, Ivy returned with Doc and his big black medical bag.

Doc frowned as he knelt down and examined Laurie's leg. "I don't understand it," he said. "Stinkbugs don't attack people."

"Well, this one did," Laurie said sourly. "And it thought I was lunch."

Doc shook his head as he dug through his black bag. "The wound's deep. I'm afraid it's going to need some stitches."

Laurie cringed and shifted uncomfortably on the sofa. "All right, just do it and get it over with."

Getting stitched up wasn't as bad as it sounded. In fact, Doc Hiro had to stitch me up twice this past summer; once when I slipped and fell by the canal, and once when I broke a glass bottle while we were sterilizing water.

As Doc threaded his needle and prepared to sew, I grabbed Laurie's hand and gripped it tightly. In an effort to keep her mind off the pain, I babbled about how brave she had been and how proud the general would be of her actions. Sweat beaded on her brow as Doc Hiro tugged repetitively on the thread. Ten minutes and twenty-nine stitches later, the task was done and the bleeding had stopped.

Before we left, Ivy informed Laurie and her team of the 0600 meeting.

"We'll be there," Laurie answered without hesitation.

Despite her injury, Laurie wouldn't miss the meeting. We all knew we were required to do whatever the general asked, regardless of physical pain or emotional baggage. Teamwork was everything in our fight against the Draco. Our survival depended on it.

Ivy stood, and I joined her. "We have to get moving," she

said. "Allie and I have to make a report and figure out how to handle our not-so-friendly bug. We'll see you shortly."

"Everything'll be fine here." Doc nodded to reassure us.

We arrived safely at the general's dwelling at 0300 hours and were immediately asked to sit at the round table. I sat quietly while Ivy explained the entire event. The general ran his hand through his hair several times, as he often did when he concentrated. He asked a lot of questions about the bug and inquired about Laurie's status twice. Ivy didn't seem to think anything of it, but I knew the general had special feelings when it came to Laurie.

From the beginning, physical relationships had been discouraged among sector personnel, and pregnancies were absolutely forbidden. Fortunately our sector hadn't had any pregnancies, but any time a group of teenagers got together things were going to happen, regardless of rules. Those who had relationships kept them private to avoid the repercussions. Since the general and Laurie didn't want to set a bad example, they kept their romance behind closed doors. Or so they had thought ...

I had been attending to my job in the armory when I noticed Laurie slip quietly into the general's office. Most everyone else had left the building for training exercises and I was cleaning up after several long hours of work. After I put my tools away, I pulled on my coat and headed toward the main room.

As I passed by the general's office I noticed that his door was slightly ajar. I could hear him and Laurie whispering, so I stopped next to the doorframe and eavesdropped. When I peeked through the slim opening I saw the general touch Laurie's face and give her a soft kiss on the lips. For a long moment they just looked at each other. Then Laurie reached out and pulled him closer and they kissed again for what seemed like a long time.

As the kiss deepened, the general began to rub his hips against Laurie's body. She slipped her hands into his back pockets and pulled him tighter.

"Laurie, I need you," he said hoarsely.

About two years before, I had seen an X-rated movie in my friend's basement. It was so fake and silly that we had laughed through the whole thing. This was entirely different and I was mesmerized. I knew I shouldn't have been watching, but I couldn't help myself. Something about it was so unlike the movie; it was real and raw, and I was completely overwhelmed by the intimacy of what was taking place.

Within seconds the general's pants were down around his ankles and Laurie was sitting on his desk half naked. They kissed passionately as the general slid his hand under her shirt and caressed her breasts. Laurie parted her legs and wrapped them around his waist as the general pushed himself inside her.

"I love you, Henry," she whispered as they began to move together.

He looked into her eyes. "I love you, too."

I had watched way too much and felt guilty. I knew I had no right to watch them and I finally pulled myself away, but what I had witnessed changed my view of sex forever. It wasn't fake and silly, as I had thought. It was something much more private and intimate, and human.

"We need to work out what this means," the general was saying as I brought my attention back to the meeting. "Why would a stinkbug be loose?"

"Maybe it's a trap," I offered.

Ivy raised her eyebrows. "If it's a trap, it might have a homing device."

The general nodded in agreement. "If you're right, we don't want the soldiers to find their little pet trapped in a can. Something like that would lead to a full-blown search. We should keep the bug for observation, though. See if you can find a place where we can contain it safely and the soldiers can't track it down."

"How about the vault inside the bank on State Street?" Ivy offered. "The walls might be thick enough to block any potential tracking devices."

"Yes, that makes sense." The general raked his fingers through his hair again. He looked tired. "But before anyone goes near that bug, I want to run this proposal by Nathan when he returns."

CHAPTER 6

While we waited for the arrival of the recon team, Ivy and I sat at the table in the general's office drinking consecutive cups of coffee. The caffeine overload was sending my anxiety levels into overdrive. I couldn't stop worrying about the guys running into another loose bug that might be roaming around. By 0400 hours I was pacing up and down the hallway, driving everyone crazy.

Ivy rolled her eyes. "Would you please sit down and read a book or something?"

"I can't. I feel better when I'm moving." I made an about-face at the green couch and headed back down the hall.

The four kids from Bushnell's Basin were still in the main room, silently observing me work off nervous energy. They had cleaned up and filled their stomachs, but the hollow expression on their faces told the real story.

As I continued to pace, the general pulled Ivy into his office.

I paced conveniently near his door and overheard him speak to her about becoming the lead officer for the newcomers. Our current residences were near capacity, so I knew a new location would need to be chosen. I always understood that Ivy would move on to another household someday, but I still wished she could stay with us in the yellow house. It had been nice having an older girl to talk to.

At 0430, we finally heard the knock of the familiar entrance code. Without thinking I headed for the window.

The general came out of his office and grabbed my arm. He shook his head. "Allie, you know the protocol," he said gently.

I had forgotten that only the guards or officers could answer a knock at the headquarters. When the general gave Josh and Jon the okay, they immediately readied their weapons and approached on either side of the window. It always amazed me how alike the twins were. Even their mannerisms were similar.

One at a time, Jackson, Nathan and Martin came through the window while the rest of us stood in the background, relieved to see them safe and uninjured. But I knew something wasn't right. Jackson was avoiding eye contact by looking at the floor, and Nathan and Martin had unusually grim expressions.

Without speaking a word, the recon team filed into the general's office and shut the door. According to procedure, Ivy and I had to wait until after the senior-level debriefing before receiving any news. I suspected it wasn't going to be good. Again I found myself pacing up and down the hall trying to pass the time.

Ivy tried to strike up a conversation with the Bushnell's Basin group, but they weren't in the mood for talking. They were beginning to look like scared rabbits, ready to run.

At 0500 hours the door swung open and Martin poked his head out. "Ivy and Allie, you're needed in here, now."

Martin took his seat at the general's round table with the others. On top of the table were a couple of maps, a small gold sack and six small green balls.

The general looked over at Ivy and me. "Nathan, please recap the mission for Ivy and Allie."

Nathan began, shifting from side to side in his seat and looking uncomfortable. "When we arrived it was pretty quiet, so we circled the camp twice before finding activity. At the south end, we spotted two soldiers just outside the stinkbug pens. The bugs were hissing and agitated for no apparent reason. Also, the soldiers weren't wearing body armor, and they were snacking on *octcha* so we assumed they were off duty." Nathan pointed to the small balls on the table.

Normally the Draco military wore incredible defensive armor. We had learned that it was made from some sort of thin liquid metal that moved easily with their bodies and was completely impenetrable. Back in August we discovered a lost glove made of the same material. We tested it endlessly, hoping to find a way to damage it, but every caliber of bullet and explosive we threw at it just bounced off. Our prisoner had told us not to waste our time, that the technology was too far beyond us, but Nathan thought differently and kept trying everything he could think of.

"Is that real *octcha*?" I asked, pointing toward the balls.

We didn't know much about *octcha*, other than it was essential to the Draco and that it came from a plant on their home planet. We also knew that if they didn't consume the important nutrients contained in the *octcha* they would eventually die, in the same way that a severe vitamin-C deficiency could eventually kill one of us.

Nathan looked at me and nodded. "Yes. As the soldiers ate, the hissing noises grew louder and the bugs began to slam themselves against the fencing. One of the soldiers walked over and banged on the cage as a warning, but it only upset the bugs further. It was so strange. I've never seen stinkbugs become so aggressive. When the soldier turned his back, a section of fencing came loose and the swarm of bugs was on him in an instant. They were like a pack of starving carnivores that had finally found food. Within seconds they'd stripped the flesh from his body, leaving nothing but broken bones and a clump of silver hair."

Nathan paused and looked at me to gauge my reaction. I gave him a small nod to let him know I was okay.

He continued. "By the time reinforcements arrived, the second soldier had lost a leg and a section of his torso. I doubt he survived. The additional soldiers had to fight to get the swarm back into the cage." Nathan began to absently play with the *octcha* on the table. Then he looked toward the general.

The general nodded. "Please, go on."

Nathan took a deep breath. "After the bugs had eaten, the hissing stopped and it was easier to hear the soldiers talking. They were clearly worried about not having fed the bugs for almost two weeks. Then I heard a soldier say there wouldn't be any more bug food until the human remains were processed from Bushnell's Basin. Apparently the bugs gorge themselves daily on processed dead bodies, which keeps them docile and trainable. The soldiers seemed surprised at how the bugs transform into completely different creatures when they're starving."

I suddenly felt nauseous. It was hard to absorb the sickening thought that our family and friends had become bug food. I looked at Ivy. It was obvious she didn't know what to say either.

The general cleared his throat. "I know this has been hard to hear, but you can see now that it's critical we learn as much as we can from our little friend in the garbage can. First, we'll store the bug in a safe place where it can't be tracked. Ivy has suggested the bank vault and Nathan agreed that would be the best place. Second, we need to find an alternative food source for it, preferably something nonhuman. Lastly, we need to find a way to kill the creatures. Ivy, Nathan and Allie, these projects are now your assignment."

We all nodded to confirm our new orders.

"Martin and Jackson, you're assigned to monitoring the stinkbug situation at the Draco camp. I want to know exactly how many bugs they have and when they're feeding them."

Martin and Jackson nodded.

"Since we now know that the double alarm means that the Draco have located a group of humans, we'll also need to ramp up our security watches. It's almost oh-six-hundred hours. We can discuss this further at the sector-wide meeting."

Along with the newcomers, we quietly made our way across the village and over to the St. Louis Grammar School, located in the business district. As we assembled in a classroom with multiple exit options, Jon and Josh took up their positions outside the building, where they stood guard and kept us forewarned of any possible threats. Once we had settled into our seats, the general kicked off the meeting.

He began by introducing the newest members of our sector: Karen Clark, Valerie Brown, Chuck Lee, and Ed Oppenheimer, ages twelve to seventeen. The newcomers would take up residence in the blue house on Lincoln Avenue, and Ivy would be the lead officer for the team.

The general then told the story of the stinkbugs and their food source, stressing his concern over the threat of the double alarms.

I heard a few mumblings among the ranks over the gory details, but since the general never withheld bad news, the group took the reports in stride. It almost seemed like we were getting used to this sort of thing.

The general wrapped up the meeting by adding, "I want to be crystal clear about what we're facing. Our main priority is to be on full alert at all times. My greatest fear is that the Draco will start a house-by-house search in our sector. Every dwelling is required to have a guard on lookout during the daylight hours, using rotating shifts. The commanding officers will need to set up the schedules, and I'll review them when I make rounds tomorrow."

After the meeting, we had a spaghetti dinner. Pots and pans

banged together and terse commands drifted from the school kitchen. Laurie and her team always prepared the meals for group occasions. Having come from a big Greek family, Laurie had been cooking her whole life and she was great at it.

"You guys need any help?" I asked, poking my head into the kitchen.

"Thanks, but we're good. Zack went to find more oregano and garlic," Laurie said as she limped down the long kitchen on her injured leg.

Serena was lifting a heavy pot onto a propane burner when Zack returned with a small jar in his hand. "Found some dried garlic," he said, "but we're out of oregano."

Laurie rolled her eyes. "Oh great. Well, I'll just have to improvise."

Once the dinner was served, everyone dug into the homemade meal, with the exception of Squirt. When I set the plateful of spaghetti in front of him, he turned his head, refusing to look at it.

"Come on, Squirt, give it a try," I pleaded, but he just shook his red head and squeezed his eyes shut.

"Here, try this," Laurie said as she set down a new plate in front of him with spaghetti, olive oil and a little grated cheese. "I think the red sauce is grossing him out."

She was right. Squirt began to pick at the spaghetti and then finally ate it.

The food situation was always a little tricky for us. Since the Draco used grocery stores and restaurants as traps, our meals consisted mainly of non-perishable foods that we found in kitchen pantries and office buildings. As time went on, edible food was getting harder to find and we knew the local supplies wouldn't last forever.

After dinner everyone returned home except for Nathan, Ivy and me. We headed back to the hungry stinkbug.

CHAPTER 7

We wasted no time retrieving the garbage can and dragging it to the bank. Nathan pulled open the heavy vault door, and we pushed the container into the center of the room and removed the board. As we peered down at the creature, it silently cowered against the side of the can, almost as if it was trying to get away from us.

"I wonder why it's so quiet," I said.

Ivy tapped the side of the can with her hand. "Hey, stinky, what's the matter? Don't you still hate us?"

The bug turned its ugly head away and ignored her.

"Strange." Nathan bent over to observe it more closely.

Ivy pointed toward the front of the bank, where the dangers of daylight were beginning to creep through the large glass windows. We had no choice but to close up the vault and head for home.

The air was warmer than usual for late October and the sun

was rising rapidly in a cloudless blue sky. It looked like it was going to be a perfect day—if you were a Draco soldier.

When we arrived in the basement, Martin and Squirt were sitting at the table. Squirt was leafing through one of his Dr. Seuss books, and Martin was leaning over a pile of papers, working on the guard-duty schedule. The embers in the woodstove had long since grown cold and the candles had been snuffed out.

"Allie, you've got the first shift, then Nathan, then Ivy. I'll take the first shift tomorrow," Martin said as he got up from the table. "Pull the alarm if you hear or see anything out of the ordinary, and I mean *anything*. Understood?"

I nodded. "Got it, I'm on it."

The alarm Martin referred to was simply a string at the top of the stairs, which, if pulled, set off a bell in the bunkroom. It did the trick for an early-warning system.

On my way up the stairs I grabbed a cup of coffee, adding two big scoops of sugar. I knew I would need the extra boost to stay awake. As I settled in on the top step, with the lukewarm mug nestled between my palms, I tried to mentally prepare for a long and boring shift. At least I hoped it would be boring.

From my vantage point I could see most of the main floor. If I wanted to, I could pull my entire shift just sitting there, but I knew if I stayed in one spot too long I would fall asleep. So, as the sun moved higher in the sky, I began to walk the house, being very careful to remain invisible to the outside world. I never crossed directly in front of a window, and I stayed away from the long sunbeams that stretched into the front rooms.

．　．　．

By 1000 hours, I had patrolled the house seven times and found myself back on the top step. I was struggling to keep my eyelids open when a long drawn-out creak from the staircase made the hairs on my arms prickle.

"It's just me," Nathan whispered as he came up the stairs two at a time. "I couldn't sleep so I thought I'd keep you company."

I took a deep breath and the hairs on my arm relaxed. "Thanks. I was having trouble staying awake until you scared the crap out of me."

Nathan seated himself across from me and squinted as his eyes adjusted to the bright light flooding the main floor. We didn't talk for several minutes. Sometimes we just kept each other company.

I had a nagging question that I wanted to ask. I knew my friend would give me a direct answer, but I wasn't so sure I wanted to hear it. After a few minutes, I finally worked up the nerve.

"How much longer do we have before they find us?"

Nathan looked at me and wrinkled his brow. "Do you really want to talk about this?"

"No, but I need to hear it from you."

"Not much," he answered flatly. "Eventually they'll find us, no matter where we hide."

"There must be *some* place we could go."

Now that the Bushnell's Basin sector had been discovered, I was having a hard time keeping the feeling of panic under control. Our prisoner had bragged that it didn't matter where we went, because inevitably we would be found and eliminated. But I hoped that wasn't true.

"If we want to survive for any length of time," Nathan said, "we'll need to move again and again." He was playing with a spider that was trying to cross the stairs to reach its web. "Once the Draco begin their colonization, our current situation will seem like a cakewalk."

"There's got to be a safe place somewhere in the world."

Nathan wrinkled his brow again. "I don't think so. Not after twenty billion Draco move in." He paused and waited for my reaction to his words. I knew he didn't want to upset me, so I kept a straight face and he continued. "At some point there'll be nowhere left to go. Until then, we'll be constantly on the run, with the never-ending challenges of creating shelter, establishing a food supply, and dealing with medical issues."

I looked at him sadly, not sure what to say.

Nathan sighed. "The only alternative is to find the Draco's weakness and fight back, but our odds would totally suck. I wouldn't recommend it."

"But you've already learned so much, Nathan. Maybe we just need to work harder at finding that weakness."

I had high hopes for some of the theories Nathan had developed, especially around weaponry. His abilities had always given me blind faith. I didn't care about the math, odds or statistics, because trying something—anything—seemed better than being hunted forever.

"Even if we could develop a weapon, the chances of our surviving would still be"—Nathan hesitated and looked away—"infinitesimal."

I hated that word, infinitesimal. Our prisoner had used that word and it was meant to beat us down. But still, infinitesimal wasn't the same as nil. I took it to mean that we still had a fraction of a chance, however small.

The general had given Nathan specific orders to learn as much as he could from the prisoner before the scheduled execution. I knew Nathan would need to spend a great deal of time with the Draco, so, with some pestering, he had agreed to let me tag along as an observer.

Our first visit with the Draco was dull. He had been chained to the wrought-iron bed and had just enough slack to use an adjacent portable toilet. As we took our seats, he sat rigidly on the edge of the mattress and stared at the wall. He seemed bored.

Nathan cleared his throat and began the session by simply talking, but the Draco continued to gaze at the wall and ignore him. Nathan offered food, water, books, pen and paper, and a bunch of other things, yet nothing interested the prisoner. With each attempt, Nathan wrote detailed notes cataloging his efforts.

"Allie, watch for a reaction. If you see even the slightest twitch, let me know," Nathan whispered in my ear.

I watched the prisoner intently for the rest of the session, but all I saw was a blank, expressionless face.

On our second visit, Nathan had tried to communicate by using what he called "the universal language of math," but again he received no response.

After two hours of failed communication, Nathan sighed and shook his head. "I don't know what else to do," he said to the Draco. "If we don't start making some progress, my superiors will put you to death."

I was very focused on watching the prisoner and I was sure I saw his eyes widen slightly. I almost jumped out of my seat. "You understand English, don't you?" I said.

He turned his head and looked at me with dark piercing eyes.

Nathan immediately focused on the Draco. He looked at me, and then back at the Draco. A smile crept across his face. "If that's true, and you value your life, you'd better start communicating."

The prisoner looked away.

"Allie, please get Martin."

I jumped up and ran into the main room to get our teammate. When I returned with Martin, Nathan turned to him.

"Maybe you can persuade him, Martin. We think he understands English, but he won't communicate."

With a smug expression, Martin balled his hands into fists. "Happy to help."

He was on the prisoner in a second, and blood was soon flying through the air. "Start communicating or die," Martin spat out between punches.

I squeezed my eyes shut and pressed my palms over my ears, trying to shut out the sounds of the beating.

"It's okay, Allie," Nathan said quietly. I felt the warmth of his arms as he wrapped them around me and held me tight. "He won't kill him. We just need all the information he can give us."

"I know," I whispered into his shoulder. "But that doesn't mean I have to like the methods we use." I held on tightly to Nathan, grateful that he hadn't wanted to do it himself.

A minute later the prisoner croaked, "Stop."

Martin stepped back and flexed his arms. "That should do it. He's just a damned civilian after all. This never would've worked if he'd been a soldier."

Nathan nodded. "Thanks, Martin. I'll take it from here."

The prisoner was crumpled on the concrete with blood oozing from his mouth and forehead. Nathan and I sat down on the floor in front of him. He made an odd croaking sound, and, very slowly, awkward words began to spill from his mouth. His speech was as deliberate as someone who had meticulously studied a language but never used it in a real conversation.

"Yes. I speak English, Spanish and Chinese. Many dialects." Speaking was obviously difficult for him and his tone was raspy.

"Why wouldn't you communicate with us before?" Nathan asked.

The captive looked at Nathan with no visible expression. "You offered nothing of interest to me."

"So, can we assume that being put to death does interest you?" Nathan said.

"That is correct. I do not want to die. Death before being assigned a mate would send my essence to a place you call … purgatory."

"You don't have a mate?" I said. "Why not?" Now that I thought about it, I realized I'd never seen a female Draco.

"I do not. Our society is matriarchal. The female of our species—our leaders—will not arrive on this planet until it is ready for colonization. I have been promised a mate at that time."

"Okay, then," Nathan said, "maybe we can negotiate a deal. You don't want to end up in purgatory without a mate, and we need something from you. Are you interested?"

"No. I do not want to die, but I am prepared to die."

Nathan thought for a moment. "We can do far worse than kill you. We can make you wish you were dead. Either way, it'll be bad for you."

The prisoner and Nathan kept perfectly straight faces as they stared at each other.

"I can call Martin back for a more intense demonstration if that would help convince you," Nathan said without a trace of emotion.

I knew that no one knew the power of a beating better than Nathan, but still his harsh tone surprised me.

The prisoner hesitated for several seconds and closed his eyes. "I understand. What do you need?"

Nathan closed his notebook and stood up. "I need to learn your language."

The prisoner opened his eyes and nodded stiffly. "Agreed. But you should understand that this will not change the fact that the probability of your survival is infinitesimal."

I brought my thoughts back to the present.

Beside me, Nathan looked at his watch and shifted on the step. "Hey, I think your shift is over now," he said. "It's my turn."

"I'll stay up here with you for a while." I wanted to return the favor of Nathan's company and talk some more.

"Sounds good. Thanks." Nathan gave me a half-smile.

We chatted for a while and then sat quietly for the next

hour. Nathan started to drift off, but I was wide awake so I decided to let him sleep.

Several minutes later, his arms flew up around his head in a defensive posture. "No, don't! Stop!"

I reached over, grabbed his right arm and shook him gently. We'd been through this drill before. "Nathan, wake up."

He opened his eyes and looked around wildly, his forehead covered with tiny beads of sweat.

"Did you have that dream again?" I asked.

"Yeah," he whispered.

Using my sleeve, I wiped the sweat from his face. Nathan had suffered from the same nightmare for as long as I had known him. He wouldn't talk about it, but given his upbringing it was pretty easy to understand why his sleep was troubled.

Nathan slid over to my side, grabbed my hand and laced his fingers with mine. "Allie, thanks for always being there for me," he whispered.

We had always supported each other. Nathan had taught me a hundred tricks to avoid being killed, and I had wiped away the sweat of a hundred bad dreams. I rested my head on his shoulder and he tightened his grip on my fingers. Sometimes I wondered if he felt safer in this new life than he did before the invasion.

We sat there quietly, until sometime later when Ivy came up the stairs yawning and stretching.

"My turn," she said. "You guys better get some shuteye, because as soon as my shift's over we're heading out to observe the bug."

I was happy to be back in the warmth of my own bunk.

Squirt and Nathan occupied bunks on the same side of the room as I did, while Martin and Ivy had bunks on the far wall. Martin snored, so I was glad he was on the other side of the room.

CHAPTER 8

By 1800 hours Ivy's guard shift had ended and, once again, it was cold and dark outside. It was my turn to cook breakfast, so I started a blazing fire in the basement stove, put the coffee on, and whipped up a pot of steaming oatmeal with brown sugar. Oatmeal was Nathan's favorite breakfast.

When Martin entered the room, he headed straight for the food. "The general's coming here for a senior officers' meeting at twenty-one hundred hours, so you guys are going to have to take Squirt with you."

"But we're working with the stinkbug today," I said, handing him a bowl. "Squirt will be terrified."

"That wasn't a question, it was an order," Martin replied flatly.

"Yes, sir."

I knew better than to argue, because when Martin made up his mind, it was a done deal. We would just have to find a way to keep Squirt entertained while we did our work. My main concern was his nightmares. He had just started to sleep through the night and I didn't want the bug to stir up his internal demons.

As we headed back to the bank with Ivy, I noticed it was a perfect night—for us. The thick gray clouds and biting breeze would be miserable conditions for the Draco soldiers. They struggled with the dark, and they also loathed the cold. Our prisoner had told us that because of our northern location, soldiers were often assigned to our part of the country as punishment for misbehavior, or simply to gain experience, while the more seasoned veterans remained in the temperate sunny regions. Nathan said that we were lucky to have the slackers in our area, although we never forgot that they were still killing machines.

The bank wasn't far and we arrived within a few minutes. Once inside, I lit a small candle and Squirt played with Big Bear behind the teller's counter. I told him that Nathan and I would be in the vault, and he wasn't to come in under any circumstances. If he needed something, he should wave from the doorway and one of us would come out.

Ivy swung the heavy vault door open and the three of us stood silently for a moment before summoning the nerve to enter the pitch-dark room.

Nathan entered first, setting his sack of supplies down and lighting a portable Coleman lantern. We never used flashlights because we didn't want to take chances with anything that gave off electromagnetic energy. Not ever.

As we approached the trashcan, the stinkbug instinctively moved to the far side of the container.

Nathan peered down at the bug. "It's weird. It still isn't interested in us. I'd like to see what it does if we take it out of the can."

"No way," Ivy said firmly. "That thing is dangerous. What if it decides to go after us?"

"It doesn't seem to be much of a threat anymore," I said, watching the bug continue to press itself against the side of the can.

"I can secure it with a rope, like when someone ties their dog to a stake in the yard. If it has another personality shift and becomes vicious, the rope will hold it back," Nathan explained.

Ivy looked at Nathan and nodded grudgingly. "All right. I suppose we can always recapture it if we need to."

Nathan got to work right away. He pulled a long rope from his sack, looped it and made a noose knot. Then he carefully lowered the loop into the can. The rope slid over the hard shell of the bug and onto the metal bottom. The stinkbug didn't seem at all interested in what was taking place. Nathan tilted the container slightly so the bug moved over one end of the loop. Tugging the rope, he was able to tighten the loop securely around the hard shell. He ran to the far side of the vault and tied the other end of the rope to one of the iron bars.

"Stand back," he said.

He tipped the container over, gently dumping the stinkbug onto the concrete floor. Ivy and I jumped when the bug's shell landed with a thump. We backed up a few steps as the bug stretched its legs, but for the most part it seemed docile. We stood quietly and observed it for a few minutes. The bug took a few steps and lifted its head to sniff the air, then took a few more steps and sniffed again.

"I wonder if it's hungry," I said.

"Notice how the typical stinkbug stink's missing?" Nathan said. "No food going in means no feces coming out. It's probably starving but for some reason it's lost interest in us as its next meal." He pulled an assortment of containers and food scraps from his bag. "I've brought some samples to test on the bug."

The samples consisted of hotdogs, beef jerky, leftover spaghetti, candy, canned spam, and several types of canned fish. Nathan prepared the food by putting a small amount of each onto a piece of paper. When he had all the samples ready, he lined them up like little soldiers, and took out a pen and pad for notes.

"Here we go," he said, "test number one."

Nathan used a stick to push the hotdogs over to the bug. The creature completely ignored them. Then, one by one, he pushed over the candy, tuna, salmon, sardines, beef jerky, spam, and anchovies. The bug didn't even seem to notice them.

"No dice." Ivy sighed.

Lastly Nathan slid over a small pile of leftover spaghetti. The stinkbug immediately reared its head and frantically backed up until it hit the wall on the far side of the vault. When it couldn't go any further, it crouched down and cowered.

"Ha! It hates the spaghetti as much as Squirt did," I said.

Nathan smiled. He pulled the spaghetti back and the bug

seemed to relax a bit. He packed the food back into his sack and zipped it up.

"I need to know exactly what ingredients are in Laurie's spaghetti," Nathan said. "Then we need to test each item individually."

Without warning, the bug lifted its head, hissed viciously, and rushed toward the vault door. When the creature reached the end of the rope, it was jerked back violently. It made sickening sounds as it struggled against the leash in an attempt to charge the opening. All three of us watched in horror as the bug went from docile to ferocious in a split second.

As I looked toward the doorway, I saw a short dark figure, wide-eyed and silent, clinging to a stuffed teddy bear.

CHAPTER 9

I ran over to Squirt's side. "You shouldn't be in here." I grabbed his hand and pulled him back to the tellers' area. His small body was quivering, and I tried to reassure him. "It's okay, Squirt. The bug's tied up and can't get to you."

I noticed that the hissing noise had stopped the second we were out of the vault. The others immediately joined us, concerned over what had just taken place.

Ivy squatted down and gave Squirt a calm smile. "Hey, I'm heading over to Laurie's house to get the ingredients she used in the spaghetti. Why don't you come with me? You can visit Michael and Sam."

Squirt smiled back and nodded his red head, his fear forgotten at the thought of seeing his friends.

Ivy grabbed his hand and headed for the door. "We'll be back in a few minutes," she said over her shoulder.

Nathan and I returned to the vault and watched the bug use

its many legs to examine the rope. Once again, it ignored us.

"Weird," Nathan said under his breath as he jotted down another sentence in his notebook. "After Ivy gets back with the ingredients, let's run the tests and finish up here. I'd like to go home and check on the meeting." He winked at me and grinned.

We had made a game out of eavesdropping on the senior officers' meetings, and since this one was being held at our house tonight we knew exactly what to do. The private gatherings were only for the general and his highest-ranking staff, which included Jackson, Alex, Martin, and Laurie. These meetings were where they discussed the future of our sector.

Twenty minutes later Ivy returned with a plastic grocery bag, but without Squirt.

"Laurie was heading out to the officers' meeting when we ran into her," she said. "She said it wouldn't be a problem if Squirt spent the next couple of nights with the boys while we worked with the bug."

"Perfect," Nathan said.

He began to rummage through the plastic bag. He pulled out dry spaghetti, canned tomatoes, olive oil, grated Parmesan cheese in a jar, and lots of spices in various containers. Again, he arranged the food on pieces of paper and lined them up. He made separate piles of spices at the end of the lineup, including, basil, red pepper flakes, salt, black pepper, thyme, onion powder, and dried garlic flakes.

"What's this?" he asked, holding up a small bottle of oil.

"That's oregano oil," Ivy replied. "Laurie ran out of dried oregano so she substituted the oil."

Nathan opened the bottle, took a whiff and raised his eyebrows. "Smells good."

After organizing the food samples, Nathan began the tedious testing process. One by one, he used the stick to push the small portions over to the bug, and one by one the bug ignored them. Then he splashed some of the oregano oil onto a scrap of paper. As soon as the oil hit the paper, the bug started to move about nervously. When Nathan pushed the oil-soaked sample toward the bug, it immediately backed up. As the paper moved closer, the bug clicked its legs on the floor and scurried away.

"That's odd," I said. "Why would the bug act that way over oregano oil?"

"I don't know. We need to do some research." Nathan quickly packed up the supplies. "Come on, let's go hit the books."

We left the bug securely tied up in the vault and the three of us made our way home, hoping to find some answers.

As we moved through the dark village, I noticed weeds pushing their way up through cracks in the street. It seemed odd that there were so many of them. Our village looked sorely neglected; it appeared as if no one had lived here for ten years, rather than only ten months. Nature seemed to be reclaiming the space, almost as if she was protecting the area and helping us hide.

I wondered how different this place would look once Earth became another overpopulated planet in the Draco colonies.

As we walked back to the house I thought about our sessions

with the prisoner. He had displayed almost no emotion, yet he had seemed surprised by Nathan's ability to pick up the strange throaty language so rapidly.

"Your capacity to learn our speech is impressive," the prisoner told Nathan after a long language session. "Your grasp of syntax is also excellent. Is there anything else you would like to be taught today?"

I had the distinct feeling that he didn't want us to leave.

Nathan packed up his bag. "Sure. Tell us how we can stay alive," he said with a cynical tone.

The prisoner leaned back against the iron bed frame. "That is not possible."

Nathan sighed. "There must be someplace we could co-exist without being a bother to your civilization."

"That is not our way. You cannot live with us. You cannot fight us. You cannot run and hide. There is nowhere for you to go."

Nathan considered his line of questioning for a moment and then took a different approach. "Why don't you tell us why you came here? What were the circumstances?"

"I am a government inspector. I was sent to assess the current situation because the troops were behind schedule with their cleanup of the indigenous population." The prisoner narrowed his eyes and made a deep grunt of dissatisfaction. "The military personnel assigned to this region are substandard. They are to blame for my current state of incarceration."

"Why do you blame them?" I asked.

The prisoner turned to me. "The final phase of my assessment was to conduct a physical walk-through of a number of buildings, yet the local officers had refused to accompany me that night. They insisted that I wait until morning. Now I understand why."

"So you went out by yourself, at night?" I said.

"Yes. I did not realize the area was so heavily infested with insurgents and I did not believe that going out alone was a threat to my safety."

"Maybe you shouldn't have assigned rejects to the northern locations," Nathan said acidly.

"Possibly. Our kind prefers the heat found in the southern territories, therefore the north is somewhat ... neglected." His facial expression clearly showed he had no fondness for the military. We felt the same way.

"All right," Nathan said, "that explains why you're here, but how did you happen to choose our planet? There must be more hospitable worlds to take over."

The prisoner shook his head. "We come from a colony of forty-nine planets, most of them located near the center of the galaxy. Over-population is an ongoing issue, therefore we are on a continuous search for the next world to inhabit."

"The center of the galaxy is pretty far from here," Nathan pointed out. "Couldn't you find something closer to your home?"

"No. We have exhausted all options in that quadrant. Our main focus is to find planets that can be colonized quickly at little cost. We are willing to travel great distances to find these attributes. Other than your northern climates, Earth suits us well, with its plentiful resources and, most importantly, a previously established infrastructure."

"So you took Earth because it was cheap and fast?" Nathan rolled his eyes.

"Primarily, yes." The prisoner looked bored as he continued with his story. "We observed you for three decades and patiently waited for this arm of the galaxy to be free from interstellar traffic. Once the area was clear of potential external influences, we began proceedings to eradicate the indigenous population. As you know, it took a very short time to eliminate the majority of your species."

"What sort of interstellar traffic are you referring to? And why did you need to wait for the area to clear?" Nathan probed.

The inspector looked at Nathan directly. "Mostly freighters and foreign military ships. You see, not all intelligent species consider our way of life acceptable. We take what we need and colonize quickly. We don't ask."

"Exactly how many other 'intelligent species' are there?" Nathan asked.

"Many thousands. Depending on which acuity rating you set as the baseline. The galaxy is a large place."

"Have all the places you've colonized been successful?"

"Yes."

"Do you consider the colonization of Earth successful?"

"My job was to make that determination. Thus far, the botanical transfers and energy-web setup have been going according to schedule, although we made a mistake in assuming the indigenous population would be easy to force into extinction. Many of you have been more adaptable and resourceful than expected."

I found it interesting that the prisoner never actually answered the question. I guessed that eliminating us was like trying to get rid of ants. Just when you thought you'd killed them all, a whole bunch more showed up.

CHAPTER 10

We quietly entered the yellow house through a rear window and tiptoed into the kitchen. With so much at stake right now, we were all anxious to listen in on the meeting that was taking place below.

"I'll go pull some books on herbs and natural medicine, leave them on the table and meet you back here," I whispered.

Nathan nodded and I darted downstairs to set the stage. I lit a couple of candles, then quickly found four books and left them on the table. The officers' meeting was taking place in the bunkroom, and I could hear muffled voices on the other side of the door.

I made my way back upstairs and into the kitchen. Ivy and Nathan were sitting on the floor with their ears pressed against the laundry chute. I sat down between them, turned my ear toward the opening, and listened to voices that were so clear we could have been in the bunkroom ourselves.

"We can't run and hide for the rest of our lives," Martin was saying in a heated tone.

"And if we stay here, they'll find us. If they find us, it'll be Bushnell's Basin all over again. Is that what you want?" Laurie shot back.

"Of course not, but Nathan's making progress with his research." Martin's voice was getting louder. "We're getting closer to being able to fight those fucking bastards. Now's not the time to run and hide."

"We need to look at the situation from both angles," said another voice that I recognized as the general's. "We can still move to a safer location while we continue to work on weaponry. Besides, an effective offense isn't our only hurdle; we still need to find a strategy for defense. If we don't find a way to defend ourselves against the lightsticks, we won't stand a chance."

"Well, I vote to stay and fight," Martin said.

"This isn't a democracy," the general said, clearly irate. "We'll do what I decide, and I'll choose the path that will keep us alive for the longest period of time. Engaging the enemy is not our main concern, especially since we don't have the ability to fight at this point. Does everyone understand?"

I heard the officers murmur, "Yes, sir."

"Martin, do I have your support?" the general said.

After an uncomfortable silence, Martin reluctantly answered, "Yes, sir."

"Jackson and Laurie," the general said, "find Will and brief him. The three of you need to be ready to leave the village in two hours. Check in with me before you take off."

"Yes, sir. We'll be packed and ready to go," Jackson said.

"Time is tight, so you'll need to move quickly," the general said. "Meeting adjourned."

Nathan jumped to his feet. "Quick, let's get downstairs."

We scrambled down the stairs and positioned ourselves casually at the table as though we'd been reading for hours. As the officers exited the bunkroom, I couldn't help but notice they didn't look like teenagers anymore. They looked serious and committed, and ready to do anything for our cause.

The general stopped at our table. "How did you guys make out with the stinkbug?"

Nathan looked up from his book. "We're starting to make progress, General, but we need to do some research. I'll have a full report ready for you in about two hours."

"I'm looking forward to it. Stop over whenever you're ready." The general turned his attention to Ivy. "We've moved the Bushnell's Basin group into the Lincoln Avenue house. When you're through here, they're waiting for you. But they're pretty fragile right now, so take care with them."

Ivy nodded. "Yes, sir. I'll be there as soon as we finish up."

As the officers left, Nathan opened his notepad. "Okay, let's get to work. We need to find out what we can on oregano oil."

It wasn't hard to find the data we were searching for. Oregano oil was fairly common and was listed in three of the four books I had pulled down.

"Here's a good description." Ivy pointed to a passage from a thick book and read aloud. "'Test-tube studies have shown that oregano oil can inhibit or destroy many strains of bacteria, fungi, and parasites.' It goes on to list several successful studies done with infected mice that were cured with small doses of the oil."

"Here's more information," I said. "This book states that high levels of oregano oil can be toxic to humans, but it's safe for low-dose, short-term use. It recommends placing one drop of oil under your tongue each day. It also says that carvacrol is the primary component of oregano oil. The research suggests that the oxygen molecules in carvacrol somehow kill the germs by dehydrating them."

"This is good." Nathan said. "One possibility is that stinkbugs have a bad reaction to the oregano oil, similar to the bacteria." He started taking down detailed notes. "Squirt didn't eat the spaghetti sauce, therefore he didn't have the oil in his system. Our hungry bug became aggressive when Squirt entered the vault because it sensed he was oil free."

"So if we take some oil every day the bugs might avoid us," I said.

"I'll have to run some tests to find the proper dosage, but yes I think they will. My guess is we'd only need a tiny amount, based on what we received in the spaghetti sauce."

Ivy clapped her hands together. "Yes! Score one point for Sector Three."

"This was pure luck." Nathan scowled at Ivy's enthusiasm. "We only scored a point because of a freak accident."

"Maybe we had a little divine help for a change," I suggested, hoping God was back on our side.

Nathan frowned. "We need a lot more than a little divine help. Besides, if God really wanted to help he'd give us some decent weapons." His voice was thick with sarcasm. "Even better, God should get rid of the Draco altogether."

I knew that Nathan considered himself a scientist and a man of facts, which didn't leave much room for faith, religion, and other things that are impossible to prove. I knew I had hit a sore spot with him. I suspected that he'd turned his back on God long before the Draco showed up.

CHAPTER 11

Ivy was anxious to address her new team, so Nathan and I helped carry her belongings over to the house on Lincoln Avenue. We said a quick hello to the newcomers and headed back towards the general's quarters.

The clouds were still thick, and a light mist was settling on the village, making the night unusually murky. Nathan moved quickly, darting from shadow to shadow, and I had trouble keeping up with him.

"Why are you in such a hurry?" I whispered.

"I want to get there before Jackson's team meets with the general. Don't you want to find out what's going on?"

"Sure," I answered breathlessly, running to keep up with him. A familiar clicking noise sent a ripple of fear up my back and I stopped short. "Nathan …"

Nathan turned and looked at me questioningly.

"Listen," I whispered.

He cocked his head for a moment. "Stinkbugs. And there's more than one. We need to hide—now!"

He grabbed my hand and pulled me toward a thick clump of bushes. Just as we dived behind the dense branches, a single bug crawled up the center of the street.

"Look, another four bugs about twelve feet back." I pointed north. "And another three over by the white house."

The bugs actively sniffed every item they came across as they made their way down the street. We had never seen this many bugs come through our village, especially at night.

As the lead bug approached our clump of bushes, Nathan whispered, "Don't move."

It poked and sniffed at the branches, but didn't hiss. I held my breath and hoped the oregano oil was still active in our bodies.

A faint breeze rustled the branches on our bush and the bug backed up, seemingly repulsed. As the creature headed back toward the road, a land vehicle passed slowly in front of us. It looked like an ultra-modern version of a Hummer, only without a top, sort of like a convertible. Four Draco soldiers occupied the seats, one in front and three in back. The soldiers in the rear directed streams of bright light at the buildings and surrounding landscape. Their gestures appeared bored and stiff, as if they were forcing themselves to go through their nighttime duties.

Nathan smiled wryly and pointed toward their heads. They weren't wearing helmets, which meant they wouldn't have the ability to detect our movements.

The soldiers began talking and we strained to listen in,

although their speech was much too rapid for me to follow. The inspector, our prisoner, had spoken slowly during his language lessons with Nathan, so I had managed to learn a few words, although I have to admit I wasn't the best student. The sentence structure was too difficult for me and much of it didn't translate well into English.

As the bugs traveled further down the road, the land vehicle followed at the same unhurried pace. After they moved well past us, Nathan shook his head.

"What were they talking about?" I asked.

Nathan gave me a look that implied I should already know the answer to that question.

"Just tell me," I said, annoyed.

"Well, they used some choice words to describe our cold climate. Then they talked about their beloved home planet, where the hot suns never set. They described it as the best place in the galaxy." Nathan grinned at me. "They also seem to feel that being assigned to this region of Earth is humiliating."

I smiled too. "Slackers."

Nathan stepped around the bush and carefully checked the road. "Looks like the path's clear, let's go."

We ran across the metal canal bridge and made our way down Schoen Place, taking care to stay close to the buildings. When we arrived at the general's quarters, Nathan rapped the code on the entrance window. Per protocol, Jon and Josh answered our call and allowed us to enter.

Alex was there to greet us as we descended into the main room. He had just turned seventeen and had been newly promoted to the position of colonel due to his exceptional skill with guns. Alex had been my main supporter when Colonel Twist had given me the job of armorer, and he had spent countless hours teaching me how to shoot and take care of guns. In the old life, Alex and his father had attended shooting competitions all around the country. He was a tough mentor and a loyal friend, and he was used to winning.

Alex looked concerned. "The general's expecting you. I almost sent out a search party. We thought you'd be here earlier."

"So did we," Nathan replied, "but the night patrol and their little pets slowed us down."

Alex nodded. "Got it. Allie, you'll have to wait out here."

I shrugged and headed for the coffee pot.

At my level I was accustomed to being excluded from conversations with the general. I sat on the couch with my mug, while Max tried to nudge me into giving him a belly rub.

After what seemed an eternity, Alex opened the door and asked me to join them.

As I entered, the general was giving out orders. "First we'll stop at the old herb store down the street to see if they have any more oregano oil. Nathan, take Allie and warn the three houses on the south end. Alex and I'll warn the rest. Everyone should still be protected by the oil in yesterday's dinner, with the exception of Squirt. Nathan, you'll need to go to Laurie's house first and give him a dose. Let's head out."

The four of us, along with Max, sprinted to the herb store. Once inside, we each held a tapered candle and looked around. Rotting herbs and old dried-up tea leaves filled the small brick-lined interior with a dusty haze. I held my sleeve over my nose to cover up the rancid smell of once-fragrant plants. Hundreds of small bottles, bags, and storage bins lined the shelves and counters. With so many products to go through, we each took a section of the store to search.

Several minutes later, Nathan's voice drifted from the back room. "Found it. Looks like there's twelve bottles." He brought the bottles to the main room and placed them on the counter.

"Good," the general said. "That's more than I was expecting. We can leave a bottle with each team and store the remaining oil in my office. Also, be sure to give each group the dosage instruction, and emphasize that they need to make the oil *last*. We don't know how hard it'll be to find more." He divided seven bottles between us and had five left over for storage. "Report back to my office when you're done."

Nathan and I headed south, while the general, Alex and Max went to the northern residences. We guessed the night patrol had moved on to the next town, because we didn't see them again.

At 0200 hours we were back in the general's outer room, sitting with Josh and Jon. The general and Alex hadn't returned and I was beginning to worry. Nathan and I had had more ground to cover, so technically they should have arrived before we did.

I turned to Josh. "Where's Jackson?" I asked.

Josh hesitated. "He's on a scouting mission."

"Where to?"

"Sorry. That's confidential."

He didn't have to tell me because I'd already guessed the

answer. Most likely Jackson, Laurie and Will had gone on the dangerous mission of scouting out a new home for our sector. I looked at Nathan and saw his brow wrinkle with concern. I knew we were thinking the same thing—Jackson's team didn't have any extra oil.

When the general and Alex finally arrived, they called us into the office for a meeting. I was grateful to be included. Alex poured coffee for everyone as we sat down.

"We're a few minutes late because we sent two volunteers to the Brighton sector to tell everyone about the oregano oil." The general looked directly at Nathan and spoke deliberately. "The breakthrough with the oil was a big win for us, but I need you to do more."

"Discovering the oil was nothing more than dumb luck," Nathan said matter-of-factly.

"But it was still a step in the right direction." The general glanced over at me. "Nathan, I know Allie's been helping you in your research and that's why I'm letting her be part of this meeting. What we do next is going to have a huge impact on the future. I've already sent Jackson and a small team to find a safer, more remote location for the sector to move to, but in the meantime I need to know exactly where you are with weapons and defense development."

Nathan cleared his throat. "It's not good news. Having the Draco glove has helped to determine which types of weapons won't work, which is basically everything we have. The body armor's made from some kind of fabric containing liquid metal. When the fabric encounters mechanical stress in the form of mass and energy, it hardens, deflects the energy, and protects the wearer. Once the energy's dissipated, the suit instantly returns to its normal flexible state. The whole process takes about a millisecond."

"Do you have any theories on what type of weapon *could* penetrate it?"

Nathan nodded. "Two, but they're both long shots. The first is based on the makeup of the liquid metal. Since the material's made up of tiny particles suspended in a fluid—essentially a nanotechnology—we might be able to force even smaller particles through the suit without triggering the solidification process."

The general frowned. "But how could something that small cause any damage once it passed through the suit?"

"It wouldn't, if we were just pushing one particle through. But if we were pushing hundreds of millions of particles through it would annihilate anything inside the suit. But we'd have to create a particle stream with huge energy for this theory to work."

Nathan shook his head. "I honestly have serious doubts that we could do this, even if we had access to unlimited resources. Nikola Tesla wrote about something similar in the early nineteen hundreds. He called it the 'death ray' but I don't think it was ever demonstrated."

"What about your other theory?" the general said.

"My second theory's based on simple cause and effect. If mass and energy cause the suit to harden briefly, think about what might happen if we applied *sustained* mass and energy."

"I suppose the suit would harden ... and stay that way for as long as we kept applying energy," the general said.

"Yes, the soldier would be frozen. We wouldn't injure him but he'd be immobile."

"Obstacles to this theory?" the general asked.

"A laser would do it, but we need to find the right type of laser. After that, our main obstacle would be finding a portable power source capable of extreme output. Building a high-powered portable laser won't be easy."

"Just tell me if it's possible."

Nathan answered carefully. "Yes, as long as I can get the necessary resources. I should be able to get most of it over at Nazareth College."

"According to our intel," the general said, "the Draco plan to level that area to make room for some kind of energy facility, so you'll have to get whatever you need as soon as possible, Nathan." The general ran his hand through his hair. "And what about defense development? How's that going?"

Nathan shook his head. "Nowhere. I need a lightstick to test out my theories and I don't know how we're going to get one."

"Let me take care of that," the general said as he jotted down notes. "Nathan, I need you to put a hundred and ten percent of your time and energy into weapons and defense. Up until now you've just been working on your theories in your free time, but you have to come up with working solutions. I need you to work like your life depends on it—because it does. Everyone's does."

Nathan looked directly the general. "I'd get there faster with a team."

"Who do you want?"

"Allie, Ivy and Ed."

"Why Ed? He's not that stable after the Bushnell's Basin incident," the general pointed out.

"I don't know anything about his mental state, but I've seen him at a few science fairs. I could use him."

"Done. I'll assign someone else to take your daytime shifts so you can spend more time on this. For now, pull your team together and bring them here at oh-four-hundred hours. By the way, you did a great job with the stinkbug, but don't waste any more time on that right now."

"Got it. What should we do with the bug?"

The general sighed. "Get rid of it."

CHAPTER 12

The wind picked up and icy droplets stung our skin as Nathan and I made our way back to Ivy's house. A few moments later, we rapped at the entrance and Ivy lifted the window.

"What are you guys doing here?" she said.

"We need to talk," Nathan said.

"Sure. Come on in." Ivy led us to the basement where a crackling blaze in a brick fireplace warmed the room. Her new team—Karen, Valerie, Chuck and Ed—sat on the floor playing a game of Monopoly.

The three of us sat down at a small card table in the far corner.

"Nice place," I said, as I looked around at the sparse furnishings.

"It'll do for now," Ivy said. "We plan on moving some comfortable couches down later tonight."

"Let's get down to business," Nathan said. "The general's tasked me with producing a working weapon and defense system ASAP. He made it a top priority and he's allowing me to pick my own team. I need a total of four players."

"Okay," Ivy said. "Since you're here with Allie I'm guessing you've picked Allie and me. Who's the fourth person?"

"Ed." Nathan looked over at the skinny sixteen year old with the thick glasses.

Ivy raised her eyebrows and looked curiously at Ed.

Ed's head popped up immediately. "M-me? Why me?"

"Yeah, why him?" Ivy asked dryly.

"Ed, explain Einstein's general theory of relativity to us," Nathan said.

"All right." Ed pushed his glasses higher on his nose. "The general theory of relativity demonstrates that time is related to matter and space, and since time cannot exist in the absence of matter and space—"

"Okay, that's enough. You're giving me a headache." Ivy rubbed her temples. "When do we get started?"

"Right now," Nathan answered. "But first we have to dispose of our friendly little bug."

"Sounds good." Ivy stood up. "I'm ready. Ed, grab your coat."

As we traveled through the damp night on our way to the bank, no one said a word. The burden of what the general was asking us to do weighed heavily on our minds. In the past, Nathan had spent his free time on weapons development, but there had always been other projects with higher priorities. Now things were different. Not only did he have to spend all his time on this one project, but he also had three full-time assistants to help him. That had never happened before. And I knew that the general never made major decisions like this lightly.

When we arrived at the vault, Ivy grabbed the heavy door and pulled it open. The dark room was oddly quiet, so Nathan lit the lantern. As Ed hovered anxiously in the doorway, the rest of us walked in cautiously. The bug sat motionless on the floor with the rope still around its middle.

Ivy knelt down to get a better look at it. "Maybe it's dead."

Nathan walked over to the unmoving creature and gave it a nudge with the tip of his shoe. It was stiff. "At least we won't have to decide how to kill it. It probably starved to death."

"They're horrible things," Ed said, as he adjusted his glasses with a shaking finger. "Just as we were getting ready to head to a safe place, the soldiers brought dozens of them to Bushnell's Basin. No matter where we went we couldn't hide from them."

We understood his pain all too well.

"I'm sorry, Ed," I said.

"Where was this safe place?" Nathan asked Ed, lifting his brow.

"Someone told us about a new place. It was supposed to be safe from the soldiers."

"Who told you that?" Nathan asked warily. "What was the person's name?"

"I don't remember." Ed shrugged. "He was a survivor who showed up from another sector."

"Was he a complete stranger, or did you know him?"

Ed put his hands on his head, visibly upset under Nathan's interrogation. I looked over at Nathan and shook my head. We didn't need a meltdown from Ed right now.

Ivy began untying the rope from the iron bar. "Let's get rid of this thing so we can get to work."

I helped Ivy tow the bug out into the middle of State Street while Ed and Nathan pried up a manhole cover. We kicked the bug into the hole and paused to listen to the satisfying thud when it hit bottom. The Draco had unknowingly just lost a valuable asset and I couldn't help but wonder if Ivy was right. Maybe we *had* scored a point against the enemy. Having any kind of a victory made everything seem a little less hopeless.

"Where are we going now?" Ed asked.

"Over to the fire hall, on Monroe Ave. That's where we keep the Draco glove and where we'll do our work," Nathan replied.

Ed adjusted his glasses for the hundredth time. "Interesting."

During our brisk walk to the fire hall, I thought about our language sessions with the Draco. After three months, I had begun to think of our captive as 'the inspector,' rather than 'the prisoner.' And once I started calling him that, Nathan picked up on it too. I'd also noticed that the inspector was beginning to look thinner and weaker, and his long silver hair had lost its shine. He had consumed the food we brought him, but reluctantly, and it didn't seem to be sustaining him. I was worried about him, and I also wanted to try to understand him better.

"Doesn't it bother you?" I asked him one day. "I mean, when you wipe out an entire race, don't you feel *anything* when you kill so many innocent people?"

"We must do what is essential for the expansion of our species. I believe you call it 'survival of the fittest.'"

I thought for a moment. I appreciated how nature worked, but not this.

"That isn't right," Nathan said. "When Darwin used that phrase in *Origin of Species*, he meant better adapted for the immediate, local environment. He didn't mean it the way it's commonly understood, that only those in the best physical shape would survive. And anyway, you're not better adapted for this environment."

The inspector looked mildly surprised.

I smiled at Nathan's reasoning. "What I wanted to know," I said to the inspector, "was do you ever feel guilty after wiping out an entire population?"

"No," he said flatly.

"Why not?"

"Because you are a species with a very low acuity classification. You are barely sentient. Do you feel guilty when you step on an insect or eat a hamburger?"

Nathan looked offended. "In some ways we're more sentient than you are. It all depends on your definition of sentient."

"What does sentient mean?" I asked Nathan.

"It means having consciousness. Or having the perception of senses."

The inspector nodded in agreement with Nathan's definition. "Most of the sentient species in the galaxy use an acuity classification to grade intelligent races. Your species has only had conscious intelligence for roughly fifty thousand years, therefore your rating is far below what we would consider meaningful."

"But what about our potential?" Nathan asked. "If you'd left us alone we would've kept on growing and evolving."

"That is very unlikely. We observed you for over thirty years and concluded that your path was one of self-destruction. Your species is far too focused on the individual at the expense of the general population. Greed and self-serving acts are inherent in your nature."

I thought back to the night we captured the inspector. "If your species is so caring about the general population, why did the soldiers let you go out that night alone? We would never let one of our people go out alone. That sounds self-serving to me."

Nathan smiled at me and winked.

"You are partially correct in your assessment," the inspector replied. "I admit, in the area of understanding the individual's wants and needs we are still struggling to evolve. We focus primarily on the continuation of our species as a whole."

"Does that mean you don't care about each other as separate beings?" I asked.

"I believe the correct term is 'empathy.' We do not regard the individual as important, in part because we do not understand how the other individual *feels* …" The inspector seemed to be at a loss for words and did not continue. He took a deep breath and closed his eyes for a moment. I noticed that his hand was trembling.

"Is there something else I can get you to eat? Something that would make you feel better?" I was concerned about his health. I knew he was a cold-blooded killer and that I shouldn't care, but over the weeks I had become used to him.

He looked at me strangely. "No, thank you. What I need would not be possible for you to acquire. Besides, you do not need to worry about me. Your time is running out on this planet, so you have more important concerns."

Ivy interrupted my thoughts when she leaned over and whispered in my ear. "Sometime soon we need to pick out some new clothes for you. You've outgrown the ones you have."

I looked down at myself and suddenly realized that the sleeves of my jacket were three inches from my wrists, and my pants were a good four inches too short. It's funny how you don't notice your own development when it happens. I was excited to think that I might finally be growing up.

I smiled at Ivy. "Yeah, I guess these are a little small."

We were almost to the fire hall when Ivy stopped unexpectedly and held up her hand, signaling us to freeze in our tracks. She tipped her head toward the west to listen for sounds hidden in the night breeze.

"Do you hear that?" she said.

I turned my head and thought I heard voices in the distance, but I didn't want to take the time to figure out who or what it was.

"We should take cover, come on," I whispered.

I led the way to a dark nook in the side of the building on the corner of Monroe Avenue and Main Street. All four of us crammed into the tight space and waited.

Ed whispered, "I don't hear anything."

"Quiet," Nathan said. "Something's coming."

Two dark objects moved at a quick pace in our direction on Monroe Avenue. I shifted to get a clearer view. As the objects moved closer, it was clear that they were people on bikes.

"It's Sara and Haley," I said, relieved that the dark figures were members of our sector.

The girls were on the return trip from the Brighton mission, but I could tell something was wrong even from a distance. As they approached, I ran out into the street to flag them down. They pulled over immediately. The black muck on their faces was smeared from tears, and they were breathless from pedaling hard.

"Gone ... they're ... gone," Sara choked out between gasps.

"Who's gone?" Ivy asked.

"The whole Brighton sector," Haley answered as she tried to hold back a flood of tears. "When we arrived everything was calm. The sector had a new leader and he was going to take them somewhere safe. People were actually smiling. But then the Draco came with hundreds of stinkbugs and it was over in minutes. We didn't even have a chance to tell them about the oil."

Sara held out the package of precious bottles. "We probably wouldn't be alive now if it wasn't for this." Her voice shook as she spoke. "They captured about a dozen kids and fried everyone else. Then they threw the bodies, like garbage, into huge collection bins."

"Thank God you got out of there," Ivy said, giving them

both a hug. "You need to debrief the general right now. Come on, let's go."

Nathan frowned. "Did you say Brighton had a new leader?"

Haley nodded. "They said his name was Tompson. He came from another sector with information about a safe place."

Nathan looked at me. I could see he was worried, but he let the subject drop. Right now we needed to get the girls back to the general's quarters.

As we made our way down Schoen Place, I began to feel the familiar sensation of panic creep up again. The Draco had butchered the sectors on either side of Pittsford, which meant they were methodically closing in on us. Time definitely was running out. I had to get a grip on my emotions. I reminded myself: *Bravery is being the only one who knows you're afraid.*

CHAPTER 13

As soon as we arrived, the general pulled Sara and Haley into his office. The rest of us waited quietly in the outer room with Max and the two guards. After several minutes, Ed began to rock back and forth in his chair, pressing his fingers to his temples. I understood how he felt, and I suspected that hearing about the Brighton sector had triggered a rush of bad memories for him.

"We're next. I know it. I know it. It's only a matter of time. They'll get us too," Ed muttered to himself. "There's nowhere to hide."

Nathan grabbed Ed's arm and looked him straight in the eye. "Ed, look at me. We're going to work together as a team and find a way to stop them. You have to use all that energy you're wasting on stress to help us find answers."

Ed glanced at Nathan and nodded, but he began to wring his hands. "Okay, okay, I get it. I'll try to stay focused."

Ivy crossed her arms and frowned. "Listen, Ed. If you snap, you're off the team. We don't have time for your neuroses. This is too important."

Ed seemed to mentally will himself into a calmer state. "I understand. Just kick me in the butt if I get too weird. I can control it. I want to be on the team and I know I can help."

The general's door opened and Alex escorted Sara and Haley out of the office. The girls looked worn out.

"The general wants to see you guys now," Alex said.

In passing, we said goodbye to the girls and filed into the office. Out of the corner of my eye, I noticed Alex exchange a long, worried look with Ivy.

The general and Martin were seated at the round table.

The general stood up. "What's all this about a new leader in Brighton, Nathan?" he said.

Nathan shook his head. "I think it's too coincidental that a stranger showed up in both places, Bushnell's Basin *and* Brighton, right before the soldiers arrived with an army of stinkbugs."

"Well, from now on *we* sure as hell won't be receptive to any outsiders," the general said with an edgy tone. "Now, I asked you here because we're promoting each of you tonight. I want you to have appropriate ranks for the responsibilities you have now."

Normally we would have been excited about receiving promotions, but this wasn't the time or place for a celebration. In the past, when someone moved up in rank we held a special ceremony at St. Louis Grammar School, but formalities were no longer an option.

"These are special circumstances, so we'll be bending the rules a bit," the general said. "Allie, you're now gunnery sergeant. Ed, you've been promoted to lieutenant, and Ivy, you've been promoted to major."

The general turned to Nathan. "Nathan, I'm giving you a new position. You're now part of my senior team. You'll be our chief science officer. I know I don't need to tell you how important your work will be to our long-term survival. The bottom line is, we need results and we need them fast. I want daily updates."

After the general dismissed us, we wasted no time heading back to the fire hall. The team was anxious to get to work and dig into Nathan's theories. The thought of devoting ourselves to that work made me feel like there was a light at the end of the tunnel, even if it was infinitesimal.

Alex had transformed the large open basement of the fire hall into a shooting gallery, which allowed us to practice without creating too much outside noise. This was where many of the sector members practiced their shooting skills, and also where Nathan worked on his projects. We had stacked up old tires, phone books, and hay bales along the far wall, and hung a variety of targets. We had lined the walls and ceiling with layers of thick carpet for additional soundproofing.

It may seem silly that we worked so hard to develop weapons skills we couldn't use against the soldiers, but it made us feel stronger knowing that we could at least *try* to defend ourselves if we had to. No one in Sector Three was going down without a fight; it was as simple as that.

Most of our weapons had either been given to us by Colonel Twist or found in the neighborhood houses. It was quite amazing to see what people had hidden in their homes once we started digging around. Our sector had collected all kinds of firearms, many of them illegal in the old world. We had thirty-four pistols (two with silencers), fifty-seven long guns (eighteen of them semi-automatic, three fully automatic), and a wide assortment of swords, knives and explosives. We had also accumulated a heavy supply of ammunition, accessories and cleaning supplies.

As we descended the stairs to the basement of the fire hall, Ivy lit two Coleman lanterns. I prepared a series of guns for impact testing. I always treated our weapons with great respect because I understood their potential. Alex had told me more than once: "Used properly, every weapon has one thing in common—the ability to kill."

Nathan took Ed over to the target area to show him the Draco glove.

"I've never seen body armor up close," Ed said as he carefully examined the gray glove. "Very interesting, but I don't see how this could function without a massive power source."

Nathan nodded. "I wondered the same thing, but there's no obvious supply of energy. Take a look at the webbing. See the thin black wires stretching around the wristband? I'm not sure what purpose they serve."

Ed looked at the glove again and fingered the delicate black wires. "Do you think they're structural?"

"No," Nathan replied. "The wires don't seem to have much strength. If I didn't know better, I'd think the glove was some sort of capacitor, but that still doesn't make any sense without a power source."

"What's a capacitor?" I asked.

"A device for collecting and holding an electrical charge," Ed said. "But this doesn't look like any sort of capacitor I've ever seen."

"Are you guys ready?" I asked, pointing toward the assembled weapons.

"Yeah, we're ready." Nathan placed the glove back in the target area. "Everyone stand back. Allie, would you do the honors with the twenty-two?"

"Sure."

I picked up the .22-caliber pistol, held it with both hands, and carefully aimed it at the glove. The gun wasn't particularly heavy and it was an easy shot. I pulled the trigger. The crack of the bullet exploding from the barrel was followed directly by a high-pitched *plink* as the bullet bounced off the glove and fell to the floor. This was typical of all of our tests with the glove. As soon as the bullet struck the glove, its energy was instantly dispersed, leaving the bullet essentially dead.

Ed ran over, picked up the mangled bullet and examined it. "That's amazing! But there absolutely *has* to be some kind of energy to counteract that much force. I wonder if we could somehow measure the potential energy usage."

Nathan eyes lit up. "Let's try attaching a voltmeter and see what happens."

Ivy began rummaging through several supply cartons and finally pulled out a small black box with dangling wires. "Is this what you're looking for?"

Nathan took the box and looked it over. "Yeah, this should work."

Ed looked at the meter skeptically. "Doesn't that run on batteries?"

"The digital ones do, but this is analog. It's safe for us to use." Nathan clipped the wires to the black webbing on the cuff of the glove. "Everyone step back. Allie, are you ready?"

"Ready."

I fired again, hitting the glove squarely in the center. And again the bullet fell to the ground, its energy spent.

Nathan, Ivy an Ed ran over to the meter to read the results. They looked at the small screen and then glanced at each other. Nathan had an expression on his face that I had seen many times before. That look meant that he didn't believe something because it didn't make scientific sense, like when I mentioned anything about faith or God.

"Oh, man!" Ed's eyes just about doubled in size.

"That can't be right." Nathan frowned. "We need to run more tests."

"What?" Ivy asked. "I don't get it. What's not right?"

Nathan simply shook his head. "Let's try it again, with a higher-caliber gun. Allie, try the nine millimeter."

"Got it." Again, I held the gun with two hands and aimed carefully. This gun was slightly heavier and had more kick, so I positioned myself securely. As the bullet exploded from the barrel, I forced my forearms to maintain control.

Nathan, Ivy and Ed ran over to the meter again.

"Wow!" Ed shouted.

"Would you guys mind explaining?" Ivy asked.

"Look at this reading." Nathan tilted the meter towards her. "It took ninety-eight thousand volts to deflect the nine-millimeter bullet. The twenty-two caliber bullet only registered sixty-seven thousand volts."

I walked over to the group. "I don't understand. How is that possible?"

"It's not." Ed pushed his glasses up the bridge of his nose. "It takes a lot of power to neutralize the energy from a bullet … yet there's no obvious power source … yet there is power coming from somewhere. It's a paradox."

We all looked towards Nathan, hoping he had the answer, but he just shrugged and shook his head.

"Well, it has to be coming from somewhere." Ivy waved her hand above her head. "That type of energy can't just materialize out of thin air."

Nathan's eyebrows went up and a smile gradually emerged. "It sure can. I don't know why I didn't think of it before."

CHAPTER 14

Ed tapped his foot on the floor. "Pray tell. What's the big secret?"

"Okay, I know this might sound a bit far-fetched," Nathan said, "but stay with me. When I was reading about Nikola Tesla's death ray, I also read about his work on wireless energy transfer. Tesla had successfully transmitted millions of volts through the air."

"Hey, that's really interesting and I don't want to spoil our party," Ivy interjected, "but the sun's coming up. We need to go silent and get home."

"All right, let's meet back here at eighteen hundred hours," Nathan said. "We have a lot to do. It's going to be a long session tomorrow night, so get some rest, everyone."

As the sun began to peek through the trees, Ivy and Ed headed north towards their new home, and Nathan and I cut through a back lot to get to ours.

Once we reached the security of our basement, Nathan stopped at the bookshelves and started rummaging through titles. I knew this meant we wouldn't be going to bed for some time, so I poured some coffee and grabbed a package of crackers. I wasn't tired anyhow.

Nathan placed volume *T* of an encyclopedia on the table, along with a stack of smaller books on Nikola Tesla. I sat down and began flipping through the pages of the first book on the pile.

Nathan opened the encyclopedia. After a few minutes he pointed to a long paragraph. "Here's something. In 1899, Tesla achieved a major breakthrough by transmitting a hundred million volts of high-frequency electric power wirelessly over a distance of twenty-six miles. He lit up a bank of two hundred lightbulbs and ran one electric motor."

"That was more than a hundred years ago. Why don't we have anything like that today?"

"It's hard to say. He might've been too far ahead of his time … or it could've been politics, or greed. Take your pick, the conspiracy theories are endless."

Within a few hours we had a pile of books loaded with scraps of paper bookmarking the pertinent information. We continued to read until our eyes burned from lack of rest, and at 1200 hours we finally gave up and headed to our bunks.

I felt like I had just dozed off when someone shook my arm. "Allie, time to get up," Nathan whispered.

"Ugh, I just fell asleep," I said, rubbing my eyes.

"I know, but we have a lot to do. We need to get moving."

I looked up at Nathan and noticed that he looked as tired as I felt, so I staggered out of bed and quickly cleaned up. Then we loaded our backpacks with books and headed back to the fire hall.

The first thing I did was fire up a pot of extra-strong coffee. Halfway through my first cup, Ivy and Ed joined us. Ivy smiled as she carried in a bulging shopping bag. Ed's hair stuck up every which way, which made him look like he had just rolled out of bed.

I handed Ed a big mug of black coffee. "Looks like you could use this."

"Thanks," he muttered, almost incoherently.

"Nathan, may I borrow Allie for a few minutes before we get started?" Ivy asked, although it wasn't really a question because she grabbed my arm and started to pull me away before Nathan had the opportunity to open his mouth.

"Yeah, sure," Nathan said as he unloaded books from his pack, but we were already halfway across the room.

I followed Ivy into a small storage room, where she lit a candle and placed it on an old wooden shelf. The room was musty, and had a cobblestone floor with old, crumbly cinder-block walls. The space didn't look anything like the rest of the basement, which was relatively modern. I felt a slight draft. On the floor I noticed a rusted metal plate embedded in the stone.

"This old room seems so ... out of place. It's not like the rest of the fire station," I said.

Ivy shrugged her shoulders. "I think the fire station was rebuilt years ago. Maybe this is an old room from the original station. Or maybe this was part of a root cellar or something."

Ivy rummaged through the contents of the shopping bag and pulled out a pair of straight blue jeans, a purple sweater, and white sneakers. "You can't keep wearing those pants or everyone will think you're waiting for a flood. Here, try these on." Ivy smirked and handed me the jeans.

"I guess I didn't notice how short they were," I replied, embarrassed. I quickly slipped out of my old worn clothes and into the new ones, and, mysteriously, each piece fit. I couldn't begin to guess how she did that. "How did you guess my size?"

Ivy flicked her hair back and gave me a serious look. "Women just know these things."

"Oh." I wondered when I would start to know these things too.

When Ivy and I returned to the other room, we found Nathan and Ed poring over stacks of books.

Nathan looked up and stared at me for a long moment. "You look ... different," he said.

Ivy smiled and gave me a jab with her elbow.

We dived back into our work. The hours flew by but our progress was slow. Nathan and Ed ran additional tests on the glove and continued to achieve similar results, while Ivy and I dug further into the books to look for more clues.

At 2200 hours Ivy yawned loudly and stretched her arms.

"This is super dry reading," she said, "and I'm having trouble understanding what's important and what's not. For example, this book states that a guy named Marconi claimed that extremely low frequency waves had the ability to penetrate metallic shielding."

Ed looked over. "You know, the navy uses—the navy *used* to use—very low frequency waves for communication because they can penetrate water."

"Here's something else," I said. "This book has a short section which states 'Tesla found a frequency wave that acted as a dampening field to nullify electrical power.'"

Nathan stopped what he was doing. "Does it specify if he used an extremely low frequency wave?"

I looked at the book again. "It doesn't mention it, but it does say that Tesla's research was the basis for Marconi's work, and it goes on to say that Marconi claimed that his beam could disrupt electrical devices and overload circuits. Then, mysteriously, his research was lost after the Second World War, so there isn't much additional information available."

"This bit of information might give us a third theory to work with. It shouldn't be too hard to test out. What do you think, Ed?" Nathan said.

Ed nodded. "Fairly easy stuff. I've done experiments with a wide range of frequencies."

"Let's get a shopping list together and then we can search for the necessary components," Nathan said.

Ivy glanced around the room anxiously and then looked upward. "Did you hear that?"

We immediately froze and tried to listen to what was happening on the main floor. I clearly heard two sets of footsteps moving across the floorboards, yet there was no way to tell if they were human or Draco. I looked around and considered the fastest way out. The basement of the fire hall had several exits, but it would be critical to choose the right one.

A creak came from the top of the stairs. "Nathan?"

I was never so relieved to hear Martin's gruff voice.

Nathan let out a deep breath. "We're down here."

As soon as I saw Martin and Alex appear on the stairs, my relief fizzled. They each carried a high-powered rifle, and wore a belt loaded with a high-caliber handgun, knives and grenades. They were ready for a fight, and that made me worry.

"The general asked us to stop by to deliver some news," Martin said.

"What is it?" I asked.

"The scouting team came back." Martin opened his mouth to say something more, but instead slammed his fist into the pile of books, scattering them onto the floor.

"What happened?" Nathan asked in a low tone.

"Jackson didn't make it," Martin said through gritted teeth. "Those fucking bastards."

Alex cleared his throat uncomfortably. "A swarm of stinkbugs cornered the team behind the old Cottage Hotel in the town of Mendon. As the soldiers approached, Jackson was able to distract them just long enough for Laurie and Will to get away. It's a miracle he was able to pull it off."

"What happened to Jackson?" Ivy asked tentatively. "Was he captured?"

Martin took a deep breath. "He was hit with a lightstick. Laurie saw him go down."

The thought of Jackson being fried was bad enough, but the idea of his body becoming bug food caused tears to pool in my eyes. The Draco were closing in on us and killing humans every inch of the way. I felt that panicky feeling threaten to bubble up again.

"I'm sorry," I whispered shakily.

"We're all sorry," Nathan added.

"Are Laurie and Will all right?" I asked.

Alex nodded. "Other than shook up, they're fine. They continued the mission and headed to the Bristol hills. After they found a small group of suitable homes, they came back. The general believes this'll be a good place for us to spend the next couple of months. At least it should get us through the winter."

Martin pulled out a piece of paper and placed it on the table. "Here's the moving schedule. The general has one team moving each night, starting tonight. We should be able to get everyone out of here within a week. Each team will travel with Max. When the team arrives safely at the new location, a green tag will be hooked to the dog's collar and he'll be sent back to the general. When Max returns with the green tag, we'll know it's safe to send the next team. If Max comes back without the green tag, or doesn't return at all, we'll know something got fucked up."

The four of us hovered over the handwritten sheet, trying to see where we fell on the schedule. Six teams appeared on the paper. Laurie's team was listed first, and Squirt's name had been added to her group. With the exception of Ed, the Bushnell's Basin survivors were divided up among the next three teams.

"There are a few names missing," Nathan pointed out. "Nine, to be exact."

Martin nodded. "That's right. Your group and the general's team will be the last to move. Once everyone else is safe and sound in the new location, we'll pack up your equipment and make the final trip. In the meantime, the general wants you to keep working. What you're doing down here is top priority."

I noticed Ivy exchanging a long look with Alex again. He gave her a reassuring nod and touched her arm.

"If you're interested, at twenty-four hundred hours we're going to have a moment of silence for Jackson at the First Presbyterian Church. Then we'll see Laurie's team off," Martin added.

"Of course we'll be there," Nathan said. While he may not have been one for religious gatherings, I knew Nathan believed in honoring the dead.

After Martin and Alex left, I felt paralyzed and didn't know what to do next. The whole group was quiet and seemed to have lost momentum.

Nathan cleared his throat. "Look," he said, "the only answer is for us to get back to it and work harder and faster. Sleeping and eating are secondary. Come on, let's get to it."

Somehow his words snapped us into action, and we jumped back into our work with new speed and energy.

Nathan quickly wrote up a shopping list and handed it to Ed. "Add whatever else you think we need for this project."

After Ed jotted down a few more items, Ivy and I threw on our backpacks, grabbed the list, and headed out the door. We began a hurried run down the road to Nazareth College, a mile away. The small college was only a short distance from St. John Fisher, where the Draco soldiers had their base, so we knew we would need to be extra cautious. Most of the leaves had fallen from the trees and the air was getting noticeably colder, so with a little luck the night patrols would be few.

Within fifteen minutes we were on campus, heading into the science center. Once we located a supply closet, in short order we found everything we needed. Our heavy packs slowed us down a bit on the way back, but since we saw no sign of the night patrol we still made good time.

After returning to the fire hall, I waited for Ivy to secure the rear door. Near the stairs I noticed a rack of books and quickly read through the titles.

"Check this out," I said to Ivy. "It's *The Official Firefighters Guide for Disaster Control.*"

Ivy walked over as I pulled it from the shelf. "Does it have advice on how to handle hostile aliens?" she asked cynically.

I paged through the table of contents. "No, but it does have a section on how to handle UFOs." I flipped through the pages. "Looks like plenty of information on how to approach a UFO crash site, but nothing on how to handle an invasion."

"No way," Ivy replied in disbelief. "The government didn't believe in UFOs. Who wrote this book anyhow?"

I checked the small print on the first page. "Looks like it was sponsored by FEMA."

"What? Let me see that." Ivy took the book and read the inscription carefully. Her voice took on a much more serious tone. "This was written in 1994, which means the government knew about aliens, or at least the potential threat of aliens, for a long time."

"I guess if FEMA took the threat seriously enough to write

this section, the military should've been all over it," I said. A spark of hope formed in the back of my mind. Maybe we still had some military forces out there somewhere.

Ivy handed me the book and I tucked it under my arm to show Nathan and Ed.

CHAPTER 15

At 2340 hours the team headed to the church to say goodbye to our comrade Jackson. As we approached the entrance I saw Josh and Jon, already positioned outside the building and performing one of their duties as sentries. We gave them a silent wave.

Inside the chapel a few candles were lit, and about twenty-five members of our sector were sitting near the dark pulpit. Laurie and her team came in right behind us, with packs on their backs and additional duffle bags hanging on their bikes. As a precaution, they parked the bikes inside, behind the last row of pews.

Laurie had bloodshot eyes and appeared worn down, but I had no doubt she would make sure the first relocation happened safely.

When Squirt saw me, he ran over for a big hug.

"Hi, Squirt. Are you and Big Bear ready for your trip?"

Squirt nodded and pointed to his overstuffed bag, where one of his favorite Dr. Seuss books was poking out.

Zack walked over and ruffled Squirt's hair. "He insisted on bringing those books. He won't go anywhere without them."

I grabbed Squirt's hand and we quietly took our seats in the third row of pews. A few minutes later the general arrived with Martin and Alex. Our leader looked weary, yet he took his place in front of the group, stood up straight and projected confidence.

"We've had far too many gatherings where we've had to say goodbye to one of our team members," he began. "We'll remember Jackson as a brave soldier, a good friend, and someone who fought hard to protect us all. It's up to us to make sure his death isn't in vain. Never forget, we have the right to life and we have the right to a place to live. Our mission will continue and we will not waver. Everyone, please take the next three minutes of silence to remember our teammate, Jackson."

I bowed my head and asked God to protect Jackson's soul, but, truthfully, I couldn't understand why God had allowed it to happen in the first place. Every time we lost one of our own, it reminded us that we were slowly losing the battle against the Draco, despite the few successes we'd had. That panicky feeling still lurked somewhere in the back of my mind, only this time I pushed it into a cold dark corner and I let my hatred for the Draco take over.

After the brief service we helped Laurie and her team prep for their journey. I smudged Squirt's face with black muck, told him he looked a real officer and that I was proud of him. When

I gave him a goodbye hug, his eyes were big and round and he held Big Bear so tightly that the animal was flattened out.

Zack came over and took Squirt's hand. "Don't worry, Allie, we'll take good care of him."

"You better, or you'll have bigger things to worry about than an army of soldiers." I gave Zack a big hug.

By the time the team was ready to depart they looked like six shadows. Even Max the dog had been painted to blend with the night. As I watched the first group quietly leave the village, the inspector's words came to my mind again: *The probability of your survival is infinitesimal.*

As we cut through back lots on our way back to the fire hall, Nathan cleared his throat and vocalized, "*Untata ghanaj.*" The sound came from deep in his throat.

"What? Are you okay?" Ivy looked at him strangely.

"I'm quizzing you," Nathan said. "*Untata ghanaj.* What does it mean?"

Ed snorted. "I have no idea, but it sounds like you have indigestion."

I struggled to recall the lessons with the inspector. "I think it has something to do with eating," I offered.

"It means 'I am very hungry.' Now repeat after me. *Untata ghanaj.*"

Nathan continued to quiz us and make us repeat words all the way back to the training room. When we arrived, I heated some cold coffee on a camping stove and we began sorting through the science equipment from the college. Nathan refused let up on the language training and continued to quiz us as we worked. I knew better than to complain, because if he wanted us to learn the language of the soldiers he wouldn't give up, and that was that.

Ed sighed and rolled his eyes. "Look, I already know three languages, English, Spanish and German. But this language is ridiculous. It's awkward and it sounds so … throaty. Not only that, there are too many words that don't translate into anything. And I don't see how this is going to help us develop weapons."

Nathan looked at Ed. "There might be some words that don't directly translate, but they can be understood as broad concepts. Look, I want you to understand something that Sun Tzu taught: know your enemy and know yourself and you can fight a hundred battles without disaster. We need to understand our enemy better. Period."

Ed held up two glass tubes and eyed them. "Far be it from me to disagree with the master, Sun Tzu," he mocked.

The hours flew by as we worked on the construction of a rudimentary laser along with trying to absorb a few alien words and phrases.

At 0500 hours Ed stopped working, scratched his head, looked around and scowled. "We're out of carbon dioxide," he said. "I could use another canister to increase the power level in the laser."

Ivy looked over at me. "I guess that's our cue. We better get going if we want to make it back before daybreak."

I put down the wires I was working with and grabbed a backpack. "We'll be back in a few minutes."

Nathan looked up and we locked eyes. "Please be careful."

I smiled back at him. "Always."

Ivy and I ran back to Nazareth College and headed straight for the Science Center. The remaining carbon dioxide canisters inside the supply closet were large and heavy, so I grabbed the end of one and she grabbed the other, and we made fast work of exiting the building.

"Okay, let's get out of Dodge fast," Ivy said as we stepped outside. "The sun will be up soon."

We hurried across the parking lot and onto an overgrown grassy area.

Ivy stopped suddenly. "Wait," she said breathlessly, setting her end of the canister down. She turned her head and listened to the night air.

"Crap," I whispered as I set my end down.

"Land vehicles. Move, over there."

Ivy pointed toward a large oblong rock. I was sure the gray boulder was once a nice piece of landscaping, but now it was just a big rock, engulfed in weeds. We left the canister hidden in the long brown grass, darted behind the boulder, and crouched down. Within a minute, two land vehicles traveled along the main road, at an agonizingly slow pace, not twenty yards in front of us.

"I could run faster than those things are moving," I whispered.

"Stay perfectly still," Ivy warned. "They have their helmets on."

We watched anxiously as they passed by at the pace of a turtle. After they had finally moved beyond the college and out of range, we stood up and stretched our stiff legs. I walked over to the CO_2 container and was just about to pick it up when the familiar high-pitched alarm went off. Then it sounded again.

In the distance we heard the land vehicles power up and move away at a significantly faster rate. A horrifying thought flashed across my mind. I stood frozen as the blood drained from my face and once again I felt the panic begin to bubble up from its dark corner.

Ivy grabbed my shoulders and looked me square in the eyes. "What is it? What's wrong?" she demanded.

"The double alarm. What if they found …" I choked out.

Ivy shook her head. "No, no, I don't think so. We've been so careful."

"But the glove, it draws electricity. Maybe they detected it. Nathan said there's no need to worry, but what if he's wrong?"

"Shit!" Tears sprang into Ivy's eyes. "But you've done hundreds of tests on the glove, and the energy burst's only a few milliseconds. That's too short …"

There was no time to debate it. We sprinted as fast as physically possible, toward town, toward the fire hall.

CHAPTER 16

We didn't slow down until we hit the intersection of Main Street and Schoen Place.

"Allie, go get the general and I'll meet you behind the shop next to the fire hall," Ivy said between gasps.

I nodded, trying to catch my breath. "Got it. I'll see you in a few minutes."

I ran to the general's quarters and skidded to a stop at the blackened window. Wildly, I pounded out the entrance code. Josh unhooked the latch and allowed me to stumble in. I saw the general, Alex and Martin hovering around Max, who was wearing a green tag and wagging his tail. The group had been smiling, but their faces immediately fell when they saw me.

I tried to explain as I struggled to suck in air. "Draco ... two land vehicles ... double alarm ... we think they're headed to the fire hall ... Nathan and Ed ..."

As soon as I mentioned Nathan and Ed, the group flew into

action. They grabbed their gear and all the weapons they could carry. I ran to the armory and picked up my preferred handgun, a SIG Sauer P250, and stuffed two extra clips in my pocket. It was a heavy gun for someone my size, but it didn't matter; I was good with guns and, like, my teammates, I wouldn't go down without a fight.

We left the general's headquarters and bolted toward the fire hall, taking care to stay hidden within the shadows. As soon as we reached the small shop on the corner, we carefully made our way to the back of the building, where we found Ivy pressed against a brick wall watching the soldiers on the far side of the street. When I saw her face, I knew things were bad. She looked terrified, and almost nothing ruffled Ivy.

Just past the fire hall, two land vehicles still vibrated despite being parked. Ivy pointed between the buildings to an area where several soldiers stood. They had removed their helmets and appeared bored, as if they were waiting for something that was taking too long.

"Two of them went inside with a bunch of stinkbugs," Ivy whispered. "But Nathan has the oil in his system. He'll hide and they won't find him."

"Oh, God," I whispered shakily. I knew the fire hall didn't have many places to hide and there was nothing any of us could do to help them.

Several minutes passed as we anxiously watched the exits. Finally, two soldiers along with a swarm of bugs emerged from the front of the building and rejoined their comrades. One of them held our test glove in his hand and they discussed the situation using their odd guttural sounds.

"What are they saying?" the general asked me.

"I'm not sure. Something about an empty building ... and I think they're blaming each other for losing the glove." I turned my head to hear more. "I think they said something about securing the site, but I'm not sure."

Before any of us realized what that meant, one of the taller soldiers reached into his vehicle, picked up a long tube, and pointed it at the fire hall. In a split second a brilliant blue electrical bolt crackled from the tube, expanding long fingers outward toward the brick walls. The instant the bolt touched the building the fire hall went up in a massive inferno of blue-and-white flames. We were hit with a blast of heat and flying grit, and then everything went foggy.

As the debris settled, I realized I was sitting on my butt. Someplace in the background, I heard the Draco vehicles power away. Then I heard the voices of Ivy and Jon, only I couldn't make out what they were saying. Something was in my eye and I tried to wipe it away. I looked at my hand and it was covered in blood.

The next thing I knew, someone was pulling my arm and making me run across a parking lot. As I struggled to keep up with the person who was pulling me, someone else grabbed my other arm and pulled harder. I couldn't think straight and I couldn't see past the red haze.

When we entered the basement of the yellow house, I was pushed into a chair. My head was pounding.

"Allie? Allie, are you okay?" Ivy was attempting to wipe blood from the right side of my face.

"I think I'm fine," I said, trying to collect my thoughts.

As the reality of what had just happened settled in, I couldn't breathe. "No, no, no!" I screamed. I started to choke and hot tears spilled down my face. Ivy tried to console me, but no matter what she said, I couldn't stop crying. I had just lost my best friend and now everyone I had ever been close to was gone.

After cleaning the wound, she taped a bandage to my forehead. "You know how smart Nathan is, Allie. I'm sure he thought of something."

"How could we have been so stupid?" I sobbed and choked between words. "They had no warning and they were stuck in there when the building exploded."

It seemed obvious that if Nathan and Ed had managed to get out, they would have come here and we would all be together by now. It was much more likely that they had found a clever place to hide—inside the building—just before they were incinerated.

I couldn't stop the flow of tears, so Ivy put me to bed and said something about Alex standing guard outside. I just wanted to close my eyes and never wake up. The pain of losing Nathan was horrible and I wasn't sure I could go on without him. When I finally faded into a dismal black cloud of sleep, I vaguely recall hearing the general's voice issuing orders in the next room.

I woke up at 1800 hours and blinked my eyes several times. They were swollen and felt like they were full of sand. Last night's events hung like a flat lifeless picture in my mind. Nathan and I had spent so much time together over the years that I couldn't imagine life without him. On top of that, without him the sector was doomed to a life on the run for however much time we had left.

I felt weak and couldn't begin to drag myself out of bed, so instead I stared at the wall.

Some time later Ivy came over and sat by my side. "You should get up and eat something," she said softly.

"I can't," I said, sounding as miserable as I felt.

"All right, but you should know that the general's accelerated the moving plans. Everyone goes tonight except us. We're going tomorrow night, so you'll have to get up eventually and pack. I'll help you."

"Fine," I replied. But I didn't care. I closed my eyes.

I opened them again when I was woken by thunder. It was 1700 hours. Had I really been in bed for almost two days? I sat up, touched my still sore head and looked over at Nathan's empty bunk. I felt sick.

Ivy was in her old bunk and Martin's familiar snoring filled the room. They had both slept right through the thunder. I crawled out of bed, stretched my stiff muscles and began shoving my limited belongings, including the SIG Sauer, into a backpack. I was angry now, really, *really* angry. I briefly thought it was interesting that I had already moved on to the second stage of grieving. I guess I was just getting good at it. Doc Hiro had once said that after what we'd been through some people might even skip a stage.

After filling my pack, I poured myself some cold coffee, sat down and patiently waited for Martin and Ivy to get up. To pass the time, I calculated the various ways in which I could take my revenge on the Draco. I knew there was little I could do without losing my life, but I really didn't care. After all, God had turned his back on me and left me completely on my own. And I didn't feel like running anymore; there was no sense in prolonging the inevitable.

I was sipping the cold coffee quietly when another clap of thunder caught my attention. This time the vibration shook the house and caused a cloud of dust to drift down from the tops of the bookcases. Seconds later, another big boom rattled the walls and caused several books to fall to the floor.

I stood up and gripped the table. No way was that just a clap of thunder.

Martin and Ivy came running from the bunkroom.

"What's going on?" Martin demanded.

I threw on my backpack. "I don't know, but you better get your stuff so we can get the hell out of here."

Footsteps pounded across the floor above. As we looked up, Alex charged down the stairs.

"The soldiers are leveling Nazareth College. We need to get moving. The general wants us to meet at his quarters."

Within seconds our small team was ready to go. We proceeded cautiously as the sun cast long shadows from the western sky. At the intersection of Main Street and Schoen Place, the explosions became noticeably louder. In the distance, ominous blue-and-white flames towered in the dark sky. As the team made the turn at Schoen Place, I didn't follow and kept walking straight.

Martin stopped. "Allie, what are you doing?"

"I'm going to the college. If I'm not back in an hour, leave without me," I said over my shoulder.

"Don't be an idiot!" he said. "You can't go there, you'll be killed."

"I'm going, period." I didn't care what Martin thought. I didn't care about anything. I felt like I was dead already and nothing was going to change my mind.

"Goddamn it, Allie, I order you to get your ass over here!"

I shook my head and just kept walking. If I lived through this, I'd have hell to pay for disobeying a senior officer. Either way, I didn't care.

I heard Martin's footsteps close in on me. He grabbed my arm and spun me around. "What's your fucking problem?"

I wrenched my arm free and started walking again. "Leave me alone!"

"Fine, have it your way, but we won't wait for you," Martin barked. He turned and headed back toward the general's quarters.

"Allie, wait!" Ivy sprinted to catch up to me. "What are you doing?"

"I'm not sure yet."

"Well, I'm not letting you go alone."

Another explosion shook the ground. I ignored it and picked up my pace.

"I know what I'm doing is crazy, but it's something I need to do."

"But you'll be killed," Ivy pleaded. "Please, let's go back."

"I'm okay with dying. Sorry. Can't go back." I kept moving.

"Then I'm going with you," Ivy said, walking faster to keep up.

"Your call. You know the risks." I didn't want to put Ivy in this situation, but it was her choice.

Ivy stayed at my side the entire distance without saying another word.

When we reached the campus, we saw that most of buildings had been leveled, making the landscape look more like a warzone. I wanted to get closer to where the explosions were taking place, so we zigzagged our way to the back of the campus until we spotted a small group of Draco standing by their vehicle. The four soldiers were talking loudly over the crackling sounds of burning debris and appeared to be having a good time.

"They don't have their helmets on," Ivy pointed out.

"Fools." I replied as I thought about how vulnerable they were.

We crouched down and ran over to a car with flat tires, roughly twenty-five yards away from the action.

The taller soldier positioned the familiar black tube at his side and fired a bolt at a remaining storage shed. The ground trembled and the structure went up in a column of blue–and-white fire. The soldiers simultaneously broke out laughing and chanting a strange song. The soldier who had made the shot walked over to the vehicle and pulled out four small tubes containing blue liquid. I was certain he was the same bastard who blew up the fire hall.

The taller one handed out the tubes and they all laughed again. Ivy and I watched curiously as each soldier broke off the end of the tube and the liquid became a blue vapor, which they inhaled through their mouths.

"What are they doing?" I whispered.

Ivy raised her eyebrows. "I think they're getting high," she said. "Look at their faces."

She was right. After breathing in the vapor, the soldiers kept their eyes closed for several seconds and appeared euphoric. Slackers, I thought.

"This is almost too good to be true," I whispered. "Actually, it's perfect."

I pulled the gun out of my backpack and stood just high enough to rest my arms on the trunk of the car. Ivy stood to my right, eyes wide. I aimed carefully at the head of the taller soldier who had handed out the shots; I wanted him dead.

I was about to pull the trigger when someone grabbed my left forearm. "Allie, wait."

I turned and looked Alex square in the eyes. "You shouldn't be here," I warned him.

"Come on, Allie, we're on the same team. We have to stick together." Alex pulled out his pistol and skillfully aimed the barrel. "I'll take out the one on the far left first, and then I'll get the one next to him. You take the other two."

I nodded, thankful to have Alex's help.

"On three. You ready?" Alex asked.

"Ready." We had performed drills very similar to this and I felt totally at ease and focused. My gun sight was perfectly aligned between the eyes of the Draco soldier on the far right.

Alex counted down. "One, two ... three."

We pulled the trigger at the same moment. The two Draco

soldiers left standing were covered with a heavy spray of red blood. They looked at each other and reached for their lightsticks. We pulled the trigger again. They never had the chance to touch their weapons.

As far as I knew, no one had ever killed a Draco soldier before, and now four of them lay dead on the ground with their brain matter splattered over the pavement. Killing unprotected slackers may not have been much of an achievement, but it was something. It was a start.

I used to go out of my way to avoid stepping on a bug. Now I was blowing heads off. Score another point for Sector Three.

Ivy tapped my shoulder. "Time to go. It won't be long before the whole outpost's after us."

"Wait," Alex said. He ran over to the dead soldiers and grabbed a lightstick.

CHAPTER 17

I knew I was in hot water when I saw how angry Martin and the general were, but killing a few Draco soldiers was well worth a tongue-lashing or anything else they cared to do to me.

"Dammit, Allie, you can't disobey orders whenever you feel like it," the general said with a deadly serious expression. Max sat quietly at his side and looked worried in a way that only a dog can.

Martin glared at me. "You know, Allie, this isn't just about you. Do you realize you fucking jeopardized Alex and Ivy's lives too? We should leave you behind as punishment."

The general shot Martin a look that indicated he had gone too far.

Ivy positioned herself protectively between Martin and me. "Look, it was our decision to go down to the college. No one forced us."

Martin rolled his eyes. "Christ, all *three* of you must have snapped."

"I haven't snapped," I said, crossing my arms in front of me. "It was time for some payback, plus I wanted to do something that left a mark."

"You left a mark, all right. Four dead Draco won't go unnoticed," the general added acidly. "We can expect their military to bring in backup soldiers from other outposts to pick apart every square inch of this area. And you can bet there won't be any more undisciplined soldiers without their helmets on."

Alex looked at his watch. "We really need to get moving."

The general nodded. "Alex is right, grab your things, everyone. We're leaving now."

Outside, Jon and Josh stood guard by the bikes parked alongside the building. In addition to the backpacks we each carried, we carefully strapped duffle bags packed with supplies, guns, ammo and food to the handlebars. We couldn't take everything, so our supplies had been narrowed down to only the items that were considered essential.

We each took a bike, and Jon and Josh led the way onto Main Street and over the canal bridge. The crisp night air had been tainted by a burning smell, and we could still hear the crackle of smoldering debris in the distance. The first few minutes of our journey were smooth going, until Max put his tail between his legs and barked at something ahead.

Jon and Josh immediately stopped and pulled out their pistols, causing us all to apply the brakes to our heavy loads.

In the dim moonlight, I could just barely make out a thin

dark silhouette moving clumsily towards us. The figure slumped a few times but continued to approach. Max stopped barking, put his ears back and let loose a deep growl. Whatever it was, it was much too small and awkward to be a soldier.

The click of hammers being readied on the sentries' handguns caught my attention.

"Wait," the general whispered.

The figure fell to its knees in the middle of the road. When whoever it was looked up, I noticed a slight glint of light reflecting off of a pair of glasses.

"It's Ed!" I said, jumping from my bike.

Ivy and Alex were right behind me as I ran toward the crumpled figure.

"Ed, are you all right?" Ivy asked as we approached him, but it was obvious he wasn't.

In the light from a crescent moon, we saw that Ed had cuts and bruises all over his face, his clothes were torn, and he was covered with dirt. We grabbed his arms and helped him to his feet.

"Trapped, we were trapped," he said breathlessly. "I finally found a way out ..."

A hundred frantic questions cluttered my head, but I needed to know one thing first. "Ed, is Nathan alive? Where is he?"

"Y-yes. He's alive, but he needs help. I didn't know what to do," Ed responded weakly.

My heart was pounding wildly and I struggled to get my mind wrapped around what was happening.

"Where is he?" I asked, this time gripping Ed's arm tightly as if it might force him to give me the answer.

"Below." As Ed pointed down at the pavement, the shrill Draco alarm sounded, not twice, but six times. The ear-piercing noise was coming from the direction of the college. In the distance, several land vehicles powered up and hummed at high speed in our direction.

We ran back to our bikes and helped Ed onto the bar of Alex's bike. We traveled as fast as we could until we reached the village crossroads. The guards came to an abrupt stop and pointed straight ahead. Another group of Draco land vehicles was approaching from the south and would soon meet us head on.

"Oh shit," Ivy said, as she quickly looked east and west. "They're coming from all directions. We're surrounded."

"We'll have to dump the bikes and go on foot," the general said.

"No!" Ed shouted. "Don't do that. It's suicide. They'll track us down in minutes. Trust me, I know where we're going." He pointed west, down Monroe Avenue and straight towards the oncoming Draco.

"Are you absolutely certain, Ed?" the general said. "We might have a small chance if we make a run for it."

"Yes, I'm certain. Trust me," he repeated. "They already know we're here, so we can't hide. There's only one safe place."

I knew Ed was right about one thing. The first rule of survival was to find a place to hide *before* they locked onto your coordinates, not after.

Ed led us a short distance to a large old house on the left side of Monroe Avenue. The Draco vehicles were dangerously close to lightstick range. It seemed insane to be riding directly toward the approaching enemy, but Ed was certain and we were out of options.

Moving as fast as we could, we pulled into the driveway and dropped our bikes. We grabbed as much gear as we could carry and followed Ed through a side door, into the kitchen.

"Follow me," Ed said, "I've been here before and I know the way."

Out of breath, we all hurried down to the basement. Ed squeezed behind the furnace and entered a tiny hidden room. It was too small to hold all of us, so Ed told us to wait while he and Martin opened a trapdoor in the floor and climbed down into what appeared to be a subbasement. One by one we followed them down into the dark abyss. The general was the last one through and he closed the overhead door tightly behind him. Max whined, as apprehensive about his whereabouts as we were.

We groped our way through the blackness until Ivy lit a couple of candles, which gave off just enough light to see the stairs stretching beneath our feet. The steps were awkwardly steep and seemed to be made of stone, and the air was damp and cool. My footing was more than a little unbalanced, as I carried my heavy duffle bag as well as my backpack. I steadied myself by placing a hand on the wall to my right, which felt coarse and slimy to the touch.

After about fifty steps we came to a landing area, made a sharp right turn, and headed down ten more steps.

"This is the bottom," Ed announced, his voice echoing eerily.

The air was damp and I was sure I could hear running water. As we began to unload our heavy bags, a long intense rumble came from above. Several rocks, along with a cloud of dirt, rolled down the steps and clattered around our feet. Max put his ears back and whined.

We all looked up. We knew instinctively that the house above us had just gone up in a blue-and-white inferno.

"At least they'll think we're dead," the general said gravely.

Martin's eyes narrowed. "That's just great. Now we're trapped down here. Allie, this is all your fault."

"Not now, Martin," the general warned.

Alex lit a small lantern, which improved our visibility to about forty feet. A mysterious cavern glistened before us. Huge cream-colored stalactites hung from the cathedral-like ceiling, and to the right, bits of light danced off of a free-flowing stream. The surroundings were so strange and unearthly that we stood silently, in awe of our new environment.

I turned to Ed. "Where's Nathan?"

Ed pointed north. "He's over there."

A small dot of light flickered about two hundred feet away. I wanted to believe that Nathan was over there, but I was terrified it was all some kind of trick.

The ground was slick and damp, so I took careful steps, using my arms to keep balance. After about fifty feet the ground became higher and dryer, so I sprinted toward the dot. The first thing I saw was a small candle burning inside an old glass jar perched on top of a wooden crate. Then I saw Nathan lying on weathered boards, which were covered with an old dirty quilt.

I knelt down and he slowly turned his head and looked at me. Only it didn't look like Nathan. He had two black eyes, a swollen nose crusted with blood, and a fat lip. Dirt was caked and smeared all over him.

"Allie," he whispered hoarsely. He tried to smile, but the effort clearly hurt him.

"Nathan, don't talk." I grabbed his hand and gave him a light kiss on the check. He was alive and that's all I cared about. "Everything's going to be okay now."

He closed his eyes for a few seconds. "I'm glad you're here. For a while I didn't think we were going to make it."

I held Nathan's hand tightly. He opened his eyes and we looked at each other for a long moment. I regretted accusing God of turning his back on me, and I felt equally bad for not holding out hope that Nathan had survived.

A tear rolled down my check as I made a silent promise to myself, to God, to Nathan, and to what was left of humanity: I would never lose hope again. I was learning that hope was something that could keep you alive, and I intended to use that power.

The others soon joined us and we went to work checking Nathan over. He appeared to have a broken leg, a broken nose, various cuts and bruises, and was running a low-grade fever. With our limited medical supplies we cleaned his wounds and gave him some Tylenol, but we had no way to gauge how bad his leg was, or what type of infection was lurking in his body. We needed Doc Hiro.

Ed was in much better shape, having only small cuts, bruises, and a sprained ankle. We offered them both some food, but

Nathan refused to eat and would only accept water. Ed, on the other hand, was ravenous and gulped down two cans of tuna fish and a box of crackers.

After taking care of the injuries, we gathered around the camping lantern on the high ground, near Nathan.

"Ed, tell us what happened at the fire hall," the general asked gently.

Ed adjusted his glasses and took a shaky breath. "Well, we were working on the laser when we heard the scuffle of stinkbugs moving across the main floor. We barely had enough time to gather our supplies and hide in the small storage room. That's when Nathan found a metal plate in the floor. He pried it up and we discovered an opening that led to this cobblestone root cellar. Obviously the soldiers didn't find us, but just to make sure we weren't hiding somewhere, they turned the fire hall into the inferno of hell."

"How did they track you in the first place?" the general asked.

"They traced the power surge from the laser. We thought the energy burst would be so short that they'd miss it." Ed cleared his throat and adjusted his glasses. "But apparently we were wrong. We tested an extremely low frequency wave in conjunction with a rudimentary laser. The laser serves as a carrier beam for the ELF wave," he explained, "enabling us to fire both beams simultaneously at the glove. We had success for a full second, but then, somehow, it failed."

The general shook his head. "You had success? What does that mean?"

Ed scratched his head. "Well, it means the body armor didn't harden. We managed to stop it by creating the disruption in the electromagnetic field."

"Wait a minute. Are you saying you can deactivate their body armor?" Martin asked.

Ed sighed. "Briefly, yes, but we still have a lot of work to do. Plus, we need to work out how to overcome the power issue."

Ivy looked around. "I still don't understand how you ended up down here."

"It happened so fast that I'm not sure myself." Ed leaned over and rubbed his ankle. "When the soldiers blew up the building, the vibration broke loose a section of the cobblestone. Behind the wall we found a passageway with a set of stairs. We were carrying our equipment into the passage when the building collapsed. The force sent us flying down the steps and we got pretty banged up. Most of our stuff was damaged, but at least we weren't dead."

Josh looked toward the immense cathedral ceiling. "I don't understand how a cavern this big could exist below the village with no one knowing about it."

"Well, someone knew about it a hundred and fifty years ago. I found a pile of antique lamps and tools, some with dates on them." Ed pointed beyond the steps where we had entered the cavern.

I suddenly recalled an old memory of my mom making a presentation at the university.

"My mother once told me that the Underground Railroad had passed through Pittsford," I said. "Tunnels and caves were used to hide the slaves while they waited for transportation."

I wished I had paid more attention and could remember what else she said.

"I always thought the stories about caves under the village were just urban legends," Ivy said.

"If the stories are true, there should be more than just two tunnels to the surface," Alex pointed out.

"Well, if they exist, they're not easy to find," Ed said. "It took me almost two days to find the one that the soldiers just collapsed."

Considering Ed was injured, and not exactly the physical type, it was a miracle he had been able to find anything.

"Nathan needs Doc Hiro," the general said, "so we need to find a way out quickly. Martin, Jon and Josh, go search the northeast side of the cavern. Alex, Ivy and I will cross the stream and go south. Look for changes in air currents." The general stood and picked up his weapons. "Allie will stay with Ed and Nathan. This area will be our official basecamp. I want everyone to meet back here within two hours."

After the teams departed, Ed complained about his ankle so I gave him some aspirin, but it was Nathan who had me truly worried. Despite the medication, his fever had gone up and he was beginning to perspire. I wet a cloth in the nearby stream and put it on his forehead.

"So, tell me about your laser," I said, trying to distract him.

He perked up a bit, but spoke slowly. "It was awesome, Allie. We managed to send the low-frequency wave through the laser and temporarily interrupt the armor's ability to draw power. It only lasted for a moment, and I wouldn't have believed it if I hadn't seen it for myself."

Ed sat down next to us. "Yeah, except now our laser is a tangled mess at the bottom of the stairs. Not only that, but it was much too large for practical use, and it definitely wasn't portable."

"Could you make a smaller one?" I asked.

Ed rolled his eyes. "No. A laser like ours needs massive amounts of energy. That's what got us into trouble in the first place."

"We have a few hypotheses to test out which might help solve that problem," Nathan said slowly. "But first, I need to better understand the power source the Draco are using."

"Oh no, I don't think we should mess with that. Well, it could work, but it would be dangerous and there would be all kinds of obstacles." Ed began to fidget nervously. "I should check on our equipment first."

Ed slowly hobbled back to the pile of damaged supplies, mumbling to no one in particular, and began to pull out various pieces of broken gear.

Nathan tried to laugh, but winced in pain from the effort. "Don't worry. He gets like that when he's anxious. He'll be all right."

I picked up Nathan's hand and gave it a squeeze. "Nathan, there's something I have to tell you."

He looked at me and waited patiently.

"After the fire-hall explosion, we thought you were dead." I hesitated for a moment and took a deep breath. "The general sent everyone to the new location, except, instead of leaving the village, I decided to go to where the soldiers were destroying the college. Martin ordered me not to go, but I went anyhow.

Then Ivy didn't want me to go alone, so she came with me. I know it was stupid, but I was looking for some payback."

"What happened?" Nathan asked, his voice barely a whisper.

"We found four soldiers. They were busy leveling the buildings and didn't have their helmets on. Then Alex showed up and … well, we killed them. It wasn't hard." I looked at the ground. "By the way, bullets are very effective when the soldiers are unprotected."

"That's good information." Nathan was quiet for a long time. "You know, if you had listened to Martin's orders you'd be well on your way to the new location, and I probably would have died down here."

"But I also almost got us all killed. And I never should have assumed you were dead. I should have looked for you."

"You had no choice. You *should* have assumed I was dead."

"We always have a choice. I should have been searching for you, but instead I put everyone at risk. I won't make that mistake again." I squeezed Nathan's hand.

CHAPTER 18

In just under two hours, Martin, Jon and Josh returned. All three had dirt smudged on their hands and clothes, which seemed strange to me because every surface in the cavern was solid rock.

"What did you find?" I asked.

Martin brushed small chunks of soil from his sleeve. "We'll wait and see what the general's group finds and then we'll discuss it."

Ten minutes later the general returned and we sat down for a meeting.

The general pointed beyond the stream. "We didn't find anything on the southern end of the cavern. On the southeast we found another set of steps, but the top was bricked up solid." He looked at Martin. "Any luck on the northeast end?"

Martin nodded. "We found a tunnel that goes up pretty steeply. Looks like it might lead to the canal, although further up there were dirt and rocks blocking the passageway. There was an opening, but it was too small for any of us to crawl through. My gut says we were close to the surface."

"Ed, didn't you say you found some old tools and lamps down here?" the general asked.

"Just a couple of rusty old shovels, a hammer, a bucket, and about a dozen oil lamps," Ed said.

"Okay. My team'll take the hammer and one of the shovels, along with a high-caliber pistol," the general said. "We'll get to work breaking through the brick wall. Martin, you take the other shovel and the bucket, and see what you can do about breaking through to the surface."

"Sir, we'll need Allie. She's the only one small enough to fit past some of the rocks," Martin said.

Somehow it seemed like this was Martin's way of getting back at me.

The general looked at me. "Allie, can you do it?"

"Yes," I said without hesitating. I wasn't going to let Martin scare me, although I didn't really care for the idea of crawling through a hundred-and-fifty-year-old tunnel.

We gathered our gear and I tagged along with Martin's crew. At the opening of the tunnel, Josh explained how far I'd have to travel before reaching the blockage. He assured me that he and Jon would be right behind me. Martin, who was the biggest and the least likely to fit through, would be last in line.

"I'll carry the bucket and shovel. When you can't go any further, tell us which tools you need to clear the way," Martin said as he handed me one of the old oil lanterns.

"Got it," I said, hunching over as I entered the passage-way.

The lantern dangled from my left hand and cast a murky glow on the rocks around me. I took small steps for about thirty-five feet, but as the tunnel narrowed and became more vertical, I resorted to crawling. As I traveled upward, I came across clusters of smaller rocks and loose dirt, which made my progress even slower. A few feet further, I smelled the familiar scent of topsoil. I wasn't normally claustrophobic, but being buried alive due to an unexpected cave-in crossed my mind more than once.

"I'm just about as far as I can go. Send me the bucket and I'll start digging," I said to Josh, who was about ten feet behind me.

I set the lamp down on a flat rock and surveyed the close surroundings. I spotted some small hair-like roots just to the left, so I knew we had to be near the top. Josh handed me the bucket and I tried to scoop away the dark earth, but it had been compacted over the years and was too hard.

"No good," I told him, "I need the shovel."

Josh carefully passed me the shovel and I situated myself so I could get some leverage. I jabbed the shovel upward into the earth, and after about four tries began to break loose hard chunks. Clusters of dirt and roots rolled down toward Josh, and he collected them in the bucket and passed it on down. We continuing doing this until he'd filled the bucket about twenty times.

Sweat was rolling down my temples and my arms felt like lead weights. "I don't think I can go any further."

"You've made the tunnel a lot wider, Allie. I should be able to fit up there now. Slide back and I'll take over from you."

I crept backwards, and Josh and I squeezed past each other to switch places. He picked up the shovel and started hacking away. He was strong and worked hard, sending back buckets of dirt twice as fast as I had. When he became tired, the three of us rotated so Jon could take over.

Two hours after we started, Jon broke through. The roots of bushes and weeds had formed a dense network, which had taken most of our time to penetrate. It took us another twenty minutes to make the exit big enough for a person to comfortably pass through.

The hole we created was surrounded by thick shrubs and tall grasses, which gave good cover. One by one, we cautiously emerged into the fresh night air and discovered that our exit was near the edge of the canal, just as Martin had predicted.

In the distance, we could see streams of spotlights crisscrossing the village, and I heard more land vehicles than I could count humming up and down the road.

Martin took a quick look around. "It's too dangerous out here, we need to get back underground," he whispered.

I was the last one to drop back into the hole, so I pulled over branches and hunks of sod to camouflage the opening. By the time we reached basecamp again, the general's team had already returned. They watched us curiously as we walked over. Glancing at my teammates, I realized that we were all covered in dirt from head to toe. Even our faces were filthy.

Martin explained our accomplishment to the group. The

general was pleased that we'd broken through, but he was still concerned about the heightened Draco activity. Then he told us about his own group's attempt to break through the brick wall.

"We barely scratched the surface," he said. "We need something much stronger than old tools, but I don't want to try explosives until we're certain the Draco have cleared the area." He hesitated and looked over at Nathan. "My biggest concern is Nathan's condition. Josh and Jon have volunteered to go to Bristol and bring back Doc Hiro."

Martin shook his head. "It's too dangerous right now. We can't send anyone out there until the area's clear."

The thought of a delay didn't sit well with me. I was losing what little patience I had. "But Nathan's getting worse. They have to leave right away or it might be too late."

"Look, Allie ..." Martin's familiar tone meant he thought I was too young to know anything. "It won't do us any good if Josh and Jon get killed because we sent them out too soon."

"Then I'll go," I said stubbornly.

"Don't do something stupid again, Allie," Martin replied, obviously thoroughly irritated with me. "You should think of someone besides yourself."

"I am thinking of someone else," I insisted.

The general cleared his throat loudly. "If the two of you are done, I have a plan. Allie will keep watch at the entrance to the tunnel. As soon as the majority of the Draco have left the village, we'll send Josh and Jon out. And I mean *majority*. If a few soldiers are still searching the buildings, the boys know how to deal with it. Once all of the remaining Draco have cleared out, Ivy and Allie will go topside and find more supplies. We'll need more food, blankets, sleeping bags, tools, and anything else you can think of."

He looked around. "In the meantime let's make this place as comfortable as we can. Alex, Martin and I will continue to work on busting through the brick wall on the southeast end. But for now, why don't you guys get cleaned up. You're a mess."

Washing up in the cool stream made me feel better. My muscles were still sore, but the clear water was refreshing. We hadn't had a clean water source since before the invasion and it was a welcome improvement.

I checked on Nathan. His skin was still warm, but he was sleeping soundly. The rest of us were tired, stressed and hungry, so Alex passed out rations of spam and crackers, and cups of water from the stream.

Ed finally decided to rejoin the group after tinkering with the laser for hours. "Hey, Allie, be sure to bring down some flashlights and batteries when you go topside for supplies," he said, as if it were no big deal.

"What?" I looked at him and wondered if he was all right. "Did I hear you right?"

"It's okay," he said. "Really. With fifty feet of limestone and dirt between us and the surface, the soldiers won't be able to track anything."

The general looked over and a rare smile crept across his face. "That's good to know."

CHAPTER 19

Every two hours I made a trip to the opening of the tunnel, and by sunset the next day I reported that the soldiers had finished their hunt. They must have felt confident that we'd been incinerated in the explosion, because their search of the village had seemed swift and superficial.

Josh and Jon wasted no time heading out to get Doc Hiro. They hoped to locate new bikes and make the forty-six-mile round trip as fast as possible.

Shortly after they had departed, Ivy and I planned out two quick supply runs to pick up necessities. We made our first trip a few hours after dusk, just as the bright moon began to cast long shadows along the ground. We spent a good part of the night searching homes for sleeping bags. Once we had located a dozen bulky bags, we managed to drag the awkward load across the village and down into the steep tunnel without incident.

It was getting close to sunrise by the time we emerged for our second trip so we stepped up our pace. We knew that the St. Louis Church still had a good stockpile of supplies, so we went there first, hoping we'd find enough goods to make this our only stop.

When we arrived, we swung by the kitchen and loaded non-perishable food into our bags. Then we located the supply closet and began rummaging through shelves of camping equipment, batteries, emergency items, and paper products.

"Looks like we hit the jackpot," I said as I stuffed a large duffle bag with a lantern, a portable cooking stove, and a few paper products. Once my bag was full I forced the snaps shut and helped Ivy finish filling her bag with batteries, flashlights, and blankets.

Ivy laughed when she found a portable toilet folded up in the corner. She held it up and smiled. "We are absolutely bringing this back."

I lifted my bag and realized it would be a struggle to haul it back. "Well, I think that's about all I can carry,"

"Oh, look, Alex would love this," Ivy said, holding up a camouflage hunting knife.

"Speaking of Alex, I saw him looking at you the other day."

"What do you mean?" Ivy stuffed the knife into her bag and pulled the strap over her shoulder.

She knew exactly what I meant.

"He likes you. It's pretty obvious."

"Yeah, but you know we're not supposed to have relationships." Ivy was trying to sound uninterested, but she wasn't fooling me.

I shrugged. "We know a lot of people who don't follow that rule. Besides, I'm pretty sure you like him too."

Ivy smiled. "We're just good friends."

"Yeah, sure."

Ivy smiled again. "Okay, I'm kind of hoping that something develops. We'll see."

By the time we arrived back at basecamp, the area was deserted, apart from Nathan and Ed, who were both sleeping soundly. Ivy and I quietly unpacked our bags, organized the supplies, and laid out the sleeping bags in a row. We also performed the all-important task of setting up the portable toilet in a small alcove about sixty feet away.

Sometime later the general, Alex and Martin returned from trying to break down the brick wall at the top of the steps. They looked worn out and discouraged.

"How'd it go?" I asked.

"No luck," said Martin. "We need an explosive."

"We'll try a grenade when we're certain there aren't any soldiers in the area," the general said. "For now, let's get a few hours of sleep. I'm sure we could all use it."

I was exhausted and ready for some shuteye, so I placed my sleeping bag next to Nathan and crawled in. I noticed Ivy and Alex over by the stream towards the south end. They were standing close together with their heads bent in quiet conversation. I looked at Nathan. He was still sleeping, but he looked terrible. Small beads of sweat had formed on his forehead and his face was still badly bruised. I prayed Doc Hiro would arrive soon.

The sleeping bags were bulky and warm, but lying on a limestone floor was hard and uncomfortable no matter how thick my bag was. After about an hour, the cold from the stone floor seeped through the material and crept into my bones. I vowed that tomorrow I would find some air mattresses.

I was jarred awake by a loud moan. It took a moment for my mind to orient itself to the new surroundings. I was still tired and my body was stiff from sleeping on the cold rock floor. Then I heard another moan. It was Nathan. I whirled around and found Doc Hiro hovering over his patient, giving him some pills.

I gasped when I saw Nathan's face. His expression was contorted in pain, and he looked even more black and blue than before.

Doc Hiro looked over and gave me a reassuring nod. "Your friend will be all right," he said. "I set his leg and straightened his nose, so the worst is over. I've given him a strong painkiller and an antibiotic, so he'll probably sleep for a while."

I was relieved to hear that the worst was over, but I was still worried.

"How do you feel?" I whispered, as I slid over and took Nathan's hand.

"Like shit, but at least I'm alive so I guess I can't complain." Nathan could barely keep his eyes open.

"Do you want some food?"

"No, thanks." He closed his eyes. "I want to sleep for a while."

I sat with Nathan until he had drifted off. The aroma of

strong coffee wafted over from the makeshift kitchen, where Ivy was cooking up a storm on the camping stove. The scent attracted me like a magnet, so I wandered over and helped myself to a big mug.

"Do you want some powdered eggs?" Ivy offered. "They're really not that bad."

"No, thanks." I looked around and noticed that almost everyone was gone. "Where did the rest of the team go?"

We both looked up when a small explosion radiated from the southeast side of the cavern, seeming to ping-pong around the high ceiling.

Ivy smirked. "I'll give you one guess. It took all five of them to set off one little grenade."

Within minutes the team returned, slapping each other on the back and smiling. When we all sat down for breakfast, the general gave an update.

"We broke through the wall and found that it opened into the basement of a house at the end of Lincoln Avenue. Then we replaced the bricks to make it look like a solid wall. For now, we should only use it as an emergency exit. We'll continue to use the tunnel near the canal as our primary entryway."

He glanced over at Nathan. "Doc Hiro's going to stay for as long as it takes to make sure Nathan recovers. I've also had a long conversation with Ed, and he assures me that the cavern's the best possible place for he and Nathan to continue their work, as soon as Nathan's fit enough. The ability to use electricity is a huge win for us, and I hope it'll speed up progress with weapons development."

"What about the rest of us?" Martin asked.

"Martin, I'd like you and Alex to continue surveillance of the Draco. Ivy and Allie, I want you both to continue gathering supplies to create a suitable living space. And please start a tracking sheet for the oregano oil. I don't want anyone forgetting their daily dose. Later in the week I'm going with Josh and Jon to check on the rest of our people in Bristol."

The next seven days whizzed by as we carried on with our assignments. The general, Josh and Jon left for Bristol as scheduled. Martin and Alex went on nightly recon missions to track the Draco movements, and Ivy and I made more supply runs than I could count.

Doc Hiro tended to his patient diligently, and by the end of the week Nathan was up and about. He looked slightly better, but his face was still black and blue and he needed to use a cane to get around. He had also lost weight. But his appetite was strong and his energy levels almost back to normal. Doc Hiro assured me several times that Nathan was making an amazing recovery.

Ivy and I became exceptionally creative with the setup of our new home. We located enough air mattresses for everyone, and Ed inflated them with a small air compressor, which he rigged up to a car battery. We brought down boards and tools, and built a nice-sized food storage area, and then created a nook for weapons storage, and another space for Nathan and Ed to work on development.

We also rounded up a supply of candles, batteries, food, propane for cooking, clothes, additional weapons, tables, chairs, and pretty much anything else we could fit through the tunnel. Our underground space was beginning to look like a well-equipped fortress.

The cavern had a constant draft, but Nathan had concerns about the airflow. He had Ivy and me walk around holding candles to determine where the fresh air was coming from. We found several natural chimneys in our search, but since we were using propane for cooking Nathan insisted on monitoring the air quality.

It was strange living in a cavern. We had no sense of time. There was no sunrise or sunset, only the perpetual glow of candles and lanterns. We kept a calendar on the wall to keep track of the date and to know when to take the oil, and we relied on our self-winding watches to tell us when to sleep.

Despite his healing injuries, Nathan jumped right back into working with Ed on the laser weapon. Each day he took time to write careful notes detailing all of their theories and experiments in a small black-leather journal.

The laser and the low-frequency beam had been fairly easy to design, but in order for them to be effective they needed a huge amount of power. Much more power than they could safely generate.

As they burned through parts, Ivy and I made trip after trip to the surface to find new supplies. One night, a small explosion within Nathan and Ed's workspace sent black smoke spewing into the cavern. No one was hurt and Nathan told us all not to worry, but I could see the frustration on his face.

Even though we had no real breakthroughs in the area of development, our lives began to settle into a comfortable routine. One night after our work was done, Ivy surprised me with a birthday cake with fifteen candles. I was fascinated by the fact that she had figured out how to bake a cake on a camp stove, but she'd always been clever that way. Everyone sang the Happy Birthday song, and when I blew out the candles, instead of making a wish, I thanked God for bringing Nathan back to us.

As we ate cake, Nathan smiled and winked at me. "What did you wish for?"

"Nothing. I'm saving my wish for now."

After the party, I crawled into my sleeping bag and looked over at Nathan, who was already asleep. His bruises had faded to a mix of yellows and greens, and his nose tilted slightly to the right, but other than that he was his old self again.

Doc Hiro and Ed were also asleep, and Martin was sitting at the table reading his homework, *The Art of War*, which was being passed around per Nathan's instructions. I had already read it, but truthfully, it didn't make much sense to me.

The sleeping bags that belonged to Ivy and Alex were empty. I suspected they were trying to find some private time in one of the many caves that stretched like fingers off the main cavern. Since we'd been living underground I'd seen many quiet conversations between them.

"Allie, are you still awake?" Nathan whispered.

I rolled over and looked at him again. "Yeah." His brow was wrinkled like it often was when he was frustrated or worried. "What's wrong?"

"The development of the laser isn't going as smoothly as we'd hoped," he said. "It's the power supply that's giving us trouble. The laser works great as long as you happen to have a generator the size of a truck."

"Aren't there any other options?"

"Maybe. I've been thinking about the Draco's wireless power source. Studying the lightstick Alex brought back helped us understand the nature of the power and how it's transmitted. Our early tests showed that it's very similar to typical electrical energy, only much stronger. The Draco use something similar to a capacitor to collect the energy, but when we tried tapping into it our equipment spontaneously fried."

"Is that what caused the explosion?" I asked, concerned.

"Yes. It's dangerous and we can't control it. At this rate we won't have a weapons prototype ready for a very long time … if ever."

"Nathan, don't think about how long it's taking, just keep working at it. Ivy and I will get you anything you need, no matter how many times you burn it up. I know you'll figure it out, you always do."

Nathan's blue eyes were thoughtful. "Allie, thanks for always being there for me … and for being my best friend."

CHAPTER 20

The start of the winter was unusually cold and snowy, but our underground haven remained a consistent fifty-five degrees. Over time we had somehow adjusted to the damp air and cool temperature, and our hideaway was starting to feel like home.

Nathan had fully recovered and Doc Hiro had long since returned to the Bristol encampment to treat an outbreak of a stomach bug. Thanks to the cold weather, the Draco generally stuck to their outpost, but when they did venture out Martin and Alex kept close tabs on their movements. The general, his guards and Max returned every three weeks to check on us and get updates on Draco activity and weapons development, but there was little to report.

Nathan turned sixteen in December, so Ivy showed me how to bake a cake on the camping stove. A few weeks later Ivy turned eighteen and I was able to use my newfound baking skills again. For almost two months the only excitement we had was our birthday parties. For most of us, boredom became a problem as the passage of time seemed to slow to a crawl.

Nathan and Ed worked almost every waking hour trying to unravel the secret to tapping into the Draco energy source, but they were very tightlipped about the results. They made numerous trips to the surface with their equipment, often returning hours later exhausted and frustrated.

Nathan became driven in his quest to find solutions and he rarely slept. When I asked him about their progress, he simply winked and said, "Stay tuned."

January brought two back-to-back blizzards, which kept us below ground for ten days and made recon missions impossible.

Nathan made use of the downtime by continuing to teach us the Draco language. He said over and over: "Communication is just as important as weapons, and in some cases more important."

It seemed like a good way to fight off the monotony of being stuck underground, so this time I focused intently and applied myself to learning the vocabulary and syntax. I surprised myself by picking it up quickly.

In February, an ice storm brought down dozens of trees and forced the Draco soldiers outside for three days to clear debris from the roads. It was the worst winter any of us could remember; yet we remained comfortable and well protected from the elements, as well as the enemy. Up on the surface, I hoped the Draco were miserable.

By April, the village had thawed after the long gray winter, and Nathan had taught the entire team key phrases from the Draco language. Between what I had previously picked up from the inspector and my newfound diligence, I was almost fluent. Sometimes I would go a whole day without speaking any English, instead only making the Draco throat noises.

Nathan and I had lengthy conversations in the foreign language, which I know were far from perfect but at least we understood each other. This tactic was annoying to our teammates, particularly Martin.

My new level of expertise also meant I was allowed to go on recon missions to help interpret, but with little happening around the village most of the trips were boring. The only helpful bit of information I deciphered was that the Draco were still *toc uuk* (twelve months) from beginning the colonization process. We also learned that the soldiers were receiving pressure from their leadership to finish up the task of eliminating the indigenous humanoids and preparing the planet surface.

The few conversations we overheard indicated that the military was frustrated by the pockets of survivors who had managed to endure this long. Despite our apparent lack of progress, it gave us great hope to know there were still others like us out there, somewhere.

By May the weather was still chilly and wet, and the Draco continued to avoid the outside environment, allowing us plenty of time for weapons training.

Per Nathan's instructions, Alex gave advanced lessons in shooting to me, Martin and Ivy. Each night we went topside, to a ravine behind an old brown warehouse just outside the village. This was one of our favorite practice areas because the ravine was low enough to help muffle the noise, and far away from routine Draco activity.

Alex was a tough mentor and graded us harshly on accuracy and form. As our target-shooting skills developed, Nathan instructed Alex to determine which rifle was best suited for each of us. Once he'd done this, Alex secured a one-pound weight above each person's scope. These became the only weapons we were allowed to use.

I was given an M4 rifle. Alex said I had a gift for it, but I wasn't so sure. The M4 needed a little extra maintenance and cleaning, but had less recoil than some of the other semi-automatic weapons. It weighed 6.9 pounds with thirty rounds, and 7.9 pounds with the extra weight strapped on.

During the first few weeks of practice with the adapted M4, my arms ached and my right shoulder developed a big purple bruise from the kick. But after repetitive training sessions, the soreness finally went away and I developed strong arm, shoulder, and core muscles.

For months we continued to practice in the remote ravine. Alex created competitive games and kept detailed accounts of our scores, and although none of us could beat Alex's numbers, I surprised everyone by coming in second more often than not. The general continued to visit and encourage our progress. He also brought updates on our friends in Bristol, who had remained undiscovered by the roaming patrols and were all doing well.

As we practiced topside, somewhere below our feet Nathan and Ed burned up more electronic components than we could count. But despite the repeated failures, they refused to give up and kept testing ways to draw from the Draco energy stream.

Over the summer, Nathan's bad dreams returned. They started out small, but the harder he worked on the development project, the worse the nightmares became.

One night I woke to find him thrashing around in his sleeping bag. I glanced around at my teammates and saw that everyone else was still sleeping soundly, with the exception of Ivy and Alex. They were missing again.

I reached over and gently shook Nathan's arm. "Hey, wake up."

Nathan blinked a few times and looked over at me.

"The dreams are getting more frequent," I said, propping myself up on an elbow. "Nathan, what's going on?"

"It's just stress." His blue eyes almost looked sad. "Everything's about to change."

He was starting to worry me. "Why? What's changing?"

"I'll explain in the morning." He rolled over and went back to sleep.

I thought about what he could have meant by change. I closed my eyes, but it was a long time before I found sleep again.

CHAPTER 21

When I finally woke, everyone was up and active. Nathan and Ed were working hard and speaking in hushed tones over in their workspace. Alex's AR-15 rifle was propped up in the middle of their cluttered table, looking very different to how it had looked the previous night.

Curious, I got up, wiped the sleep from my eyes and walked over to their work area. "What are you guys doing?"

"You'll have to wait for the unveiling," Ed replied smugly, stepping in front of me to block my view.

Nathan just smiled and winked at me.

A moment later Alex wandered over. "Hey, what's going on with my rifle?"

"We'll show you after breakfast," Nathan stated firmly as he covered the table with a blanket and shooed us all away.

I whipped up a big pot of oatmeal and brown sugar, and one by one the team came over and grabbed a bowl. Ivy and Alex sat next to each other at the table with their arms touching as they ate. Their relationship had obviously become more serious and I made a mental note to ask Ivy about it later.

"So, Nathan, what's the big secret?" Martin said.

"No secret. We'll talk about it after breakfast."

Everyone ate faster than usual, anxious to hear any news of progress. After months of watching Nathan and Ed deal with failures, explosions, and roadblocks, any little tidbit of positive information would give us a reason to celebrate.

It was Ivy's turn to do the dishes, so I grabbed the stack of dirty plates off the table and offered to help her. She bent over at the edge of the stream, washing the dishes and handing them to me to be dried.

"When I woke up last night, you were gone again," I mentioned casually.

Ivy smiled. "Alex and I went to the south end … to talk."

"You really like him, don't you?"

She smiled and whispered, "No one can kiss like him. Best kisses I've ever had."

"What makes them so special?" Having never been kissed, I was more than a little interested in knowing why one kiss was better than another. In the old life, Ivy had had a lot of boyfriends, so in my mind she was an authority on the subject.

She leaned over and whispered in my ear, "Well, it has to do with *how* he kisses me. Softly at first, with his mouth open"— Ivy looked around to make sure no one was listening—"and he uses his tongue."

"Really?" My eyes widened with curiosity. "And then what happens?"

Ivy smiled. "Nothing," she said, but her tone said otherwise.

"Come on, tell me."

She shrugged and smiled again. "Well, he gets a hard-on in his pants." She sighed. "But he's a gentleman and doesn't want to push me into having sex. Personally, I don't think we should wait too long."

I wasn't sure how to respond to that statement. I understood about having sexual desires, but I had no idea how someone would choose the right time to act on them.

Ivy looked me straight in the eyes. "Look, we don't know if we're going to make it to the next day around here. We can't put off important things for a time we might not live to see."

"Come on, you two, it's time to see the big surprise," Martin shouted across the cavern.

We picked up the clean dishes and hurried over to Nathan and Ed's workspace.

Ivy and I stood next to Martin, Ed and Alex, eyes wide with interest, as Nathan gently pulled the blanket off the table. "*Voila!*"

Alex's rifle was sitting on a wooden stand, with a long silver tube mounted above the scope where the one-pound weight had previously been. The tube was about an inch in diameter and roughly sixteen inches long.

Nathan picked the rifle up and handed it to Alex. "How does it feel?" he asked.

Alex grinned, felt the weight of the gun, and looked through the scope. "Feels about the same as it did with the dummy weight. How does this contraption work?"

"It's pretty simple, really. Just sight your target like you normally would. Let's assume your target's a Draco soldier in full body armor. When you pull the trigger, the bullet and laser discharge simultaneously."

Nathan pointed to the silver tube. "It's important to remember that the laser carries the extremely low frequency wave. Since light travels much faster than bullets, the laser will hit the suit first and the ELF wave will nullify the electrical charge for slightly over one second. Without an electrical charge the metal particles inside the armor won't be able to harden. By the time the bullet reaches the target, the soldier will be defenseless and vulnerable. At that point, the accuracy of your shot will determine the amount of damage done."

"Wow," was all I could think of to say. When Nathan said that everything was going to change, he wasn't kidding.

Ivy clapped her hands together. "Finally! Score another point for sector three."

"How do you know if this thing works?" Martin said. "Have you tested it yet?"

Nathan shook his head. "No. Our work's based on theory and previous experiments with the glove. We want you all to test this weapon at target practice today while we fit the rest of your rifles with lasers. But you'll need to keep your guard up. The laser draws an enormous amount of energy directly from the Draco's power source. We don't know if the Draco will be able to tell who's using the energy—them or us. So be careful."

Nathan glanced at the calendar on the wall. "The general's coming back tomorrow. I think we should wait until then to talk about a strategy for testing the rifles on actual body armor. At the moment we just need to focus on getting the rifles sighted and calibrated."

"We've waited a long time for this," Martin said, smiling broadly. He rarely smiled and it made me a little uneasy.

"Don't get too excited," said Nathan. "We're not sure how the body armor will react when it suddenly doesn't work anymore. If I had to guess, I'd say it'll try to compensate by drawing huge amounts of power. How much power, we don't know. There are too many variables that we still don't understand and can't predict."

"Now listen up, because this next bit's important," Nathan said, looking at each of us in turn. "When we test this on actual body armor, we *have* to do it in a controlled environment. Ed and I have already tested the laser discharge and everything seems to be working properly. Tonight you're only going to shoot the rifle at a standard target so Alex can make the necessary adjustments to the scope. Keep the trip short and get back here as soon as you can."

We were excited to be trying something new, so we wasted no time grabbing our gear and racing up the tunnel. The crescent moon provided just enough light to travel the familiar path along the canal, under the Monroe Avenue bridge, and over to the ravine behind the old brown building.

Ivy and I tacked up a target on a thick tree truck. As we stepped off to the side, Alex prepared to take the first shot, using what little moonlight there was to focus.

"Hey, take a look at Martin," Ivy whispered in my ear. "I'll bet he can't wait to get his hands on that thing."

I glanced over at Martin, who was watching Alex closely. He shifted his weight from foot to foot and balled his hands into tight fists. I hadn't seen Martin that wound up in a long time.

Alex pulled the trigger and the bullet exploded from the barrel at what seemed to be the exact same moment the laser hit the target. The human eye couldn't make out which force hit the target first, but we knew it would have been the laser.

Ivy and I ran to the target. "It's just above center," I said.

"Looks like the scope's slightly off and the laser isn't perfectly aligned, but we can fix that," Alex said, examining the position of the scope. "At least we know the laser's working properly."

"Too bad we don't have actual body armor to test it on," Martin said sourly.

"Nathan said that would come later, when the general comes back," Alex reminded him with a firm tone. "Here, why don't you take the next shot and get a feel for it."

Martin took the rifle and sighted the target, but just as he was about to pull the trigger Ivy jerked her head around and held up her hand.

"Wait," she whispered. "I hear something."

I looked around, but saw nothing. "Maybe the soldiers tracked the power surge," I said in a low voice.

Alex walked over and pulled down the target. "Come on, let's get out of here. We've done what we came to do."

As we started back towards the bridge, I noticed Martin hanging back and staring in the direction of the road. He still had the rifle in his hands.

"Martin, come on," I urged, but he didn't move.

In the distance, the low hum of a land vehicle slowly making the turn onto Monroe Avenue caught our attention.

"Martin, we have to go *now*," Alex said.

"Dammit, what's wrong with him?" Ivy asked.

Martin waved us over and sprinted toward the side of a brown building. He stopped at a clump of gnarled shrubs just fifteen yards from the road.

"Martin, are you crazy? We need to get the hell out of here," Alex shouted.

Martin turned and addressed us in a harsh voice. "Look, I'm the senior officer here and you'll follow my orders. Get over here."

We looked at each other, unsure what to do. We knew Martin was acting like an idiot, but were so accustomed to following orders within the ranks that we felt compelled to obey him.

Alex shook his head and marched over to Martin. Ivy and I were right behind him.

"Martin, you're crazy," Alex said. "If they tracked the power surge they probably know exactly where we are right now. They'll be ready to fry us the second they get here. We've got to go. Now!"

"Oh my God, here they come!" Ivy said, her voice shaking.

We were out of time and had to find a place to freeze. We ducked behind the dense branches beside Martin.

"Everyone get down," Martin ordered as he crouched low and positioned his rifle between two crooked branches in the center of the shrub. "And for God's sake don't move."

As the land vehicle approached, it was clear they hadn't detected us yet. They were moving at a leisurely pace, almost as if they were bored. The two soldiers seated in the front were well protected with full body armor and helmets.

I knew Martin would have to move his arms to aim the rifle properly, and the instant he did that the Draco would pick up the motion and know exactly where we were. From there, it would take about half a second before we were fried. I wasn't ready to die. Not tonight. My heart pounded and my eyes were glued to Martin and his rifle.

When the soldiers finally crossed in front of us, Martin shifted his arms to the left and took aim.

"Shit! Martin, don't do it," Alex hissed.

The vehicle immediately slowed down and the soldiers looked in our direction as they scanned the area. As soon as the vehicle came to a complete stop, Martin pulled the trigger.

CHAPTER 22

The driver instantly slumped over and the vehicle powered down. The other soldier briefly assessed the situation, stood up, pulled out his lightstick and began sweeping with the beam.

Ivy covered her mouth with her hand. "Oh my God," she said through her fingers.

Martin fired again and missed. "Goddamn it, the sight's off." He pulled the trigger again, and again he missed.

As the light beam moved closer, everything seemed to happen in slow motion. Alex reached over, yanked the gun from Martin's grip, and smoothly butted the stock to his shoulder. He pulled the trigger. The laser and bullet hit the body armor dead on.

The second soldier dropped his lightstick and fell over his partner. Both bodies lay slumped lifelessly across the front seats.

The night became deathly quiet. For a few moments we remained frozen in our positions, unsure what to do next.

Finally Ivy turned toward Martin. "What the *hell* is wrong with you? That was a ridiculously dangerous game you just played with our lives."

"Nothing's wrong with me. I was doing my job—destroying the enemy."

"Except you almost killed all of us in the process," Alex shot back.

Cautiously, I walked over to the dead soldiers. "Look at their helmets." A series of colored lights were blinking wildly on the sides of the smooth domes. "That can't be good."

The others moved closer for a better look.

"It could be some sort of alarm system that monitors their vital signs," Ivy said, with more hope than conviction.

"What if it's not? What if it's transmitting the information back to the outpost?" I looked around frantically. "This place will be crawling with soldiers in seconds."

"All right, time to go," Martin said. "Let's get out of here."

"Let's at least grab some souvenirs," Ivy said. She reached into the vehicle and scooped up the two lightsticks.

"And we need one of those helmets so Nathan can study it," I said, climbing into the vehicle.

Martin nodded. "Good idea, but hurry up."

I tried to remove the driver's helmet, but it wouldn't come loose. The headpiece didn't seem to twist on, snap on or lock in place. Then I realized that earpieces extended from the inside shell of the helmet to the inner ear, and they were holding it firmly in place on either side. I was burning too much time. My hand shook as I wedged it under the lower edge of the helmet, removed both earpieces with my fingers, and with a small tug pulled the helmet off. Then I grabbed a glove and pulled that off too.

Ivy looked off in the distance. "Time to get out of Dodge. Quick, they're *coming*!"

The ground vibrated and we heard the hum of several land vehicles traveling up Main Street.

As I was climbing out of the vehicle I noticed a small gold bag on the floor. It looked like the one that had held the *octcha* we'd seen months before. I grabbed the bag and stuffed it into my pocket.

We took off, running wildly, trying to stay out of range as the land vehicles crested the hill. We ran down to the canal, brushing past thick overgrowth and around trees. Branches scraped my face and arms, and my legs muscles burned as we kept up the relentless pace. Once we reached the tunnel, each person jumped in and slid recklessly down the incline. I was the last one through, and I made sure the opening was camouflaged with grasses and sod.

We ran into the living area, still high on adrenaline. Nathan and Ed looked up from their work, surprised to see us.

"We weren't expecting you back this ear—" Nathan had caught sight of the helmet and glove I was carrying. "Where the hell did you get that?"

Alex explained the circumstances surrounding the skirmish and Martin tried to defend his actions. Ivy and I added our two cents' worth and soon everyone was talking at once. But it didn't matter who said what, because Nathan was furious.

"Attacking the enemy should have been the *general's* decision, not *yours*." Nathan pointed at Martin.

"I was the senior officer and it was my call. Besides, we brought back valuable Draco equipment." Martin pointed at the helmet.

"The helmet and glove are great, yes, but that doesn't change the fact that the repercussions from your actions are going to be devastating. The soldiers are going to be crawling all over this area, and the next time we surface they'll be ready for us. Hell, for all we know they might even be able to reprogram their body armor so that our frequency wave is ineffective." Nathan threw his arms angrily in the air.

Ivy gasped as the color drained from her face. "The general's coming back tomorrow with Jon and Josh."

Alex closed his eyes. "Shit. They'll be walking into an ambush."

Nathan sat down and pressed his palms against his temples. "And there's no way to send a warning," he said in a low voice.

"We'll have to sneak out and warn them," Alex said. "We can't let them come in blind."

Nathan nodded. "You're right. We don't have a choice. Let's get to work."

CHAPTER 23

Ed continued to fit our rifles with lasers while the rest of us sat at the table and worked out a strategy to intercept the general and his team. We prepared a solution for every scenario we could think of. If the soldiers came from the west, we formulated plan A. If they came from the north, we had plan B. If we ran into a trap, we had plan C, and so on. We had six plans in total and we memorized them top to bottom.

Several hours later, after we had finalized our strategy and Ed had adapted eight rifles, the only thing left to do was sight-in the lasers. Alex handed out earplugs while I lined up dozens of books, one behind another, on the far side of the stream. On the outermost book covers, Ivy drew simple bull's-eye targets with a black marker.

As Alex test-fired each rifle, massive vibrations bounced through the cavern and caused a big stalactite on the west side to crash to the floor of the cavern. After the adjustments had been made to the lasers, I inspected the targets and discovered that the bullets had traveled through about ten inches of thick books, reaffirming the power of our weapons.

At 1200 hours we collapsed into our sleeping bags and fell into an exhausted slumber.

A short time later, Martin's loud snoring woke me. Glancing over my shoulder, I noticed that Ivy and Alex were missing again. When I looked over at Nathan, I was surprised to find him staring back at me.

"It's too noisy in here to sleep," he whispered.

I smiled. "Maybe we should've left the earplugs in."

Nathan didn't smile back. His brow was creased in the familiar worried expression.

"What's wrong?" I asked.

"I'm worried about tomorrow. The odds of us all surviving aren't good."

I understood his anxiety. Since the six of us had been living together underground, we had grown close, like a family. The idea of losing someone was unthinkable.

Nathan rolled onto his back and stared at the ceiling of the cavern. "Allie, you don't need to go tomorrow. You and Ed could stay back and let the officers take care of this one."

"I have to go. I can handle it," I said, his words offending me. "Besides, our chances are better if we all work together, you know that."

"I know you're more than capable, but having working weapons is a game changer for us. We won't be dodging the Draco anymore; instead we'll be engaging them directly. They'll suffer some losses, but so will we. That's the nature of war." Nathan turned his head and looked at me intently. "Allie, I don't want to lose you. I can't lose you."

I reminded myself: *Bravery is being the only one who knows you're afraid.*

"Don't worry, you won't," I said confidently, but deep down fear was tearing at my gut and it took me a long time to fall asleep again.

When I opened my eyes again I saw that most of the group was already up and moving around. I stretched, stood up and went over to the stream to wash up.

The mood was solemn as we went about the task of selecting dark clothing, preparing breakfast, and trying to ready ourselves mentally. The general was scheduled to arrive at 2300 hours, which gave us two hours to sit down and review the various contingencies of our plan.

While Martin and Nathan were quizzing us on our roles, Ed began to stutter and rock back and forth in his seat.

I looked at Nathan. "Maybe we need a break."

He glanced over at Ed and nodded, obviously concerned about him. "We're as ready as we'll ever be. Come on, let's wrap up."

Just before it was time to go, we carefully loaded our weapons. I tucked my hair up into a black baseball cap and hooked three spare ammunition clips to my belt.

As Nathan triple-checked each of our laser devices, I walked over to Ed to help him strap on his weapon. I noticed he was sweating. "Are you sure you want to do this, Ed?"

"Y-yeah. I'm p-positive."

"Come on, let's go," Martin said, waving for us to follow him to the tunnel.

Just before we began our ascent to the surface, Martin turned to address the group. "If anyone isn't up for this, we won't hold it against you. Now's the time to speak up."

He looked directly at Ed, but didn't get a response. Instead, Ed pushed his glasses up his nose and stood tall. I didn't expect Ed to back out. We were a team and we had each other's backs.

"One more thing," Alex said. "If anyone gets fried, let's agree now to do everything we can to bring back the body. No one becomes bug food. Period."

We silently nodded our agreement and entered the tunnel, single file.

Once we were topside, we broke into three groups. Ivy and I headed south toward the far end of the village, where we hoped to intercept the general and his team. We both had extra rifles strapped to our backs, ready to hand off to the general and his team as soon as we found them.

I looked over my shoulder to the west and saw Alex and Ed flanking us. They were darting in and out of the shadows, keeping watch for soldiers. Martin and Nathan were positioned about five hundred feet behind us, covering the rear.

Along our route we saw at least a dozen Draco and four times that many stinkbugs. The soldiers were conducting a methodical search, building by building, just like they had in Bushnell's Basin. Since we'd been taking the oil, the bugs seemed to go out of their way to steer clear of us. The soldiers were almost as easy to avoid due to their bright lights, predictable movements and humming vehicles. We simply skirted the areas where they worked and stayed out of range of the detection devices.

Ivy and I reached the cemetery at the south end at 2200 hours and quickly found a hiding spot under a dark pine tree with huge sweeping branches. The cemetery was an excellent place to wait, with old craggy trees, large tombstones, and uneven terrain. I felt much safer knowing we had teams to the north and west, monitoring the movements of the soldiers and allowing us to concentrate on intercepting the general.

We settled in on top of a bed of soft brown pine needles and waited. As the minutes ticked by, the moon slowly rose higher, illuminating the surroundings more than we liked. When midnight approached, we still hadn't seen any sign of the general's team. It wasn't like them to be late.

Half an hour later, Alex and Ed crept up behind us.

Alex pointed toward the village. "Don't go anywhere near Main Street. About thirty more soldiers arrived and brought in new equipment. We've no idea what they're up to. Once the general arrives we'll need to move fast."

Ivy nodded. "Got it." Alex reached over and squeezed her hand for reassurance.

I looked over at Ed and noticed he was blinking nervously. "Ed, are you okay?"

He absently adjusted his glasses. "I'm g-good."

"He'll be fine." Alex gave Ed a firm slap on the shoulder. "We have to return to our post, but don't worry, we've got you covered."

Ivy and I changed our position and moved to the far end of

the cemetery, hoping to find a better sight line to the general's path. We crouched in a concealed area just past a small brick maintenance building on the edge of an overgrown field, which ran parallel to the cemetery.

Fifteen minutes later, Ivy tapped me on the shoulder and pointed southeast. In the distance I could barely make out a group of dark figures traveling through the tall weeds. We waited until they moved in a little closer and we could confirm that there were three people pushing through the overgrowth. I looked at Ivy for direction.

She nodded. "Go."

Ivy covered me as I ran. The group was highly visible from several directions so I needed to intercept them as fast as possible. As I came closer, Josh and Jon spotted me and lifted their rifles into firing position. I stopped short when I saw the long barrels pointed in my direction.

The general motioned for them to lower their weapons. "Allie, is that you? What're you doing here? What's wrong?"

"We can't talk here. Follow me." I turned quickly and led them to the maintenance building.

As we approached Ivy's position, she stood up. "There's no time to explain, sir. Something's happened and the village is swarming with soldiers. We need to show you the safest way."

Ivy and I pulled the extra rifles from our backs and handed them to Josh and the general.

The general inspected the adapted rifle and then looked at us. "Are these what I think they are?"

I nodded and pointed to the lasers. "Nathan and Ed fitted

the rifles with lasers that deactivate the soldier's body armor. Just shoot as you normally would," I told Josh and the general, "but make sure you aim to kill."

"Shit," Josh said, as he carefully examined the weapon. "Are you sure they work?"

"Yeah, we're sure," I answered dryly.

"We need to move," Ivy said. "Let's go." She motioned for me to lead the way and then fell in behind the guys to cover the rear of our group.

I took the specific path we'd mapped out and rehearsed so many times. As we approached the village, I saw how dramatically things had changed since passing through earlier that night. More soldiers than I could count were moving in and out of the buildings. Hundreds of stinkbugs, with their heads to the ground, were roaming the streets sniffing for human scent.

Another flurry of activity was taking place around two enormous gray vans parked in the middle of Main Street. They were almost two stories high and took up the entire width of the road. I'd had never seen vehicles like that before. They were obviously meant to transport something quite large, but I had no idea what that could be. According to our intel, it was much too early for the Draco masses to arrive.

Dark gray clouds sporadically covered the moon, giving us brief periods of darkness that we used as cover to cross the main roads. We were closer to the soldiers' activity than we cared for, but we had no choice if we wanted to get back to the tunnel.

Staying in the shadows, we made our way around the

construction site where the old library was once located. The Draco had erected the framework for a new building, which looked about eight stories high. The area seemed to be deserted.

We moved past the building and through the rear lot, which bordered the canal, and ran smack into two fully armed Draco soldiers standing near the water.

CHAPTER 24

The soldiers immediately looked our way, alerted by their motion detectors. They appeared as surprised to see us as we were to see them. Then I saw the familiar blue vapor tubes and almost laughed out loud. Slackers.

The soldiers hesitated for a fraction of a second, giving us plenty of time to shoulder our rifles. They dropped the blue tubes and reached for their lightsticks, but it was too late. In the blink of an eye, we opened fire and the two Draco soldiers dropped to the ground, bodies jerking.

I estimated that we put six to seven holes into the chest of each soldier, leaving no doubt that they were dead. But now we had bigger problems. The racket we'd made by repeatedly firing our rifles had echoed throughout the entire village.

"Run!" the general shouted.

As we bolted, I heard the hum of land vehicles powering up. Two seconds later the high-pitched Draco alarms sounded.

We ran down to the canal and into an area that was dark and overgrown with foliage. Our tunnel wasn't far, but I worried about the other teams that were covering us from a distance.

Ivy pointed to the hill above us. "Take cover, two soldiers on the ridge."

We quickly crouched behind an old park bench just as the deadly light beam began its sweep in our direction. I thought for sure this was the end, but then I heard the crack of rifles from the far side of the hill. When the two soldiers fell to the ground I knew it was Martin and Nathan.

"Move! Now!" the general shouted.

We bolted to the west and that's when I saw it; the deadly glow was just a few feet in front of me. I stopped short and started to back up. Shit. I wasn't ready to die.

The beam was about to touch my feet when something shoved me hard and propelled my body a good six feet to the side. I smacked the ground on my back and everything went gray for a moment. My chest hurt and it took a few seconds before I could breathe again, but despite my disorientation I still clutched my rifle tightly to my side.

When I looked back to where I'd just been standing, I saw a body on the ground. The side of his face was burned and the arm of his sweatshirt was charred. It was Alex.

I quickly glanced around and saw the rest of the team scrambling for cover. Then I saw Josh on the ground about thirty feet away, a thin wisp of smoke rising from his body. I thought I was going to be sick.

"No!" Ivy screamed as she ran to Alex's side.

A deep croaking laugh came from a few yards away. It

was a horrible sound that I will never forget; mocking and authoritative.

I looked up. A Draco soldier had a lightstick pointed directly at me, with his long finger dangerously near the strange markings on the side. His black eyes narrowed as he croak-laughed again. Then he spoke in his native tongue.

"Your friend is dying and you cannot help him because you do not know how. We own this world now and we will cleanse this place of your kind. Are you prepared to die?"

His need to brag gave me the extra seconds I needed to move the barrel of my weapon a fraction of an inch to the right. My confidence was renewed as my finger began to apply pressure to the trigger.

Slowly and clearly, I replied in his language, "I am not dying tonight."

As his eyes widened at my response, I pulled the trigger. The laser worked its magic and the bullet instantly penetrated his glove, causing the lightstick to fall away. In shock, he clutched his injured hand. His head jerked toward me, the smug expression gone from his face.

I moved the barrel again and shot both of his feet. He instantly fell to the ground, writhing in pain.

"You said I can't help him because I don't know how," I said in Draco as I pointed my rifle toward his head. "Tell me how." He had given me a valuable clue and I intended to learn more.

He stared back at me with disbelief and in pain, but he said nothing. It was apparent that he wasn't going to cooperate, so I didn't hesitate and shot his right knee. He let out a deep groan and grabbed his leg, blood oozing from multiple tears in his body armor.

My palms were sweating as I pointed my rifle back at his head. "Tell me now or you are dead."

The soldier clucked in frustration. I saw the fear in his eyes and recalled what the inspector had said about going to purgatory before being assigned a mate. "My lightstick ... the last insignia."

Nathan and Martin came over the crest of the hill and ran down to us.

"They're right behind us," Martin said, breathing hard. "We have to get the fuck out of here."

Nathan pointed his rifle at the soldier while I picked up the lightstick and frantically tried to find the last insignia, whatever that was. I knew Nathan and Ed had spent some time studying the lightsticks, but they hadn't learned how to use them since most of their time had been devoted to our weapons. I looked at the peculiar hieroglyphics along the barrel and punched the last one. A yellow beam instantly discharged from the end. My hands were shaking and I had no idea what I was doing, but I didn't see how I could make things any worse.

Ivy was leaning over Alex, trying to find a pulse. "No, oh God, no." she cried.

"Ivy, move away from Alex," I yelled.

Ivy looked at me with a tear-streaked face and quickly backed away. I swung the beam over to Alex and prayed there was something more than simple lightwaves traveling through the yellow haze. After a moment, it automatically shut off.

Ivy quickly crawled back to Alex's still body and placed her head on his chest. "I think his heart's beating," she sobbed. "Quickly, Allie, go! Try to save Josh."

Soldiers crested the hilltop. They couldn't see us in the blackness of the shadows, but I knew they could detect our movements.

"There's no time," the general shouted.

He and Jon picked up Josh and started to run. Martin and Ivy grabbed Alex's arms and dragged him along behind.

Leaving the wounded soldier behind, Nathan reached for my hand and we ran like hell until we rounded the bend that led to our tunnel. One by one, we fell into the opening in the ground. After everyone was through, I camouflaged the entrance and skidded down the steep incline.

At the bottom, the general turned to me. "Did they see us come into the tunnel?"

"I don't know," I answered with a shaky voice. "It's possible."

"We can't take any chances. Jon, collapse the tunnel," he ordered.

Jon pulled several explosives from his belt and scrambled back up the incline.

I turned toward Alex and Josh, where they had been gently placed on the limestone floor. The odor of burnt flesh and smoldering clothing was overwhelming. Josh's body had taken the full impact of the light and he was almost unrecognizable.

The general bent down to listen to Josh's chest. "He isn't breathing. Allie, try the lightstick."

As he moved back, I activated the yellow beam and directed it toward Josh.

When the light went off the general leaned over and listened for Josh's heartbeat again. He shook his head. "Try it again," he yelled.

Jon scrambled down the tunnel just as I was trying the yellow beam for a second time. The explosives detonated behind him, sending rocks and dust spilling out around our feet, but we barely noticed it.

The general listened again for Josh's heartbeat and shook his head. "Again, Allie."

I touched that last symbol one more time, but nothing happened. I tried several more times, but there was nothing.

Nathan closed his eyes in despair. "The capacitor's drained. And it can't pull energy from the power source down here," he said in a low voice.

For a long moment we felt paralyzed as we stared at our friend's charred remains. Josh was gone and there was no way to bring him back.

I threw the dead lightstick to the ground as tears spilled onto my checks. Jon dropped to his knees and began to sob at his brother's side. Ed hugged himself and rocked back and forth. Martin kicked the limestone wall and swore up a storm. Nathan remained motionless, staring at Josh's lifeless face, and Ivy held tightly onto Alex's unconscious body.

The general closed his eyes and hung his head.

The smell of death was back.

CHAPTER 25

It had been twenty long months since the invasion and I thought about how much I had changed. I felt old and detached from the person who used to be Allie. The inspector had said that I had compassion, but I wasn't so sure anymore.

"Hello," I had whispered tentatively.

He had turned his head slowly and looked me. He didn't look well. He was much too thin and his skin was a sickly yellowish color.

"Are you sick? Please, tell me what you need and I'll try to get it for you."

"No. It is not possible."

"How do you know for sure unless you tell me? At least I could try to get it for you."

He looked horrible and I was more than a little worried about his health. He may have been our enemy, but I had got to know him; I didn't necessarily want him to die.

He made an odd clucking noise and somehow I knew that was the sound of frustration.

"What I need can only be obtained from our soldiers. You will not be able to secure it." He closed his eyes, as if speaking the words had exhausted him.

"I could try."

His eyes flew open. "That is the trouble with your species, you do not think logically. Any attempt you made to secure *octcha* would result in your death."

I shrugged. "Well, thanks to your species I live with death hanging over my head every day. That's nothing new."

The inspector clucked again.

Nathan entered the room and set his bag down. "What's going on?" he said.

"Your friend is thinking about going to the outpost to secure *octcha* for me," the inspector told him. "I advised against it."

Nathan looked at me questioningly.

"If he doesn't get it, I'm worried he'll die," I explained.

Nathan eyed the inspector. "Is that true?"

"Yes."

"What exactly is *octcha*?" Nathan asked as he took a seat.

"It is a nutritional food source derived from the octchalangic plant that thrives on our home planet, although the processed form is green and spherical." The inspector looked at me. "You should not attempt this."

"I don't want you to die. Besides, if I want to help you, that's my choice."

"It should not be your concern." The inspector looked at me quizzically. "Why do you think this way?"

"I don't know," I said honestly. I had no idea how to answer his question.

"That is illogical."

I stood up. "No, not really. It's called caring. I just don't want to see you die."

Nathan stood next to me. "That's just how she is. Allie looks out for those she cares about."

The inspector was quiet for a moment and seemed to be deep in thought. "This is what we call *loctorpac*, or what you would call compassion. Among my people it is considered a rare and special gift."

Later that night Nathan and I had made plans to find the *octcha*, but we never had the chance to act on them because the next time we went to visit the inspector he was gone.

I had cried when Martin and Jackson dumped his body unceremoniously into the sewers. Martin said I was being ridiculous, but the truth was that the inspector was a lot like us—trapped in an impossible situation.

After tending to Alex's burns and wrapping up Josh's body for burial, we spent the next hour answering the general's questions regarding the events that led up to Josh's death. He quizzed us relentlessly and got to the root of the matter in short order.

"Goddamn it, Martin, what the fuck were you thinking?" he shouted as he paced back and forth. "Shit. The problem is that you *weren't* thinking. This isn't Martin's personal revenge campaign. Goddamn it, you're the leader of a team, and I expect you to *act* like it."

Martin stared at the ground as the general gave him the

well-deserved tongue-lashing. Although we knew that Martin was ultimately to blame, when it came right down to it we all felt responsible for the loss of our good friend.

The general looked at each of us. "Let me get this right," he said. "Since yesterday we've killed six Draco. Is that correct?" He raked his hand through his hair and sighed. "That was fucking sloppy work and *not* how we should've gone into combat with our new weapons."

He turned his heated gaze toward Nathan. "Not to mention that we should have killed seven soldiers, not six. You *never* should've have left that wounded soldier behind, Nathan. I'm damned sure that at this very minute he's giving his superiors valuable intel."

Nathan looked at the ground and nodded.

The general sat down at the table and put his head in his hands for several minutes. Other than the sound of the flowing stream, the cavern was silent. We knew when to keep our mouths shut.

Finally, in a low voice, he said, "Nathan, do you think the Draco will rework their body armor technology based on what happened?"

"I suppose they could try, but I doubt it. At this point we don't pose a big enough threat to their overall plan. Plus, as long as they don't have one of our lasers in their possession, they won't be able to reverse engineer the process." Nathan hesitated. "Of course, that's just my best guess."

"He's coming round," Ivy said from Alex's side.

The burns on the side of Alex's face and arm had been bandaged, but the rest of his skin was uncovered and almost dead white. He blinked several times and reached up to touch the bandage on his face. "What's going on?" he said in a raspy voice.

"You're back in the cavern," Ivy said gently. "Don't try to move."

He tried to sit up anyhow, but a wave of dizziness pushed him back. "I think I'm going to be sick." He leaned to the side, threw up several times and rolled back onto his sleeping bag. "I feel like shit. What happened?"

"You were hit with a lightstick. You need to take it easy," the general answered softly.

"A lightstick?" He looked confused. "Shouldn't I be dead?"

Ivy nodded. "You should be, but Allie discovered how to reverse it."

Alex looked at me. "Thanks, Allie," he said weakly.

I walked over and stood next to Ivy. "It was the least I could do, considering you saved my life. I should be thanking you."

The general bent down next to Alex and looked at him with concern. "We need to have Doc Hiro look at you. As soon as things quiet down out there, I'll go get him."

Time passed slowly while we waited for the Draco activity topside to subside. Still feeling the effects of Josh's death and the general's reprimand, Martin was sullen and spent a lot of time staring at nothing.

Nathan and Ed redirected their focus to studying the lightsticks. They seemed to feel that given time, they could develop a defense against the deadly weapon, although their initial tests hadn't yielded anything interesting.

Alex was up and around within a few days, and although he said he felt better, he still looked unusually pale. Jon, on the other hand, seemed to be slipping into a deep depression. He refused to eat and wouldn't participate in group conversations. Losing someone close, not to mention his twin, was almost too much for him to bear.

The general kept the rest of us busy by laying down a challenge to locate another exit from the cavern. This small project managed to keep us busy for about four days, but after multiple trips to the far ends of every winding cave and crevice, we found nothing and lost interest.

I had the added job of checking on the Draco activity every few hours. By the end of the week, the Draco's huge transport vans had moved out and headed towards Rochester, and the constant patrols dwindled. As long as we timed it right, we were finally able to leave the cavern.

Using the exit located in the basement of the house on Lincoln Avenue, we made the journey to the cemetery and buried Josh next to Colonel Twist. It was hard to say goodbye to another friend, but we were thankful we could lay his body to rest and have a short service. Burying our own had become important to us.

After the service, the general issued a formal order forbidding the shooting of any more soldiers. "It's critical that we lie low and develop a meaningful plan before we attack again," he said.

The next night the general made the decision to leave for the Bristol hills and retrieve Doc Hiro. Jon insisted on accompanying him as guard, despite his depressed state. The general eventually agreed, but only because he thought it might help Jon if he stayed busy.

Within forty-eight hours of their departure, the rest of us quickly became irritable and bored. To pass the time we debated what the general had meant by "meaningful plan."

Martin crossed his arms over his chest. "Ultimately, we need to kill as many of them as possible. We need to send a clear message that we aren't going to take any more of their crap."

Nathan rolled his eyes. "We wouldn't last ten minutes if we did that. Let's not forget that they still have the superior technology. Plus, we still haven't developed a defense against the lightstick."

"To win a hundred battles is not the height of skill. To subdue the enemy without f-fighting is," Ed said. "You know, from *The Art of W-War*."

"But we'll never subdue them without fighting," Martin insisted.

Ivy stood up. "No. What I think the general meant is that we need to try things like negotiation, or bargaining. Or maybe scare them into leaving somehow."

Martin laughed. "Yeah, right. That's a great idea. We'll just *scare* them into leaving."

Ivy gave Martin a sour look.

Nathan glanced over at me. "Allie, what do you think?"

I shrugged. "I don't think the general wants to go to war. I think he's hoping for a better solution."

"Like what?" Martin asked snidely. "There is no other solution."

Even though the cavern was huge, it was starting to feel very small. After our long and somewhat heated discussion, Martin wandered off and the rest of us decided to play a Monopoly marathon.

As we played the game, I thought about how the person who won always owned the most property. I wondered if the Draco owned Earth now, or if we still owned it. Didn't you technically still own something even if it was stolen from you?

About halfway through the game we heard Martin's distant shouts echo across the ceiling, "Hey, I think I found something. Come over here!"

"Where are you?" I yelled back.

"Northeast, past the old tunnel," his voice reverberated.

Nathan shook his head and laughed. "You guys can go. Ed and I have work to do."

I looked at Ivy and shrugged. "Should we go? Might kill some time."

"Sure, why not." Almost as an afterthought, she grabbed a rifle and tossed the strap over her shoulder.

I grabbed a lantern and we headed northeast, hoping Martin had stumbled upon something interesting. As we walked past the old tunnel, the memory of Josh's death was still fresh and raw to me. It was strange how I could almost smell the odor of burnt flesh, even though I knew it was long gone.

Martin was nowhere in sight.

"Where are you?" I shouted, sending off an annoying series of echoes.

"Keep going and then look up to your left," his voice bounced back.

I didn't particularly like this section of the cavern because it was tricky and uneven. The floor had abundant stalagmites and slippery inclines, making our travel slow. But regardless of the difficult terrain, we followed Martin's echoing voice until a dim light coming from high above caught my eye. As I focused on the faint glow, I saw Martin perched on a rock ledge, waving down at us. The light had been coming from the small lantern he had tied to his belt.

"How the hell did you get up there?" Ivy asked.

He pointed down. "Come over here and look directly below me."

We climbed over a challenging rock formation and found ourselves under the ledge where Martin's feet dangled a good twenty feet over our heads. As I looked up, I saw he had climbed up a series of niches that were carved into solid rock, sort of like rungs on a ladder.

"I'm going higher," he said, as he turned and began to climb. When he reached the limestone ceiling, he continued through a three-foot-wide opening. As he disappeared through the hole, the subtle glow of his lantern was the only thing that remained.

A few minutes later, his words sounded as if they were coming through a tin can. "You won't believe this!" he shouted. "Come on up."

I reached over and put my hand on one of the rungs. "This thing is probably a hundred and fifty years old. Do you think it's safe?"

Ivy shrugged. "It might be another way out. Let's try it."

I took a cautious step onto the rock ladder and started

climbing. I tried to picture how this exit might have been used a century and a half ago. The image of women in long awkward dresses trying to scale the slippery steps somehow made the climb easier. If the Underground Railroad slaves could do it back then, surely we could do it now.

"It's a damn good thing neither of us is afraid of heights," Ivy commented as she climbed below my feet.

As we passed through the hole in the ceiling, the passageway became tighter and I had to concentrate on making sure my feet found secure footing on each rung. After about twenty more vertical steps I saw Martin crouched in an opening that appeared to have been carved into the limestone.

"Come on in," he said as he extended his arm.

I took his hand and stepped into the opening.

"Keep going." Martin pointed over his shoulder.

I took one careful step and as my eyes adjusted to my surroundings, I couldn't believe what I saw. "This is amazing!"

CHAPTER 26

Martin had pushed a heavy bookshelf out of the way to gain access. When I stepped past the bookcase I was back in our old home, in the familiar basement of the yellow house on Main Street.

Ivy stepped to my side and smiled. "Well, I guess this explains why the basement was always so drafty."

"Hey, I think there might be some blankets in the bunkroom we could use," I said as I started to cross the basement. "As long as we're up here, let's grab them." But as soon as I reached the bunkroom door, footsteps clunked across the floor above our heads.

"Fuck," Martin whispered, as he looked toward the ceiling.

"They're heading for the stairs," Ivy said, pulling the rifle from her shoulder.

Martin quickly pushed us into the bunkroom and squeezed

in behind us, leaving the door open a crack so we could see what was going on. One by one the soldiers filed down stairs. Just our luck.

Martin whispered a warning. "Don't move. They have helmets."

Three Draco soldiers in full body armor and packing weapons entered the basement and sat down at our old table. One of the soldiers tipped up a bag and emptied it onto the floor. Inside was gold jewelry, human jewelry. The precious gemstones were scattered carelessly across the floor. The largest soldier crouched down and sorted the contents into small mounds, while the other two seemed to be calculating the value of each pile.

I strained to listen to their words and decipher their meaning. They seemed to be debating how much they could get for the gold on the open market and agreed that they needed to find more to make the sale worthwhile. Undoubtedly the gold had been taken from dead bodies, but I couldn't begin to imagine why it would have value to the Draco.

The soldiers were just about done with their business when the bigger one looked over at the bookcase, which Martin had pushed aside. He stood up and looked curiously at the dislocated unit. As he moved closer, his comrades also became interested and rose from the table.

"If they find the tunnel, we're screwed," Martin whispered without moving his lips.

We knew all too well what would happen if the soldiers went into the cavern. The tunnel would lead them straight to Nathan, Alex and Ed, not to mention all of our research. My knees began to shake as I thought about losing everything we had worked for and cared about.

The big soldier poked his head behind the bookcase, looked down into the tunnel, and croaked a series of what I believed were curse words.

Crap.

I quickly sized up the odds of three lightsticks against our single rifle. I knew I was the best shot among the three of us, but even if I did my best I'd be lucky to take out all three of them before they retaliated.

"Allie," Ivy whispered, shoving the rifle into my hands. Her movement instantly registered with the soldiers and they spun around and looked in our direction.

I didn't think; I just reacted. Bracing myself against the doorframe, I sighted the targets and consecutively shot the two smaller soldiers. The short distance made for easy shots. One soldier fell back across the table, while the other crumpled to the floor. The big soldier, standing next to the opening, went for his lightstick but was dead before his hand had the chance to touch it. His body slammed against the bookcase and hit the floor with a noisy thud. The shots were easier than I could have hoped for.

Martin ran from the bunkroom to examine the bodies, while Ivy and I hovered closely behind. The arm of the soldier lying across the table twitched slightly and we all jumped. Martin turned and yanked the rifle from my grip, took aim and shot the body three times.

"Martin, stop wasting bullets," I said, annoyed. "He's not going to get any deader."

"What should we do with the bodies?" Ivy nudged the soldier on the floor with her boot. "We can't leave them here."

She was right. If the others found them they would start another search and compromise the general's return. We couldn't have that happen again.

"Their helmets are starting to blink," I said anxiously. "Whatever we do, it has to be fast."

Martin crossed the room in three big strides, grabbed the arm of the big soldier and dragged him towards the opening of the tunnel. Then he got down on all fours and grunted as he pushed the huge body through the opening. After the soldier disappeared into the hole, he took a deep breath. "Goddamn, he was heavy."

Together we pushed the other two soldiers through the opening, one after another. The bodies fell, bouncing off the rock formations and crumpling onto the stone floor of the cavern below.

"There's a lot of blood on the table," Ivy pointed out.

"We don't have time to clean it up. Quick, let's find something to cover it with," Martin said.

I ran into the bunkroom and grabbed a blanket while Ivy picked up the piles of gold jewelry and stuffed them into her pockets. After I stretched the fabric over the tabletop, Martin topped it off with a small pile of books placed neatly in the middle.

Martin waved us over to the tunnel. "Come on, let's go."

A few minutes later we were back in the cavern trying to explain the situation to Nathan, but he wasn't accepting our excuses.

"You did *what*?" he yelled.

"It wasn't our fault," I said defensively. "Martin discovered a new exit and we were just checking it out. We had no way of knowing the soldiers would show up."

"That doesn't change the fact that you disobeyed direct orders," Nathan snapped. "And you ..." He stared at Martin. "You were the senior officer!"

"Let's stay focused on our biggest problem," Alex said calmly, "which is dealing with the dead bodies."

Ed wrinkled his nose. "Well, they can't stay down here or they'll start to r-rot and stink up the whole p-place."

"Maybe we could put them in the sewers, where we put the stinkbug," I suggested. I didn't mention that the inspector was also in the sewers, because I hated that he had ended up there. The sewer wasn't exactly purgatory, but it was close.

Nathan nodded. "Yeah, that's probably our best option."

We spent the next two hours carefully stripping the soldiers down to their gray undergarments, and organizing their body armor and devices. Nathan selected the items he wanted to keep, carefully labeling and cataloging each piece in his leather journal. This new assortment of Draco gear would give Nathan and Ed months of research opportunities.

Seeing dead alien bodies up close was a weird experience. I didn't feel guilty or even sorry for them. I now thought of the Draco as something that needed to be killed. Which was exactly the way they thought of us.

"Here's some additional junk to study," Ivy said, pulling the collection of gold jewelry from her pockets and making a neat pile on the worktable.

Nathan touched the jewelry, picking up a wedding ring and examining it closely. "Why would the Draco want gold? It doesn't make sense."

Ivy shrugged.

Once the bodies were ready to be transported, we wrapped them in blankets and tied them up for easy carrying. Alex and Ed stayed behind while we hauled the soldiers topside. The village was quiet and dark, and so far no alarms had sounded. We quickly crossed to the main road and located a manhole cover. The process of prying up the cover and unceremoniously dumping the bodies took about three minutes. When I looked over at Nathan, he looked sad. I knew he was also thinking about the inspector.

As we were heading back, the ground rumbled and a loud buzzing noise came from the direction of the Draco outpost. We ducked behind the old coffee shop and watched as another large transport van glided into the village, turned onto Monroe Avenue, and headed for Rochester.

Martin shook his head. "Those things are almost the size of apartment buildings."

"Anything that huge can't be good," Ivy added.

Six hours later, while the village was still quiet, the general and Doc Hiro arrived safely in the cavern. Within minutes, the general was seething mad and his face was bright red.

"I don't fucking believe it!" He threw his arms in the air; his eyes blazed with anger. He spun around and pointed his finger directly at Martin. "This is unacceptable, Martin. I'm gone for three days and you let it happen again?"

I stepped forward. "It was my fault, sir. I killed the soldiers." I didn't want Martin to take the blame for something I'd done.

Ivy stood next to me. "No, it's my fault. I handed Allie the rifle and asked her to shoot them."

"This has nothing to do with either of you. Martin was the officer in charge and he has to take responsibility." The general locked eyes with Martin. "I'm transferring the commanding officer position of this station over to Alex. I'm sorry, Martin, but that's how it has to be."

Martin just nodded and looked at the floor, but I could tell he was furious.

Doc Hiro had just finished examining Alex, and they joined us. Doc smiled and gave Alex a slap on the back.

"He's in good shape considering he recently returned from the dead," Doc said. "The burns have already started to heal. He'll have some scarring, but it shouldn't be too bad. More importantly, I don't see any signs of organ damage. If I had to guess, I'd say the yellow beam of light had some sort of residual healing effect."

"That's good to hear," the general said. "Alex, going forward, you're now the CO of this post."

Alex looked embarrassed and nervous. He glanced over at Martin and back at the general. "Yes, sir," he said quietly.

CHAPTER 27

22 MONTHS POST INVASION
16 YEARS OLD

The next few months passed quickly as we fell into a routine around helping Nathan test out theories, making brief supply runs, and going on recon missions. The Draco had permanently stepped up their patrols, using rotating shifts every three hours, and seemed to have a heightened awareness of their surroundings. We were forced to keep our topside activities short and spend more time than we liked underground.

We learned little from the few recon trips we were able to make, although we did pick up on grumblings that the soldiers were falling further behind in their preparations for colonization. We discovered that the original twenty-four-month schedule had been pushed to thirty-six months due to the 'lag in suitable preparation of the planet surface.'

The delay wasn't hard to understand. After all, the Draco had to create a functioning global power network, establish worldwide agriculture for the cultivation of *octcha* and other plants from their home planet, and, of course, eliminate the indigenous population.

The general, Jon and Doc Hiro visited once a month, bringing updates from the Bristol hills regarding the rest of our sector. Jon stuck close to the general and didn't talk much, but he seemed to be coping somehow. We learned that Laurie had planted several large oregano gardens and had subsequently produced enough oil to supply our sector for over a year. We also learned that Squirt had grown a full two inches, although he still wasn't talking. I hadn't seen Squirt in over a year and I missed him.

So far there had been no sign of the Draco entering the Bristol area and the general was hopeful they would be able to stay through the winter, but we all understood it was only a matter of time before the sector would be forced to move on.

As the leaves turned vibrant shades of orange, red and yellow, I also turned sixteen. My body had completely changed and I no longer looked like a boy. I was taller and had filled out with curves. And ever since we'd found Nathan in the cavern, I had a renewed faith in God. I had come to think of myself as a soldier for humanity. I felt as if I had a purpose in life, and that purpose was to fight.

For the six of us, the cavern had become our home, and, with the exception of Ed, our team was healthy and strong.

Ed's fear of the Draco had grown into a full-blown phobia. He refused to go topside and hadn't left the cavern in four weeks. Doc Hiro had told him it wasn't healthy to spend all of his time in the damp underground air, but the mere mention of going to the surface threw Ed into a meltdown. We quickly learned that it was better not to even bring up the subject. As long as we kept Ed focused on research, he almost seemed like his old self.

At the end of October, the general sat down with Nathan and Ed to review their progress. The table was covered with several Draco gadgets, a helmet and a lightstick. I hovered nearby and picked up as much of the conversation as I could.

"Well, we've achieved one important thing," Nathan said. "We've learned how to deactivate a helmet after taking down a soldier."

"Excellent," the general said.

"And we're developing a theory around the physics of reflection," Nathan stated.

The general looked at him. "And the physics of reflection is …"

"Well …" Ed scratched his head. "We've worked out that the lightstick emits an infrared beam, which carries an obscure wave that somehow disables the electromagnetic field given off by the human heart. It's a similar concept to the carrier beam principle we've used with our lasers. We think the mystery wave is shorter than a gamma wave, but we haven't been able to isolate the frequency. But the good news is that we know how to reflect the infrared waves."

The general shook his head. "What does that mean in terms I can understand?"

Nathan tried to contain a smile. "If we can block or sufficiently reflect the infrared waves, we might be able to make the more destructive mystery wave follow the same pattern."

"Okay, that makes sense," the general said. "What do you need to get this done?"

"More time to research infrared reflection, and supplies to build multiple prototypes. And eventually we'll need to test it out." Nathan frowned. "At some point we'll have to test the prototype version with an actual person."

The general looked concerned. "Okay. Well, let me know when you're ready and I'll worry about finding a human guinea pig. Did you manage to test the lightsticks on other animals? Does it work?"

"Yes and no. It doesn't work on birds or insects, but we had some luck with rats. I have a suspicion the lightsticks are specifically tuned to a frequency that only works on mammals."

The general picked up the lightstick and looked it over. "So that means they probably won't work on the Draco."

"Probably not," Nathan said. "But we won't know for sure until we try."

"Put that on your list of priorities. But remember, even though it's critical that we find out, we can't let them know what we're doing. We'll have to do that test as discretely as possible."

The general set the lightstick back on the table and shook his head. "It's hard to believe this single weapon has almost wiped out the entire population of our planet."

Two nights later, seven of us changed into dark clothing, collected our weapons, and grabbed two Draco lightsticks. We were ready to test the lightsticks on the soldiers.

Just mentioning going topside had caused Ed to hyperventilate, but it turned out to be nothing a paper bag couldn't fix. We left the cavern through the Lincoln Avenue exit as Doc Hiro waved goodbye from the bottom of the steps. Ed and his paper bag stayed in his work area; he refused to even watch us leave.

We broke up into three groups to search the village for soldiers. The general and Jon took the south end, while Nathan and Alex traveled east. Ivy, Martin and I took the north side. Since we were simply scouting the area and not conducting a kill, we agreed to meet at the old yellow house in one hour to review Draco activity.

The village was desolate. We roamed the area methodically for fifty-five minutes, finally circling back to the house. We were the last group to arrive, and no one had anything of interest to report.

"Just our luck. You can never find a soldier when you need one," Alex said acidly.

The general looked at his watch. "We need to move in closer to the Draco outpost. Martin, take your team and approach from the southeast. Alex and Nathan will cover you from the east, and Jon and I will cover you from the west. Remember, we don't want to engage the enemy, we only need to find one or two soldiers working alone to test the lightstick." He paused and looked directly at Martin. "You will kill on my orders only. Don't blow it this time, Martin."

Martin nodded. He had been on his best behavior since the last Draco killing, and none of us wanted to see him get into trouble again.

As we made our way through the thick overgrowth, a frigid breeze came up from the west. I realized the cold air would keep the majority of the soldiers inside tonight. When the colonization actually took place, I wondered what kind of Draco civilians would get stuck with the unpopular northern climates. Maybe lower-class citizens, I decided. Or even criminals.

We cut through a residential area and approached the outpost from the southeast side. The first building we came across was a large three-story structure surrounded by parking lots. Several land vehicles were parked outside, but since the area appeared quiet we settled in behind some trees to wait it out. Despite the cold, we knew if we waited long enough a soldier would eventually emerge.

For two hours we waited, listening to the eerie repeating *hoot* of an overactive owl. We were stiff and bored, and my nose was cold.

"Maybe we should try another location," Ivy suggested.

"Not unless the general gives the order," Martin said firmly.

Ivy nodded in agreement. Then she quickly turned her head and pointed down the road.

In the distance, we heard the buzzing noise of a transport vehicle. We stayed frozen in our positions as the gigantic machine approached. The ground vibrated from the sheer size of the thing. It slowed to a stop in front of a small building two lots down from where we were conducting our watch.

The transport vehicle remained motionless for several minutes. Then a large door near the front end slid open and bright light spilled onto the street. Two soldiers emerged and walked over to the small building, pausing in front of the main door. Within seconds their helmets began to blink, the door opened and they disappeared inside.

I looked to the west where the general and Jon were positioned. The general motioned for us to move in closer.

I led the way as we carefully skirted the parking lot, circling until we found a good enough hiding spot behind an old dumpster, not far from the transport vehicle. Once we settled in, Martin pointed across the street to where Alex and Nathan were taking up a new position behind some trees to better serve as our backup.

Being extra cautious, we waited another ten minutes. Other than the creepy hooting owl, everything remained deathly quiet. Finally the general gave us the signal to check out the vehicle.

Martin crouched down and approached the unit slowly while Ivy and I covered him. The door had been left open, so he squinted against the bright light and took a look inside. After a few seconds he pulled back and turned toward us, shaking his head. He looked toward the general for instruction and received the signal to go inside the vehicle.

Ivy and I exchanged anxious glances. We had no idea who or what was in there; for all we knew there could be a hundred soldiers waiting with lightsticks.

Holding his rifle in the ready position, Martin entered the vehicle. He vanished for about a minute, which seemed like an eternity as I counted down the seconds in my head. When he reappeared, he motioned for Ivy and me to follow.

Ivy nodded and we approached cautiously. We were well armed, but I still felt uneasy; something about the huge vehicle was just wrong.

Martin held his finger to his lips and waved for us to follow him. We walked up a slight incline and entered a good-sized space. At first the intense light hurt my eyes, but once they'd adjusted I saw two chairs and dozens of panels with strange markings, indicating that this was the command center for the vehicle. The air was stale and had a metallic smell.

We followed Martin through another doorway that led into the interior of the vehicle. The space was huge and unlit, but our eyes were used to darkness and adjusted within a few moments. Rows and rows of rack shelving, about three feet apart, reached up to the ceiling. There was something on the shelving, but I couldn't quite make it out what it was. Martin waved us over to take a closer look.

I cautiously approached the closest rack and saw a young girl lying on her back. She looked about nine or ten years old. Her eyes were closed and she had tubes coming out of her nose. I reached over and felt her wrist; it was warm and her pulse was strong. I turned and nodded silently to my comrades.

I looked around. Every single shelf was occupied by a sleeping child. It seemed like the Draco had gone to great trouble to make sure their cargo was kept alive, so I doubted the occupants were on their way to become bug food. But still, this room looked like some kind of sick experimental lab and the thought of what these kids were headed for terrified me.

Alex's voice came through the doorway low and clear, breaking the tension in the air. "Head's up. They're coming back and they'll be in motion-detection range in about thirty seconds."

We moved back to the control room. "How many?" Martin asked.

Alex held up two fingers.

"Okay, cover us. We'll take them in here."

Alex nodded and ran back to his position on the far side of the street.

Martin motioned for Ivy and me to go back into the dark storage area where we wouldn't be seen. Ivy crouched down on the right-hand side of the opening and positioned the lightstick at her side. Martin and I crouched down on the left side of the doorway with our rifles ready.

The soldiers entered the vehicle and immediately took their seats at the controls. Martin nodded to Ivy. She touched the first insignia on the lightstick, which instantly sent an intense orange beam towards the soldier sitting on the right. I held my breath as the light engulfed his entire body.

Nothing happened.

CHAPTER 28

Within a fraction of a second, both soldiers had spun around and were looking in our direction. The beam of light continued to radiate with no effect. The soldiers' confused expressions rapidly turned to anger. The one on the left reached for his lightstick.

Wasting no time, Martin shot him twice. The first bullet tore through his hand and the second penetrated his shoulder, causing the solider to drop the lightstick and fall back against the control panel. His partner looked on fearfully, unsure what to do next.

Slowly and clearly I spoke in the alien language. "Don't touch your weapons or you'll both end up dead."

As blood dripped down the arm of the injured solider, it began to form a small puddle on the floor. His expression was one of disgust as he spoke to me in Draco. "So what they say it true. You're nothing more than primitive barbarians."

"Really?" I responded. "What does it matter if someone kills by spilling blood or by shining a light? I don't see the difference. Dead is dead."

"Ivy, go ask the general how he wants us to handle these assholes," Martin said without taking his rifle's sight off the soldier.

Ivy quickly exited the transport and the four of us found ourselves in an awkward silence.

Martin took a deep breath. "Ask about the children."

I took a moment to work out the translation in my head. "Where are you taking the children?" I croaked in the alien tongue.

The soldiers remained silent. Apparently they needed convincing before they would talk.

"If you don't answer, you'll die," I added.

"The information won't do you any good," the wounded soldier said in a monotone.

"Try me."

"You can't get them back. They're ours now, just like this planet. You won't survive."

I almost felt like I was having a conversation with a robot. "Then you have nothing to lose by answering my question. Unless of course you *want* to die."

I forced a fake smile on my face, attempting to appear like a cold-blooded killer, which in a sense wasn't far from the truth.

The soldier's jet-black eyes narrowed as he considered my proposition. Martin moved in close and held his rifle inches from the soldier's chest for additional motivation.

The soldier clucked in frustration. "We're taking them to what you call *has-put-ol*—"

Just then Ivy entered the transport and quietly announced, "Kill them. General's orders."

As our attention shifted briefly to Ivy, the soldier on the right began to reach for the control panel. I caught the movement out of the corner of my eye and immediately pulled the trigger. The bullet hit him in the head. The alien jerked in his chair and crumpled to the floor.

The wounded soldier lunged for his weapon with his good hand, but Martin shot him between the eyes long before he reached his goal.

I looked at the soldiers in a heap on the floor, surprised by how much blood spilled from their wounds. The pool of red around their bodies was growing larger every second. It looked like a gory crime scene from a movie and my gut did a flip-flop. I wondered if the soldiers had mates somewhere out in the galaxy or if they were headed to purgatory.

Both helmets began to blink rapidly. Ivy looked over at me, concerned.

The general and Jon entered the vehicle.

"We're going to have a shit-storm on our hands if we don't get those things off and deactivated," the general said.

I nodded and reached for the helmet of the closest soldier while Ivy worked on the other one. It only took a moment to get them off and unplugged from their power source, but it was a messy task, given where they'd been shot. By the time we'd finished, we both had blood smeared all over our coats.

Alex and Nathan covered our backs as we dragged the

bodies out of the transport and over to a wooded area. We couldn't leave the bodies behind with our bullets in them, which would be like leaving a calling card. Instead we disposed of the remains and left the Draco to guess what had happened to their transport drivers.

We paused alongside a large tree to catch our breath.

"It's too far to drag the bodies to the vault," the general said. "We'll take them to the residential area on Alpine Drive and drop them in the sewers."

It took only a few minutes to get to Alpine Drive, but it took us another ten minutes to find a manhole cover that we could pry open, and another forty-five seconds to dump the bodies. I worried that we were taking too long to finish the task. By now, the Draco should have found the bloodbath we left behind and begun searching for the missing soldiers. We all knew we needed to get the hell out of there.

As Martin and Alex struggled to replace the heavy cover, Ivy looked anxiously toward the sky.

"What is it?" I asked her.

"I don't know," she said, as she continued to look upward. "There's an unusual sound."

Just as we all looked up, two jet aircraft flew by so fast that at first I wondered if I'd really seen them. Then we heard the sonic boom, and there was no doubt.

With excitement in their eyes, Nathan and Alex ran over to us from the trees where they had been on the lookout for enemy soldiers.

"Were they ours?" I asked, looking back up at the empty night sky.

Nathan smiled. "I think they were F35s. Supposedly the most advanced fighters our air force had at the time of the invas—"

Before Nathan could finish his sentence three Draco airships flew soundlessly overhead at a high rate of speed, heading in the same direction as the F35s. If we hadn't been looking up, we would have missed them completely.

Since most of the Draco operations in our area were performed on the ground, we rarely saw the oval-shaped airships. Plus, their flight was silent, and if you weren't looking directly at them as they passed overhead you would never know they were there. Generally the Draco military used the aircraft for long-distance transportation around the planet. This time, following directly after the F35s, they were unmistakably in combat mode.

The general motioned for us to get moving. "They're headed south. Let's get to higher ground for better visibility."

As we ran toward the village, we spotted two columns of smoke rising from the far side of town. My hopes sank. Then we saw the Draco airships circle back toward the smoke, moving much slower now, presumably to inspect the crash area.

Nathan shook his head. "Our guys didn't stand a chance."

The general nodded in agreement. "We need to move fast. The Draco will have ground troops all over this area looking for survivors. We need to get there first."

Wasting no time, we broke into two groups and headed south. Nathan, Ivy and I took off, sprinting, because we were the fastest and would make better time than the others. The general and the rest of the group followed as our backup.

We ran us fast as we could, but I worried that we would be too late to find survivors. The pungent smell of burning jet fuel was overwhelming as we approached the Pittsford Burial Grounds. Two streams of dense black smoke were coming from an open field just past the cemetery. We quickly wove our way through the tombstones and over to the edge of the open field, where we had a good view of the twisted, smoldering wreckage.

"No one could survive a crash like that," Nathan said in a low voice.

"Look," Ivy said, pointing up at one of the larger pine trees.

A broken tree branch was draped with a piece of torn fabric and several heavy strings. The lightweight material moved with the night breeze, causing the fractured limb to creak.

We searched directly under and around the tree but found nothing. I touched a nearby tombstone and it felt sticky. I looked at my hand and it was covered in blood.

"He can't have gone far, not losing this much blood," I said, holding up my hand to show my friends. I wiped my hand on some pine needles. I'd had my fill of blood tonight.

"Okay, let's split up and search the cemetery," Nathan said.

We each went in a different direction. The grounds were difficult to search, given the tall weeds and countless headstones, but I knew that if I'd been injured and needed to hide quickly I'd go behind one of the larger monuments.

It took me less than a minute to find him. He sat on the ground, motionless, leaning back against a granite pillar dated

1789. He had dark hair, a strong build and appeared to be in his early twenties. I knelt down and lightly touched his shoulder. Slowly, he turned his head and looked at me. Blood dripped down the side of his face from a bad gash along his hairline, and the arm of his uniform was cut up and bloodied.

The pilot opened his mouth to say something, but nothing came out.

"You're going to be fine," I whispered.

"How ..." the pilot struggled to say.

"Don't try to talk." I took his good hand and gave it a reassuring squeeze. "Don't worry, we won't leave you here."

The sharp click of a handgun, about two inches from my ear, made me freeze.

"Don't fucking touch him," a deep voice threatened.

CHAPTER 29

I put my hands in the air slowly and turned. He wore the same outfit as the other pilot, but he was older, probably in his mid-thirties, and he had more stripes on his shoulder.

The man blinked a few times, as if he was trying to focus. "Is this some kind of trick? You're just a kid."

With my hands still in the air, I stood up and looked him squarely in the eyes. "I haven't been a kid for a long time. Look, your friend's hurt and needs help."

"I'll be the judge of that," the man said. "Who are you and what the hell are you doing here?"

Ivy and Nathan silently appeared behind the man and pointed their rifles at his back. For effect, Ivy chambered a round in her rifle, the distinctive sound not lost on the older airman.

"I'll ask you nicely to lower your gun, but I'm warning you, I'll only ask once," Ivy said coldly.

The man grimaced and slowly lowered his pistol to the ground. As he put his hands in the air and turned, his mouth formed a tight line when he saw Nathan and Ivy, and their firepower.

"Who are you?" he asked.

"We're the ones who're about to save your lives," Nathan said as he lowered his rifle. "Are there any other survivors, besides you and your friend?"

"No, just me and my fellow officer on this mission. Both our aircraft were shot down like toys." The pilot shook his head. "We didn't stand a chance, it was a miracle we got this far."

"Where did you come from?" Nathan asked. "And why did you come on this stupid suicide mission?"

"That's classified."

The general and the rest of the team made very little noise as they approached. The pilot seemed startled as new faces emerged from the shadows.

"Ivy, what's the status?" the general asked.

"Two survivors. One injured."

"Okay. There's no time for introductions. The Draco are already in the village with land vehicles. We need to go, all of us. *Now*."

"Wait a minute, we're not going anywhere with you," the pilot said stubbornly.

"You won't last two minutes without us," the general said. "The Draco will be here any minute and they'll bring hundreds of stinkbugs. Where do you think you're going to hide?" The general didn't try to hide the irritation in his voice. "You have ten seconds to make a decision. Come with us and live another day, or stay here and deal with the enemy on your own."

The pilot's jaw clenched. "All right, we'll go with you."

Martin and Jon picked up the injured man and carried him, and Nathan led the way back toward the village.

"Where are we going?" the pilot asked. "Shouldn't we be moving in the other direction, away from the enemy?"

Martin narrowed his eyes. "If you want to survive, shut the fuck up and follow us."

We silently made our way through the dark back streets of a residential area, ducking from house to house, shadow to shadow. The hum of land vehicles moving down an adjacent street gradually grew louder.

"Something's wrong. The land vehicles are getting closer," Alex whispered. "They shouldn't have a lock on our whereabouts from this distance."

Nathan spun around to face the pilot. "Do you have anything on your body that might be giving off electromagnetic energy?"

"Uh, just my watch, it has a tracker in case we were shot down." The pilot stripped the watch from his wrist. "Sorry."

"That's bullshit. Can the air force really be that stupid?" Nathan said. "What about your friend? Does he have anything that might get us all killed?"

Martin and Jon immediately began searching the injured pilot for anything that might contain a battery.

"He's clean," Martin said.

Nathan grabbed the watch from the pilot's hand and threw it as far as he could across the street.

"Move it," the general said. "A few more seconds and they'll be tracking our motion."

We took off running between the houses and around buildings, always staying on the darkest paths. The rest of our journey was routine and smooth. We easily avoided the land vehicles and quietly entered the house on Lincoln Avenue. Ivy and I went to work removing just enough bricks so we could pass through the opening that led to the cavern. Nathan lit a candle and we all followed him down the dark steps. After everyone was safely through, I replaced the bricks carefully and precisely.

At the bottom of the stone staircase the pilot stopped and looked around. "This is amazing," he said, his eyes wide.

I shrugged. "It's home."

Martin and Jon carried the wounded stranger over to our living area and lowered him onto an air mattress. Doc Hiro rushed over to examine him.

The older pilot eyed Doc suspiciously as he went to work on his comrade. "Does he know what he's doing?" the pilot whispered to me.

"Yeah, he does," I said.

"Don't worry, I know what I'm doing," Doc said without looking up.

"I don't want you doing anything to him without checking with me first," the pilot snapped. "You barely look old enough to be a college student."

I didn't understand where the pilot's distrust was coming from. Weren't we supposed to be on the same side?

Ed approached cautiously, pushing his glasses higher up his

nose. "Wow," he said, "strangers. Where are you guys from?"

Before the pilot could answer, the general said, "I suppose we should make some introductions."

"Agreed." The older pilot nodded and extended his hand toward the general for a formal handshake. "I'm Major Christopher Davis and that's Lieutenant Ian McGregor."

The general shook the major's hand firmly. "I'm General Henry Reynolds, and this is Colonel Alex Harris and Colonel Martin Conner."

"You're a general?" The major's smile was laced with condescension as he turned to Alex and Martin. "And you're colonels? You expect me to believe that you're part of the military?"

"You can believe whatever you like," Henry answered smoothly. "This is our world and this is how we function."

Major Davis held up his hands in mock surrender and smiled again. "Okay, whatever works for you guys. You've managed to stay alive this long, and that's no small feat."

The general made the rest of the introductions and asked everyone to have a seat at the table.

"Major Davis," he said, "the only thing we know about you is that you're air force. Why don't you start by telling us about your mission?"

"Sorry, that's classified," the major said. His face became a controlled blank slate and he was no longer smiling.

"Okay. Then how about simply telling us what's going on in the world? We've been living in the dark for almost two years. We want to know what's going on out there."

The major frowned. "There's not much to tell. What you've

seen in this village is about the same as it is everywhere. The Draco have armed forces situated in every city and town in the world, and they're continuing to eradicate the few surviving humans as they make preparations for colonization."

"What's our military doing about it? You're here, so obviously something's in the works," The general responded.

"That's classified." The blank slate reappeared.

"Okay. What about the government? Is any of it still intact?"

"That's classified."

The general took a deep breath, making an obvious effort to calm himself. "Is there anything you can tell us that isn't fucking classified?"

The major shrugged. "Not much."

"Are there others like us?" I asked hopefully.

"There are others, but not like you. We occasionally find pockets of survivors, usually starving, wounded or suffering from severe PTSD, and we try to transfer them to a safe place."

"A safe place? And where's that?" Martin asked with an edge to his voice. "Oh wait, let me guess, that's classified."

"That's correct."

Doc Hiro walked over and cleared his throat. "Sorry to interrupt." He looked at Major Davis. "Lieutenant McGregor's lost quite a bit of blood, but he'll be fine. I removed seven pieces of shrapnel and gave him thirty-five stitches. I also gave him something to help him rest, so he'll fall asleep in a few minutes."

"That's good to hear." The major stood up and shook Doc's hand. "Thank you for your help."

Major Davis seemed truly grateful. He excused himself and went over to see the lieutenant. I went with him, intensely curious about these strangers, the first people outside of our group we had seen for so long.

The major squatted next to the lieutenant. "Hey, Mac, how do you feel?"

"A little torn up, but better. I'm a little lightheaded too."

The major smiled. "Who are you kidding? You've always been that way."

The lieutenant's eyelids were heavy and he returned a weak smile. "What the hell happened? The last thing I remember was seeing a girl. A pretty little thing. She said she was taking me somewhere. What happened, was she real?"

"Yeah, she was real. Now get some rest, we'll talk later."

Within moments the lieutenant had closed his eyes and faded into a restful sleep.

I smiled inwardly. I couldn't recall anyone ever calling me pretty. We didn't talk about those kinds of things. Not in this life.

The major stood up, noticed me standing behind him and gave a brief nod. Then he glanced in the direction of Nathan's workspace, his eyes opening wider as he focused on the table. His jaw dropped slightly.

"Is ... is that a Draco helmet?" he whispered.

"Yes," I said.

He strode over to the table and touched the helmet as if he couldn't believe it was real. He scanned the table. The small gold bag caught his eye. He picked it up and dumped out the little green balls.

"And this ... is this real *octcha*?"

The general saw the major and came over in time to catch the major's question. He shook his head. "I'm sorry, Major, that's classified," he said with a sideways grin.

"And this?" The major held up a lightstick. "This is a death ray. Where did you get this? How did you get it?"

"That's classified as well," the general said firmly, crossing his arms over his chest.

The major's mouth hung open but nothing came out.

"You might want to take a look at these as well, Major," Nathan said, coming over and setting a large box of body armor on the table.

Major Davis used great caution as he touched the grey material. He looked at the general with a hard expression. "*No one* has access to these things. You'd better start explaining, General Henry Reynolds."

"No, actually I don't have to explain anything." The general remained calm.

The major's face became red, but he controlled his tone. "Oh, I think you do. We're at war to save the human race, and you have valuable intelligence which needs to be turned over to the military for study."

The general's eyebrows shot up in mock surprise. "Are you saying that you *don't* have any of this?"

"That's classified."

The general slammed his fist down on the table. "Then you can take your 'classified' bullshit and shove it up your ass."

I stood silently to the side, too stunned to talk. I'd never seen the general get this ticked off. But more importantly, I couldn't believe that after all this time, after we'd finally found other humans, we couldn't seem to communicate with them.

After a long, awkward silence, Nathan spoke up. "Look, Major Davis, we're all in the middle of the same conflict. The only difference is that in some ways we seem to be managing it more successfully than our military. We haven't survived just by chance. If you expect intel from us, you'd better start sharing information and stop treating us like kids."

The major looked over at the lieutenant, now asleep, and nodded. "I believe you're right."

CHAPTER 30

We all sat back down again, and this time I hoped for a better outcome from our talks.

"You first," the general said to Major Davis in a polite but challenging tone.

"Okay." The major hesitated for a moment and took a deep breath. "We're in bad shape. We lose soldiers constantly and most of our weapons are ineffective. It's about as bad as it could be."

"Have you tried nukes?" Ed asked.

The major nodded. "We've had limited success with nuclear weapons. The Draco don't want the planet torn up by nuclear weapons, and they definitely don't want the after effects of radiation. So each time we've used them—and we've only fired off two—within seconds they tracked down the origin and wiped out our stations. We lost more humans than it was worth."

"Where are your stations?" the general asked.

"In underground bunkers, much like yourselves, but don't ask me where. That much I won't give away."

"What about the government?" Nathan asked.

"It still exists in a small way. What's left of the government's also located underground. The president and secretary of state are still alive and leading the resistance, but the vice president, secretary of defense and most of the cabinet have perished."

A sense of optimism crept into my thoughts. I tried to push it back, but my mind wanted to know that there were others fighting for survival just like we were. There was resistance somewhere out there and we could potentially work together. We were no longer alone and that changed everything.

"Why were you flying over our village tonight?" the general asked.

"We were on a recon mission. Over the last few months there've been reports of disruptions in this area. Our orders were to determine the source of the disturbance."

Nathan shook his head. "You had to know that you were on a suicide mission. Your jets couldn't possibly outmaneuver the Draco airships."

"We knew that. But something was going on up here that wasn't happening anywhere else. We received intelligence that the Draco military had concerns over humans gaining a small foothold in this area." The major looked directly at the general. "Are your people responsible for that?"

The general shrugged. "Possibly."

"You mentioned pockets of survivors," I said. "Where are they now?"

"Some are in underground bunkers, but most have moved to extremely remote locations in Canada." The major turned his attention back to the general. "I have some questions for you. I'm very interested to hear exactly how you acquired your little collection of Draco paraphernalia."

We spent the next two hours explaining how we began with Colonel Twist, how we had gone on countless recon missions, how we had captured a Draco inspector, how we overcame the stinkbugs, and how we had researched ways to create working weapons. Although we had lost friends along the way, and our victories had been infrequent, we still *had* victories, and that set us apart from the major's experience.

The general handed the major a laser rifle.

The major examined the weapon. "How did you build these? How did you learn how to deactivate the body armor? And why isn't the power surge detected when you fire the laser?"

Nathan shot the general a look and shook his head. I knew Nathan wouldn't want to divulge the secret to his most important discovery. Not yet, anyhow. In a way, I guess we were as distrustful as the major.

"We're not ready to disclose that information just yet," the general said.

"Fair enough," the major said. "But I'd greatly appreciate seeing a demonstration at some point."

The general nodded. "Absolutely. But by now it'll be daylight topside and we need to get some rest. Tomorrow night we'll take you out for some firsthand experience."

Nathan frowned. I knew he wouldn't like the idea of going topside while the Draco activity was still heavy.

. . .

It was Ed's turn to cook dinner, and he prepared his own version of tuna casserole. He had learned to do wonders with canned goods and a camping stove.

"I haven't had tuna casserole for years," the major said, taking his second helping.

After supper, Ivy and I arranged an air mattress and sleeping bag for the major. He seemed pleased with his accommodations.

"You've done a nice job here," he said to us. "It's very comfortable down in this cave."

"Just let us know if you need anything else, Major," I said, handing him an extra blanket. "You might need this. It's chilly down here, at least until you get used to it."

After six hours of shuteye, it was my turn to prepare breakfast. I got up early, washed up in the stream, and made my usual pot of oatmeal with brown sugar, and an extra-strong pot of coffee. One by one our team members rose, helped themselves to breakfast and took a seat at the table. When the major got up, Nathan showed him where to wash up and invited him to breakfast.

I saw the lieutenant sit up and rub his eyes, so I poured a cup of coffee and walked it over to him. Off to the side, I noticed Nathan watching me closely. His brow was wrinkled and he had an odd expression.

"Hello," I said to the lieutenant, holding out the steaming cup. "Would you like some coffee?"

"Yes, please." He took the cup, placed it to his lips and took a sip. An instant grimace formed on his face and he almost choked. "You actually drink this stuff?"

"Every day." I smiled and laughed.

He looked at me curiously. "You're the girl I saw in the cemetery."

"Yes. My name's Allie."

"I'm Ian. Ian McGregor. I guess I have you to thank for saving my life."

"No, not me. You have Doc Hiro to thank for that." I pointed over to the table where Doc was sitting. "He removed the shrapnel and sewed you up."

"Well, I suppose I should thank him properly." The lieutenant attempted to stand, but he wobbled a bit and almost lost his balance. I reached out to help support him and he put his arm around my shoulder. "I guess I'm just a little stiff," he said sheepishly.

After he'd taken a few steps and stretched his muscles, he was fine. The general seemed happy to see him up and around, and invited him to join the group for breakfast. Lieutenant McGregor personally thanked Doc Hiro and then introduced himself to the rest of the group.

After breakfast I overheard the major briefing the lieutenant on the stories we had told him yesterday. He had a tone of skepticism in his voice that didn't sit well with me. A short time later the general arranged the demonstration mission, which I hoped would clear up any remaining distrust.

Based on our shooting skills, Alex and I were assigned to go with Major Davis and Lieutenant McGregor for the weapons demo, while Martin and Ivy would serve as our cover.

Alex and I gave our guests a quick lesson in the use of the laser rifles, and Ivy gave them each a dose of oregano oil.

"I hope this stuff works," the lieutenant said, pointing to the small bottle. "I feel like I'm throwing myself into enemy hands."

"Just stay with us and you'll be fine," I reassured him.

Lieutenant McGregor leaned over. "That's the second time you've told me I'd be fine."

I smiled. "Because you *will* be fine, as long as you do what we tell you."

I felt Nathan's eyes on me again. I had the distinct feeling that he didn't like it when I spoke with the lieutenant. It suddenly occurred to me that he might be jealous and the thought took me by surprise. We weren't kids anymore, and adulthood had come at us fast and hard. Sometimes Nathan became so wrapped up in his work that he didn't seem to notice that I'd grown up.

I went over to the supply area and grabbed my M4. As I was putting the rifle strap over my shoulder, Nathan came up behind me.

"Allie, please be careful," he said just above a whisper. "I don't like this. This isn't an ordinary recon mission. The soldiers will probably still be on the hunt for the pilots."

"Nathan, you know I'll be careful," I said, looking him in the eye.

He reached down and took my hand. "You know, I couldn't take it if anything happened to you." His blue eyes were filled with worry and fear. It was a look I'd seen dozens of times when we were young, when he would run over to our house to escape the brutality of his own home. We were just kids back then, but the expression in his eyes was the same.

"Come on, Allie, we're ready to go," Martin shouted impatiently from across the cavern.

"Please be safe," Nathan said and let go of my hand.

"I will." I leaned over and gave him a kiss on the cheek. He smiled and winked back at me.

CHAPTER 31

Martin and Ivy were already topside checking for Draco activity when Alex and I led the pilots up the stone steps to the exit on Lincoln Avenue. The rest of the group stayed down below to work with Nathan and Ed on defense strategies.

As our mission leader, Alex chose to take us across the metal canal bridge to an observation spot near the Pittsford Farms Dairy. He quickly found a good vantage point on a small hill behind several large trees, not far from the road. We settled into a patch of overgrown shrubs, which offered additional screening. Martin and Ivy positioned themselves alongside the building behind us, where they could provide cover if needed.

Alex looked at Major Davis. "I'm guessing we won't have to wait too long since the soldiers are probably still looking for you both," he whispered.

But as the hours slowly crawled by, the village remained quiet. The cold night air made my fingers stiff and gave me a runny nose. Major Davis and Lieutenant McGregor killed time by asking Alex and me questions about our former lives and how we all ended up together. It felt strange to dredge up the old memories, which were normally considered taboo to discuss. I found myself talking mostly about Nathan and how we had grown up together.

After a while, the conversation shifted and I began to ask the pilots about their lives. Major Davis had a wife and two children, who were in a mysterious Canadian camp. Lieutenant McGregor was single and had lost his entire extended family in the invasion. We also learned that the pilots were part of a garrison somewhere south of us, yet they still refused to disclose the location. I didn't blame them. The fewer who knew the location the better.

A brisk breeze caused the nearby trees to creak as a cold front swept into the village. I sniffled and felt a tickle in the back of my throat. I couldn't wait to get back to the cavern to warm my hands over the camping stove.

Soon a crack of thunder gave way to a steady drizzle, which the breeze blew in sideways. Moments later Martin and Ivy ran over.

"Stinkbugs were just dropped off on Washington Road. Looks like they're headed this way," Martin whispered. "The land vehicles shouldn't be too far behind."

Martin and Ivy fell back to their position alongside the building.

Noticing the major and lieutenant look apprehensively at

each other, I said, "The oil works, don't worry. The stinkbugs won't even know you're here. You'll be fine."

The lieutenant smiled at me and then focused his attention on the bugs, which were marching up the road. As they came closer, they made a distinctive shift to the far side of the street and passed by as if we didn't exist.

"I might just have to start believing you. Those things actually seem to be avoiding us," the major said with wonder in his voice.

Down the road, a single land vehicle made the turn onto Main Street and headed in our direction. It had only two occupants and they were in full gear. As luck would have it, it was the perfect scenario for our demonstration. But it wouldn't be so lucky for the soldiers.

"Excellent. Only one vehicle tonight," Alex whispered.

Alex and I carefully aimed our rifles.

The major placed his hand on my shoulder. "Are you sure about this?"

"Yes," I said without hesitation.

Alex adjusted his position. "Okay, Allie, we have to take them out before they reach motion detector or lightstick range. You take the one on the right and I'll take the one on the left. Wait until I say fire …"

Just as the vehicle came into range, we heard gunfire behind us. I spun around and saw three streams of orange light crisscrossing at the top of the hill near the building where Martin and Ivy were stationed. I watched as Ivy fired back blindly toward the deadly beams. On the street below, the land vehicle slammed on its brakes and pulled up onto our hill.

"Allie, cover Ivy and Martin and I'll take these two," Alex shouted.

I tried to find a target through my sight but visibility was low and I couldn't see anything. I heard two shots explode from Alex's rifle. I knew he hadn't missed his objective. Alex never missed.

I shot a couple of blind rounds in the general direction that Ivy was shooting in. The major and lieutenant raised their rifles and also fired off a few rounds. Martin and Ivy knew they were dangerously close to the lightbeams, so they used the covering fire to sprint south, toward the canal.

In the distance I heard additional land vehicles powering up.

"We need to move," I said. "Now!"

We ran past the stalled vehicle containing the two dead soldiers Alex had shot.

The major paused to view the lifeless soldiers. "I don't fucking believe it," he said breathlessly.

"Keep moving," I yelled over my shoulder.

We sprinted across the street and stopped alongside a brick building that was once a fancy hotel. We took a moment to catch our breath, watching the beams of light on the other side of the road continue their dance on the hill. Fortunately we were now well out of range.

Two more land vehicles came up the street at high speed. I looked to Alex for direction.

"We have more than enough firepower to take them," Alex said. "Major, lieutenant, are you up for it?"

"Hell, yeah," the major responded.

Alex gave rapid instructions and we positioned ourselves against the brick wall. We had a significant advantage since our rifles easily had double the range of a lightstick, but it was still critical to take out the soldiers before they came close enough to get a lock on our movements. Visibility was still low as the wind whipped the ice-cold rain sideways.

I looked through the scope, made a rough adjustment for the conditions and hoped it was accurate.

"Fire!" Alex shouted.

Four rifles fired simultaneously and four soldiers instantly slumped over. Their vehicles powered down to a stall. It almost seemed too easy.

"This is a fucking miracle," the major shouted, holding his rifle out in front of him.

I tapped Alex's shoulder and pointed across the street to where the deadly orange beams were now sweeping closer to us.

"Time to get out of here," Alex said, waving for us to follow him.

He headed toward the metal bridge that would take us back across the canal, but I grabbed his sleeve and pulled him back.

"What is it?" he asked.

I looked around. "Something's not right. I thought I saw a small flash of light just past the bridge."

The lieutenant put his scope up to his eye and surveyed the area. "Just past the bridge. Take a look at ten o'clock."

We looked through our scopes and saw three land vehicles parked in inconspicuous spots just past the bridge.

"They're waiting for us," I said. "They're herding us like animals."

"Let's try another bridge," Alex said.

Alex took us around a back lot and we followed the canal until we came to the bridge on Monroe Avenue. We crouched down near the bank of the canal and scanned the landscape through our scopes.

"Looks like the same scenario. I see four more vehicles and at least eight soldiers," the major said. "Obviously they're expecting us to enter the village by crossing one of the bridges."

By now the driving rain had soaked through our clothes and I was beginning to worry about the moisture affecting our weapons.

"We'll have to find a spot to swim across," Alex said.

The major looked around. "Agreed, but we'll need to find a more remote area. Someplace with good cover away from the action in the village."

We went about half a mile further down the canal, where the trees and undergrowth were much heavier. We spent several minutes surveying the area for signs of enemy soldiers. When we determined that the area was safe, the major and Alex slid down the concrete embankment and into the murky brown water. Fortunately for us, the canal hadn't been maintained and it wasn't at full capacity. Holding their weapons above the waist-high water, they waded across while the lieutenant and I stood guard. Once they were on the other side they scanned the area again and waved us over.

The lieutenant and I slid into the bitterly cold water. I was shorter than the men, so the water came up to my chest. I struggled to hold my gun above my head while keeping my balance on the rocky bottom. The piercing chill of the stagnant water stung my skin and made my teeth chatter uncontrollably. My chest felt tight and the last few steps were a struggle to take.

"Pull her out," I heard the lieutenant say. "Quickly. She's freezing."

They dragged me out of the water. My muscles ached and I felt cold right down to my bones.

"Come on, we have to move," the lieutenant said as he grabbed my arm and pulled me along.

Once we began moving again, I started to warm up and feel a little better. We ran through the trees and around buildings, stopping only to ascertain the location of the soldiers. Along the way we saw additional land vehicles moving into the village, as well as another transport van traveling toward Rochester.

After zigzagging our way through the shadows, we finally made it back to Lincoln Avenue and into the passageway that led home. As we descended into the cavern, our worried teammates were there to meet us. They caused quite a commotion with greetings and questions.

"You gave us a scare," the general said. "Ivy and Martin came back almost an hour ago. We were about to send out a search party."

While the rest of the group hurried across the cavern to get dry clothing and hot coffee, Nathan intercepted me at the bottom of the steps. He had a blanket in his hands, which he wrapped around my shoulders.

"I was really worried," he said, his blue eyes piercing into me. "Are you all right?"

I nodded. "Just a little c-cold." I pulled the blanket tighter as an involuntary shiver shook my shoulders.

Nathan put his arms around me and hugged me. His warmth seeped through my wet clothing and felt wonderful. I put my arms around his waist, soaking in his body heat, and held on tightly.

"Martin told us they lost track of you," Nathan whispered in my ear. "I was so scared. I thought something had happened to you."

"It's okay. We made it back safely."

Nathan pulled back and looked at me with concern. "It's not okay, Allie. We might be doing all right in one-to-one combat, but we don't have the ability or firepower to take on the entire outpost."

I nodded. "You're right. Nathan, they were prepared for us this time. It was like they were expecting us."

He nodded. "We have to be more careful. We can't afford to take chances like that." Nathan's eyes were pleading. "Allie, I can't lose you. You're more than just my best friend."

I opened my mouth to say something, but Nathan leaned down and kissed me. It was soft and lingering, a perfect first kiss.

I had always loved Nathan as a friend, but over the last year my feelings had evolved into something more. Now I knew that Nathan felt it too. We'd been through so much together, both before and after the invasion. We understood each other and we were undyingly loyal to each other.

I slipped my arms around his neck and kissed him back with every ounce of feeling I had.

Ivy's voice echoed across the expanse of the cavern, "Should I pour you guys some hot coffee?"

We didn't answer.

CHAPTER 32

Now that the pilots had seen our weaponry in action, they were much more open with their conversation. The remainder of the night was filled with speculation regarding our common enemy. We compared our knowledge to theirs, and gained new insight into the Draco soldiers' operations. We told the pilots about the inspector and the intelligence we had gained from him, and they informed us that although the resistance had not developed a weapon with which to fight the Draco, they had managed to decipher a little of the difficult language as well as learn interesting facts about the alien culture.

The major leaned forward as he spoke and we listened intently. "There's something else you should be aware of. We've learned that the Draco have an aversion to combat. I'm guessing this has something to do with the information you gave us regarding their fear of going to purgatory if they haven't found a mate. But regardless of the reason, it's been reported that they hire mercenaries. We haven't seen any evidence of this, but it's something to keep in mind as human survivors become more difficult to eliminate."

"Where would they find mercenaries?" I asked. I didn't like the idea of creatures that could do worse to us than what the soldiers had already done.

"We don't know. But we do know there are many other species of extraterrestrials out there. In fact, Earth had been unknown to the Draco until almost a century ago. They learned about our remote location from the Elnaki, a race that's been traveling the galaxy for millennia."

"Exactly how long have you known about the existence of aliens, Major?" Ivy asked accusingly.

"And how do you know about the Elnaki?" Nathan asked.

The major sighed. "Top-ranking military officials have known since the forties. Since then, we've had an agreement with the Elnaki that we would ignore each other. This has worked out well for everyone. They felt that we were too primitive to bring into their fold, and we knew that the general population couldn't handle the truth about ETs."

"Apparently the Draco weren't in on your little agreement with the Elnaki," the general added.

"No, they weren't. But the Elnaki warned us about other dangerous species. They promised to give us a heads-up if an aggressive race ever threatened our region of the galaxy."

"The Elnaki probably don't know what's happened here," Nathan said. "The inspector told us that the Draco had to wait for decades until our quadrant was free of interstellar traffic before they could begin the invasion."

To me, the Draco strategy seemed like something a child would try when stealing candy from the corner store—simply wait until no one's looking and then take what you want.

The major sighed. "The bad news is, according to the Elnaki there's more than one race that operates like the Draco. There are others out there who will take over a planet by wiping out the indigenous population and using the remaining infrastructure as a quick fix for an over-population problem."

"Cheap bastards," Martin said under his breath.

"Isn't there any kind of law or universal justice system in the galaxy?" Nathan asked.

The major shook his head. "We don't know. But based on what happened here on Earth, I doubt it."

As the night progressed, our conversation shifted to what we had seen on the transport vehicles. The soldier had told us they were taking the children to the *has-put-ol*, which we finally deciphered to mean "hospital." Strong Memorial Hospital seemed like the most logical place. It was also a huge teaching establishment with seven hundred and fifty beds, countless outpatient centers, highly specialized labs, offices, and state-of-the-art research facilities.

"I wonder what the Draco are doing with the children?" the lieutenant said, voicing the thought that we all had.

Nathan shook his head. "Could be anything, but I'm guessing slave labor. Kids would be easier to train than adults for long-term use."

By the time we were ready for bed, my throat was raw and I was beginning to cough. Doc Hiro pulled me aside to check me out.

"Well, you've got a low-grade fever and swollen glands. Looks like you're getting an old-fashioned cold." He handed me two white pills. "Take these and call me in the morning." Doc laughed at his own joke.

I popped the pills, swallowing them dry, and crawled into my cozy sleeping bag.

After six hours of sleep, I woke up with a splitting headache and thick congestion in my chest. As I staggered over to the coffee pot and grabbed an oversized mug, I noticed that Nathan was already at work on his latest project, and that I was the last person up.

"How are you feeling?" Nathan asked when he saw me. "You look tired."

I shrugged. "I'm getting a cold."

"Come on over. I want to show you something." He grinned and winked at me.

I held the coffee mug with both hands, allowing the heat to warm my fingers. The cavern felt particularly cold and damp as I watched Nathan take something out of a tattered shoebox.

"A present, for you." Nathan smiled and handed me my SIG Sauer. He had altered it so that it now had a small laser attached to the rail under the barrel.

As I felt the weight of the gun, a ripple of excitement overcame the fog in my head. "Is this what I hope it is?"

"Yeah. It's for close-range targets." Nathan pointed to the

new attachment. "The laser's small and only good to about forty feet, but it should do the trick."

"It's perfect." I smiled and gave Nathan a hug.

He put his arms around me and held tightly. The warmth of his body made me remember yesterday's kiss and I wondered when he would kiss me again. I hoped it would be soon.

The general headed in our direction and Nathan pulled away. "Allie, there's something I want to talk to you about," he whispered. "Maybe later?"

"Sure," I said.

"What's this I hear about Allie's pistol?" the general said.

Nathan and the general spent the next hour discussing the new mini-laser with the team. The pilots felt that having a handgun equipped with the laser was another big win and wanted to know when more could be produced.

"Do you have enough supplies to go into production?" the general asked Nathan.

Nathan shook his head. "No, and I don't know how we're going to get them. We've already exhausted everything here in the village."

The major looked at the general. "The developments you've made here will be critical to the resistance. I think we should return to base, tell our superiors what you've done here and start production of more laser weapons. We already have a good stockpile of scientific supplies, as well as an outstanding scientist who has two PhDs."

The general raised his eyebrows. "If you want more information from us, I think we should know where your base is located."

The major and lieutenant looked at each other. "You're right." The major cleared his throat before continuing. "Our base is below the old Seneca Army Depot. We currently have sixty-three men and women, some civilian and some military, working together to learn as much as we can about the Draco. And as I mentioned before, we have a brilliant scientist, who I'm certain would want to meet Nathan and Ed."

"Wasn't the Depot closed down over a decade ago?" Ivy said.

"It was," the major said. "But at one time nuclear weapons were stored there, which meant networks of underground bunkers were constructed as fallout shelters. Our operations are eighty feet below the surface, well out of Draco detection range."

Martin pulled out a wrinkled map of New York and flattened it out on the table. "The Seneca Army Depot's over fifty miles away," he pointed out sharply. "That's too fucking far to travel in one night. Not only would we have to pass right by a Draco base in the town of Geneva, but we could end up crossing the last few miles in the open in daylight."

The general leaned over the map and shook his head. "We can't risk a journey like that unless we're heavily armed. With our current inventory, we don't even have enough weapons for one per person. There has to be another way of getting what we need."

"There is," Nathan said. "The Rochester Institute of Technology would have the supplies. It's only about nine miles from here, but enemy traffic's also much heavier in that direction."

I didn't like where the conversation was going. The institute was close to the city of Rochester, where a huge contingent of soldiers resided.

The general ran his hand through his hair. "Major, as much as we want to see your facility and share Nathan's knowledge with your team, our chances of surviving a fifty-mile trip on foot would be a whole lot better if we were properly armed. I propose we make the trip to the Depot only when we can supply each person with a rifle and a handgun. If we can get the supplies from Rochester, it won't take long to produce the weapons."

The major nodded reluctantly. "I have to admit, I'd also feel better about making the trip if I was well armed. We'll do whatever we can to help."

"We'll need a full day to work out what we need," Nathan said.

Ed put this head down and began scribbling notes.

"Just let us know when you're ready," the major replied.

After dinner, my cough had progressed to a hacking sound that wouldn't go away. Doc Hiro listened to my chest and said I was developing a nasty cold, no surprise there. He gave me some vitamin C tablets and told me the damp environment in the cavern was probably making my symptoms worse.

At bedtime, I couldn't seem to find a position in my sleeping bag that didn't make the tickle in my throat worse, or cause a rattling sensation in my chest. As I tried to fluff up the pillow and readjust myself for the tenth time, Nathan looked over at me.

"Hey, what's the matter? Having trouble sleeping?" he said.

"Yeah. I'm sorry if my coughing woke you."

"That's okay, I'm not tired anyhow." Nathan's eyes were wide with excitement. "I keep thinking about going to the Army Depot and seeing their operations. I still can't believe there's a Resistance out there. When we join them, there's no telling what we'll be able to do."

I knew Nathan would do wonderful things with better resources, but right now I had other worries. "Getting the supplies for more weapons scares me," I admitted between coughs. "You know as well as I do that the Institute of Technology's only a few miles from Strong Memorial Hospital and even closer to the airport. We'll be on the edge of the soldiers' main turf."

"It's not the first time we've been on missions like this. We'll just have to be super careful." Nathan reached over and held my hand. "Try to get some sleep. You need to get healthy."

CHAPTER 33

During breakfast Doc Hiro checked me over again, and said that if I didn't get out of the damp cavern air for a day or two, my cold could develop into pneumonia.

I insisted that I was fine, but the general ordered me to spend the next twenty-four hours in the old bunkroom of the yellow house. Since no one ever stayed topside alone, a guard was assigned to stay with me in rotating shifts.

Martin took the first shift and didn't say two words the whole time. We were both angry about not being below to help with the preparation for the mission. Martin sat stoically with his rifle in his lap, staring at the stairs while I sat on my old bunk and read a book by candlelight.

Ivy came up for the next shift and brought me a couple of guns and some cleaning supplies, which I was thankful for. Boredom had begun to eat away at my patience.

"How are you feeling?" she asked.

"Better." Then I launched into a fit of coughing.

Ivy looked at me with worry reflected in her eyes. "The general and Major Davis have decided to leave straight after breakfast tomorrow."

"So soon?"

"Nathan and Ed finished the supply list and they're pretty much ready to go," she said, handing me another cleaning rag. "You need to get better fast or Doc'll never let you go."

Crap.

Several hours later, Doc Hiro paid me a visit and listened to my chest. He shook his head. "I hate to give you bad news, but I don't want you going on the mission. You're not well enough yet."

Ivy had warned me, but I still felt like a rock had landed in my stomach. "I'm feeling much better. I *have* to go. Next to Alex, I'm the best shot we have." Dammit, the team needed me.

Ivy stood off to the side and looked at me sympathetically, but didn't say anything.

Doc Hiro packed up his bag and headed for the exit. "Don't fight with me about it. Take it up with the general."

I knew better than to do that. If Doc said no, the answer was no.

After Doc left, Ivy sat next to me. "We'll be back before you know it. It's more important that you get healthy for the trip to the Depot."

I felt miserable about not being able to contribute to the mission, so I did the mature thing. I pouted.

"Try not to worry about it. I'm going back down now.

Alex'll be up in a few minutes." Ivy gave me a rare hug and left quietly.

I changed into an oversized T-shirt and climbed into my sleeping bag. The dim pre-dawn light began to illuminate the stairs, so I blew out the candle and waited for Alex to take over the next guard shift.

As footsteps came across the basement floor, I turned my head and looked toward the doorway.

"Nathan, what are you doing here?"

He smiled. "I persuaded Alex to switch shifts with me. I wanted to talk to you."

"Good, I want to talk too. I'm the second best shot we have. It's not fair that Doc Hiro won't let me go on the mission." The minute I said the words I knew I was whining, but I couldn't help myself. I wanted to contribute to the team.

Nathan sat on the other end of the bunk and leaned back against the wall. "Allie, I know you probably have a hundred good reasons why you think you should go, but the fact is, you need to get better and we can't afford to postpone the mission."

"It's just a cold and I'm already feeling better," I said as I folded my arms in front of me. "Besides, this trip is dangerous. You need me."

"Look, we've mapped out the operation and it's no different from dozens of other missions we've done." Nathan moved closer and gave me a gentle kiss on the forehead. "And you're right, I do need you," he said quietly.

I looked up into Nathan's blue eyes. "Well, I need you too and I don't want anything to happen to you."

"Allie ..." he hesitated, as if trying to find the right words.

"What is it?" I asked.

Without answering, he leaned forward and kissed me. His mouth was warm and soft, and felt amazing. My brain instantly dismissed the mission and I lost myself in the kiss.

Nathan pulled back and looked at me intently, his eyes showing an emotion I hadn't seen before. "Allie, I care about you more than you know," he whispered, lifting his hand to brush across my cheek.

"You have to know I feel the same way," I whispered back.

He put his arms around me and pulled me close. He kissed me again with a new intensity that clearly showed his desire. I leaned into him with my lips parted. Nathan made a small noise and plunged his tongue into my mouth. He tasted sweet and hot. I could feel his heart pounding through my thin T-shirt.

I recalled what Ivy had told me a long time ago: *You have to take what you can get, when you can get it, or you might lose it forever.* I knew what I wanted. I wanted Nathan.

We fell back against the bunk and I ran my fingers through his hair. Our tongues intertwined and Nathan slid his hand inside my T-shirt. I arched my back as he cupped my breast with his hand. He was driving me crazy with a need I wasn't quite sure how to define.

The bulge in his jeans pushed hard against my thigh. A throbbing sensation grew between my legs and I instinctively pushed my hips toward him.

"Oh, Allie," Nathan said raggedly. "Are you sure about this?"

"Yes," I whispered in his ear. "Nathan, I want you. I've always wanted you."

We frantically tore the clothes off of each other and then kissed again. We couldn't get enough of each other as we pressed our bodies together.

There is something primal and powerful about bare skin touching bare skin. What I felt for Nathan was indescribable, and I wanted, needed, to know him in a sexual way. I felt an urgent need growing deep inside, but I wasn't quite sure what to do about it. Moisture developed between my legs as he kissed me again and again, on the breast, on the neck, on the ear, on the lips.

"Nathan, please," I whispered in his ear.

"Allie, I need you so much," he murmured back.

Nathan carefully positioned himself between my legs. I wanted him so badly that I lifted my hips trying to find him. Nathan gave a hard thrust and moaned into my ear. I gasped as something small tore internally, but then he kissed me hard and long, and the pain began to fade into something wonderful as we moved together.

As Nathan and I clung to each other for dear life, we discovered the oldest and most basic aspect of being human.

CHAPTER 34

That night Doc Hiro checked on me and deemed me well enough to go back down to the cavern. I was anxious to get underground so I could say goodbye to the team, especially Nathan.

Once I resigned myself to the fact that I wasn't going to be part of the mission, I concentrated on the task of making sure everyone had loaded weapons, plenty of ammunition and full water bottles.

A few minutes before the group was scheduled to go, Nathan pulled me aside. "I want you to take this," he said, handing me his black leather journal.

"I don't understand. Why are you giving me this?" I flipped through the pages and saw that it was packed with diagrams, calculations and comments. He had put much more effort into his documentation than I was aware of.

"It's my notes on everything we've developed over the last

EYE OF THE DRACO

two years." He pulled me close and whispered, "If anything happens to me, I want you to take this to the Seneca Army Depot where they can analyze it. The general's the only one who knows I'm giving this to you."

Nathan had never done anything like this before. I glanced at the journal and then I looked into his eyes. I saw uncertainty hiding behind a brave exterior. A flash of fear shot through my chest.

"But nothing's going to happen to you," I insisted. "You'll be back in no time."

Nathan smiled. "Allie, I feel better than I've ever felt in my whole life. You can count on the fact that I'm coming back—to you."

I threw my arms around him and gave him a bone-crushing hug. "Oh God, Nathan, please be careful."

"I will, don't worry. I miss you already." Nathan put his hands in my hair and gave me a kiss that expressed everything he was feeling.

From a dark window in the house on Lincoln Avenue, I watched my teammates run covertly through the shadows. The moonless night swallowed them up as I said a prayer for their safety. After several minutes, I headed back downstairs for what I knew would be a long and torturous night.

Usually alive with activity and voices, the cavern was eerily quiet. Ed muttered to himself as he worked on a project, and Doc Hiro sat quietly to the side observing his behavior. Recently, Doc had become concerned with Ed's stability and was considering having him taken to Bristol. He hoped the calmer setting in the distant hills would benefit him, but Ed hadn't left the cavern in almost four months. We all knew it would be a struggle convincing him to go topside.

For the first few hours, I sat on my sleeping bag and went through Nathan's journal page by page. It was comforting to read his words and see his sketches. Most of the math was out of my league, but I understood the theory he described in his text. As I read his handwritten notes and looked at his drawings, it was almost like he was here with me, whispering his thoughts.

When my eyes began to ache from reading by lamplight, I tucked the journal under my pillow and heated up some canned soup for the three of us. I wasn't hungry, but keeping my hands busy seemed to help keep my nerves in check. Doc and Ed sat down and I served up the soup.

"Just a few more hours," Doc said, as he blew on his steaming bowl.

The next three hours crawled by at a snail's pace. Every time we heard a noise, we jumped and looked toward the stairs, but each time it was nothing.

Ed adjusted his glasses for the hundredth time. "I d-don't think it was a good idea for the team to go on a m-mission so close to the city," he muttered.

I glanced at my watch and gave Doc a worried look. He nodded his understanding. The team was well overdue.

At the six-hour point I was in a full-blown pacing-worrying-praying state. I was so anxious that I started to feel sick. As I tried to burn off nervous energy by walking back and forth across the cavern, Doc Hiro watched me with a pained expression. I knew that he was silent because he didn't want to upset Ed, but I could clearly see how alarmed he was.

Finally the sound of footsteps caught my attention and I spun around. The team was at the bottom of the stairs and headed towards us. I thought it was odd that they'd entered the cavern so quietly that we didn't hear them.

"Doc, they're back!" I shouted, as I ran over to greet them.

"You're so late. What happened?"

I looked at their faces, but not one of them would look at me. The general looked down, Martin looked over at the stream, and Alex just looked away. I'd seen this reaction before. Shit. I immediately started to count heads.

"Where's Major Davis?" I asked.

The general looked at me and shook his head. Then Ivy stepped forward and I saw tears in her eyes. I looked around again.

"Where's Nathan?" I asked in a small voice that didn't sound like mine.

Ivy reached out and gave me a tight hug. "I'm sorry," she sobbed out.

"No, no, he's not ..." I couldn't finish my sentence.

The general put his hand on my shoulder. "Allie, Major Davis is dead, and ... Nathan was taken away."

My knees felt weak as Ivy took my arm and escorted me over to the table.

"Let's all sit down now and debrief," the general said.

I sat and waited patiently while silent tears streamed down

my checks. I wanted to listen to every word of what had happened, but numbness was taking over my mind and it was hard to concentrate.

The general said that the group had retrieved the needed supplies and everything had gone as planned. The trouble began when they attempted to leave the campus of the RIT.

"We walked straight into an ambush on the south side," he said.

No one was sure how it had happened, but they were suddenly dodging soldiers and lightbeams. Major Davis was hit by a beam and went down in the tall weeds. Nathan and Alex went back to try to reverse the effects with a lightstick, but their attempt failed. The general ordered them to leave the major and run for cover. Alex obeyed, but Nathan stayed behind to give the lightstick another try.

A moment later, a swarm of soldiers descended on the area. With all the chaos, no one was certain if Nathan had been taken alive, but no one saw a flash of light either.

I turned to Lieutenant McGregor and choked out, "I'm sorry, Lieutenant."

He had a hollow expression in his eyes. "I'm sorry, too."

I wiped my cheeks and forced my mind to move on to the next logical steps. "We need to plan a rescue mission," I said firmly.

"Allie, I know what you're thinking." The general looked at me with a mix of sadness and compassion. "I've already discussed it with the lieutenant and my senior officers. We're taking the supplies, as planned, to the Seneca Army Depot so their team can start work on developing more weapons. Then we'll plan a rescue mission. We'll have a much better chance of success with their military expertise behind us."

"But that could take months," I said, fighting back more tears.

"It's already been decided," the general said as he raked his hand through his hair. "Right now we need food and some rest. We're going to the Army Depot tonight."

I felt completely helpless to do anything meaningful. The last time I lost Nathan he had almost died because we didn't look for him, and I wasn't about to make that mistake again.

I helped Ivy prepare dinner, but I couldn't bring myself to eat anything. My stomach churned with grief and I could barely look at the rice stir-fry as I served it to the others.

At 1300 hours, after everyone else had fallen asleep, I stared at the cavern ceiling and made my own plans. An hour later, I quietly got up, grabbed my weapons along with a few supplies and headed toward the dark steps. Dead or alive, I couldn't stand the thought of Nathan being in enemy hands. Realistically I knew there was little I could do alone, but I had to try something. It would be months before we would be able to plan and execute a rescue mission, and Nathan might not have months. I was stressed out and tired, but I felt my actions were justified.

As I approached the stone staircase, I stopped short when I saw Martin partially hidden in a dark shadow, leaning casually against the wall.

"Yep. I thought you might try something stupid again," he said.

I tried to think of something to say, but my intentions were obvious. "Would you believe I just needed some air?"

Martin sighed and stood up. "Look, I'm tired and I want to go to bed. The general's plan is the best thing for all of us, including Nathan. You just need to accept it. After all, you're not fourteen anymore. You need to fucking grow up, Allie."

"I am grown up," I said, annoyed.

"Then prove it and do the right thing. Now promise me you won't pull this shit again."

I felt deflated. Deep down I knew Martin was right. Getting myself killed wouldn't help Nathan, but a well-organized plan might. My emotions had clouded my judgment and I was being stupid and immature.

"I'm sorry ... I promise."

"Good, because I sure as hell don't feel like babysitting you all night."

I thought Martin was angry with me, but he put his arm around my shoulder and in his eyes I saw nothing but sadness and worry. He walked me back to my sleeping bag and made sure I crawled in.

Although I was exhausted, sleep wouldn't come. Every time I looked over at Nathan's empty space, I felt deep pain. I couldn't stop thinking about what might be happening to him. Whatever it was, I hated the fact that he was dealing with it alone.

CHAPTER 35

At 1800 hours, while everyone was washing up and preparing breakfast, I felt a renewed sense of purpose. We would make the trip to the Depot and I would devote myself to making sure a rescue mission for Nathan happened.

I looked around and noticed Ivy was missing. I approached Alex as he downed a big mug of coffee.

"Where's Ivy?" I asked.

"She went for a walk about an hour ago." He looked at me and took a deep breath. "Allie, you know we all feel the same way about Nathan. We'll find him, but it's important we do it the right way."

I nodded. I'd thought about it all night long and I knew our only chance of success was to join forces with a bigger group. There was no way we could take on an army of soldiers without a well-equipped army of our own—and a brilliant plan.

I was worried about Ivy, so I grabbed a lantern and went

to find her. It took me more than fifteen minutes, but I finally found her sitting on a rock about twenty yards past the collapsed tunnel. She didn't look good.

"Are you all right?" I said.

She looked up at me, her skin pale even in the lamplight. "Yeah, I'm fine." Then she turned her head and vomited into a small depression in the rocks.

"How long has that been going on?" I asked.

She groaned and held her head in her hands. "About a week."

I wasn't sure how to ask the question that came to my mind. I knelt beside her. "Are you sick, or is it … something else."

She looked at me with a strange mixture of emotions. "I think it's something else."

I put my hand on her arm. "Does Alex know? Does anyone know?"

"No one knows except you," she said as she clutched her stomach and fought off another wave of nausea. "We were so careful, I don't know what happened. Alex is going to be furious, and I don't even want to think about how pissed off the general will be. This is the last thing we need after what happened yesterday."

"You have to tell them. The general's about to hold a meeting to discuss the trip to the Army Depot. You have to tell them now, because it might change the strategy."

"I know that," she said with a pained look, "but I don't want to disappoint everyone."

"I'll be a lot worse if you don't tell them. Do you want me to help you?" I asked.

"No. This is something I have to do. Just give me a minute and I'll come over when I stop being sick."

I made my way back to the main living area and grabbed a cup of coffee.

Alex sat next to me and I saw concern in his eyes. "Did you find Ivy?"

I wasn't sure what to say. "Um, yes, she'll be back in a minute."

"I'm right here," Ivy said tentatively as she came up behind us. She grabbed Alex's hand. "We need to talk for a minute, let's take a walk."

Ivy took Alex across the cavern, over to the staircase. I could tell she was crying, but within seconds Alex was hugging her. About fifteen minutes later, they returned to the group and asked the general if he could join them for a private conversation before the meeting. Alex looked worried and Ivy's eyes were red.

As the general followed them over to the stream, the team began to gather at the table for the strategy meeting. "What's going on?" Martin asked as he sat down.

I just shrugged.

I could tell that the conversation over by the stream was tense. The general raked his hand through his hair and appeared to be asking a lot of questions. I recalled how strict he had always been about not allowing pregnancies. After several long minutes, he shook his head and called Doc Hiro over to join them. Once Doc entered the conversation, they all seemed to relax. Doc was smiling and he slapped Alex on the back. He didn't seem the least bit ruffled.

When the streamside discussion concluded, the group joined us back at the table.

The general took a deep breath and said, "Okay, listen everyone. Something's happened that's going to change things a bit. Ivy might be pregnant, and that makes her safety one of my top priorities. Doc pointed out to me, quite rightly, that if we don't have pregnancies, we might not have a human race. Pregnancies are *critical* to the continuation of the human race. So I'm officially changing my previous policy about this."

Then the general went straight into the structure of his new plan. We would travel on foot until we were well outside of the village, then try to find bikes to cover the next thirty-five miles. At about the twenty-mile point, Alex, Ivy, Doc Hiro and Jon would continue down Route 64 and head to Bristol.

The general insisted that Ivy and Alex remain in Bristol, where Doc could tend to Ivy's pregnancy in relative safety. He said he wasn't comfortable sending them to the Depot until we understood more about what to expect there.

"Allie, Martin, Ed, Lieutenant McGregor and I will continue to the Depot to meet with the lieutenant's commanding officer," the general said. "We already know there'll be heavy Draco traffic on the major roadways near Geneva, so we'll be traveling the last ten miles on foot. We're probably going to run into some rough terrain over the last stretch, but we still want to make it in one night. Everyone will carry their own supplies and weapons, and we should be packed and ready to go by dusk tomorrow."

As soon as Ed heard he was going to the Depot, he almost hyperventilated. The general reminded him how important his presence would be now that Nathan was gone, but that didn't help.

Doc Hiro attempted to talk Ed through his anxiety, but after several hours, nothing he said had calmed Ed's nerves. Finally Doc gave him a little white pill that seemed to do the trick. After a few minutes, Ed quieted down and stared numbly at his hands.

I spent the rest of the night cleaning and preparing our weapons, and gathering ammunition and explosives. As far I was concerned, the sooner we headed out the better. After I finished with the stockpile of weapons, I filled every bottle we had with water from the stream and lined them up in rows. Then I began laying out food items that would travel well.

"I see you're making it easier for everyone," the general commented.

"Just trying to stay busy." The truth was, I couldn't stop worrying about Nathan. If I didn't keep myself occupied, a new flood of tears would overwhelm my delicate emotional state. I also knew that remaining strong was more important than ever and I was determined to find ways to stay that way.

Just before bedtime, I stuffed my backpack with a few articles of clothing, some food, three water bottles, a hundred and twenty rounds of ammo for my M4, and a hundred rounds for my SIG Sauer. The last thing I packed was Nathan's journal, but first I flipped through the pages and carefully tore out and folded pages fifty to fifty-three. I slipped them into my back pocket.

After zipping up my pack tightly, I grabbed one of the straps and slung it over my shoulder, testing the weight. The ammo made it heavy, but at least I was properly prepared.

Doc Hiro gave Ed another pill an hour before we headed out. This did wonders to keep him calm, but Ed still made it clear that he would rather not be going on this trip.

Just before it was time to leave, I approached the general with a question that had been lingering in my mind. "Do you think it would be all right to leave Nathan a note telling him where we are? Just in case he comes back after we're gone."

The general shook his head. "I'm sorry, Allie, but it's just too risky." He put his arm around my shoulder and gave a gentle squeeze. "Think about what would happen if that note fell into the wrong hands. Besides, if Nathan came back to find the cavern empty he'd know to go to Bristol."

I nodded. "Understood."

We left the cavern at 1700 hours. Our departure was smooth and uneventful, but the further from the village we traveled, the guiltier I felt. I had convinced myself we were doing the right thing, but somehow it felt like we were deserting Nathan. In a way we were.

CHAPTER 36

The soldiers we spotted as we left the outskirts of the village appeared to be highly engaged, following protocol to the letter. I assumed that recent events had forced them to step up their operations, but regardless, we easily dodged them.

It was early December and the ground was crunchy beneath my feet. The leaves had long fallen off the trees and the crisp night air nipped at our cheeks.

Four miles outside of town, we stopped to search several garages for bikes. Once we had enough bikes for everyone and were mobile again, we were able to quickly cover the next segment of our journey.

At 2000 hours, we reached the point where Route 64 branched off toward Bristol. It was time to say goodbye to Ivy, Alex, Jon and Doc Hiro. We hoped to meet up with them in a few weeks, but we all knew that any future plans were impossible to predict. Ivy and I squeezed each other tight, but said nothing. Everything we felt was far beyond mere words.

As I watched the small group disappear into the darkness, I had a peculiar sense that I was deserting more of my friends.

During the next leg of our trip, the air turned colder and snow flurries began to drift through the air. Ed wasn't handling the stress well and his unstable behavior slowed our progress. He was muttering to himself constantly and appeared to be at the point of exhaustion. We tried giving him another pill and taking frequent breaks, but nothing seemed to help.

"Ed, be quiet," Martin snapped. "You're going to give us away with your babbling."

"S-sorry," Ed said, as he adjusted his glasses with shaking hands.

As we skirted the town of Geneva, we saw increasing numbers of patrols. The small town seemed to be a hub of activity for the aliens. Most of the sightings were land vehicles, although just after dumping our bikes to travel on foot, we saw three airships flying in formation.

The lieutenant looked concerned. "We don't usually see airships in this area."

"What do you think it means?" the general asked, concerned.

"I have no idea," Lieutenant McGregor said. "But let's try to pick up the pace."

We avoided the roads and stuck close to the deserted hills. I noticed that the more ground we covered, the rougher the terrain became.

Ed sat down without warning. "I c-can't go any f-further," he said breathlessly.

The general scanned the area and pointed to a spot on top of a nearby hill that had good sight lines. "We'll take a break up there. Only two more hours to go. You're doing great, Ed. Just hang in there."

I helped Ed up to the top of the hill, where we could sit in relative safety. After he had settled down, I handed him a water bottle and he took a shaky drink.

"Th-thanks. I'll be glad when we're b-back underground. This is m-much, m-much t-too dangerous."

The night sky was full of thick heavy clouds and the snow was starting to stick to the ground. Truthfully, I was thankful for the rest. The journey had been long and my muscles ached, so I was certain the strain had been much worse for Ed.

"Up th-there," Ed yelled, pointing toward the sky.

Two airships had appeared out of nowhere, soundlessly as always. The whoosh of air moving in the wake of the ships was the only noise we could hear as they headed north at an incredible speed. By the time my eyes had focused, they were gone.

"That's the second time we've seen them tonight. Not a good sign," the lieutenant said. "We should move on, I don't have a good feeling about this."

"Agreed," the general said, standing up.

I picked up my backpack and threw it on. It felt about ten pounds heavier than when we left. Just as we began to head down the hill, another airship flew overhead. This one was lower and much smaller.

"Everyone, *down*," the general yelled.

I hit the ground as fast as gravity would allow. When I

looked up, the ship was making a perfect one-eighty turn and heading back toward us. Ed was the only one still standing.

"They're c-coming for us. G-got to g-get out of here!" Ed said, blinking rapidly. Then he made an unexpected about-face and began to scramble down the hill.

"Ed, get back here and get your butt on the ground," Martin said between clenched teeth.

Ed ignored him and continued his haphazard descent.

"Damn it, Ed! Stop running, you're heading for the road," Martin yelled.

"We have to do something," I said. "Land vehicles aren't far away."

The airship halted about hundred feet above us and hovered silently.

"Allie, Martin, go get him," the general ordered. "Lieutenant, will you help me cover the aircraft?"

The general and Lieutenant McGregor aimed their rifles at the floating craft.

Martin and I dumped our packs, grabbed our weapons and sprinted toward Ed. A light covering of snow made the ground slippery and I had to be careful with my footing. In his frightened state, Ed was attempting to run too fast for someone of his physical abilities. Within seconds, he had tripped near the base of the hill and hit the ground hard.

I gasped. It looked like he was hurt.

"Over there." Martin pointed at two rapidly approaching land vehicles.

Ed was struggling to get up just as the two land vehicles pulled to the side of the road. When he spotted the soldiers, he froze for a few seconds, then turned and began limping back up the hill. The soldiers wasted no time. They jumped from their vehicles and began to pursue their prey.

Martin grabbed my arm and pulled me behind a large rock. "Start firing now or we'll lose him," he ordered.

I threw myself over the top of the boulder, sighted the target and began shooting. I immediately dropped two soldiers. Martin shot another in the chest three times. More land vehicles pulled up and reinforcements quickly filled in for the dead soldiers. Martin and I kept firing, trying to protect Ed, but he was making himself an easy target on the open hillside.

A small wave of soldiers formed at the base of the hill. They pulled out their lightsticks and began to make the familiar sweeping motions in unison.

"Fuck, I'm out." Martin moved quickly to change his clip.

As he made the switch I kept firing, but there were too many of them. I dropped two more soldiers just as a cluster of lightbeams reached Ed's pale skin. I heard a piercing scream and he was down. A thin wisp of smoke rose from his body and my heart sank. I knew there was no way we could get to him in time to try and reverse the hit. To make matters worse, we had problems of our own as more soldiers continued to arrive.

Immediately after firing on Ed, the Draco turned their attention toward us and began their ascent up the hill. Fifteen soldiers moved toward us, with deadly lightbeams flashing. A few more yards and we would be within their range.

Martin looked at me. "Do you want to run or stick it out?" he asked.

"Stick it out," I answered without a second thought. I looked through my scope and pulled the trigger in rapid succession.

Now that Martin had reloaded, our combined firepower took down the entire first row.

"They're idiots," Martin said through gritted teeth. "We're picking them off like ducks, yet they just keep coming."

The Draco style of warfare seemed strange. I thought back to *The Art of War*, which by now we had all read, and one of Sun Tzu's lessons: *Do not attack an enemy that has the high ground.* I guess good advice never gets old.

Seconds later the general and Lieutenant McGregor joined us and helped us finish the fight. The battle lasted only a few more minutes. The Draco soldiers were mechanical in their approach; as their comrades dropped, the remaining soldiers continued to push forward. It was almost too easy.

When the path was clear, Martin ran down to check Ed. I stayed behind the rock and covered his approach. Martin knelt down at Ed's side, looked toward us and shook his head. I felt sick inside. We knew Ed was unstable. We should have taken better care of him.

The small airship continued to hover silently overhead.

Martin returned and pointed toward the distant hills. "More land vehicles approaching from the north. We need to move."

"What about Ed's body?" I asked.

"Shit, there's no time," the general said.

The lieutenant shook his head. "We can't take him with us. Carrying his body would slow us down and we need to move *now*."

"Then we'll come back for Ed later and give him a proper

burial," the general said. "For now let's try to hide him behind those rocks." He pointed up the hill.

We quickly dragged Ed's body into a concealed area between three large rocks and I said a silent prayer for our friend. As we covered his body with some dried brush, it occurred to me that I'd almost become used to the smell of death.

"Grab your gear and follow me," the lieutenant said. "I know another way to the Depot that might be safer."

We trailed closely behind the lieutenant, but each time we progressed a few hundred yards, the airship followed our path. Again and again it tracked us in short incremental movements. It didn't matter which direction we headed, the airship followed, and then within moments a land vehicle would power in our direction.

"I wonder why that thing isn't firing on us," Martin said, looking up.

"I don't think it's a combat ship," Lieutenant McGregor said. "It's probably a drone, alerting the ground troops to our location."

"How can we make that work to our advantage?" the general said.

"We need to think of something fast, or we're going to have company," I said, pointing to the east.

The land vehicle had stopped not far from us and four soldiers were headed in our direction on foot.

Martin and I quickly positioned ourselves on the ground and prepared to shoot.

"Wait, I have another idea," the general said. "Each one of us targets an individual soldier." He quickly assigned us all particular soldiers. "But only fire if they make a move for their weapons. Follow me."

With his rifle in position, the general approached the soldiers and we fell in behind him. As we came within lightstick range, one of the soldiers foolishly lifted his weapon. The general shot him through the heart and he dropped to the ground like a rag doll.

Martin's assigned soldier went for his lightstick and Martin shot him twice. As the third soldier went for his light stick, the lieutenant shot him. They were either slow learners or really good at following orders, I wasn't sure which.

With four rifles pointed directly at his vital organs, the remaining soldier hesitated.

"Allie, I need you to translate," the general said. "Tell him that if he wants to live, he should put his lightstick and helmet on the ground and not communicate with his comrades."

I shouted out the commands and was surprised to see the soldier drop his weapon obediently and pull off his helmet. He appeared to be much younger than the typical Draco soldier. Apparently he didn't have a death wish.

As soon as his helmet touched the ground, the lights along the top began to flash.

"Allie, put the helmet on," the general said. "Tell me what you hear."

I slipped the metallic dome over my head and plugged in the earpiece. Familiar alien chatter was issuing multiple commands.

"They seem to think all the troops in this area are dead and they're sending out coordinates for reinforcements. From the number of responses, it sounds like they're sending an army our way."

"Good. Now take the helmet off," the general said.

I set the helmet on the ground and picked up my rifle.

The general walked around the land vehicle and shot out the headlights and spotlights. "Martin, search the vehicle for other weapons, and communication and positioning devices."

After a quick sweep, Martin smashed a few items with the butt of his rifle, and then jumped out of the vehicle. "All clear."

"Allie, tell this guy to go back to his vehicle and get the hell out of here."

The soldier wasted no time stumbling back to the safety of his vehicle. Without lights, he would have a hard time seeing much of anything.

"Now, everyone stay perfectly still," the general said. "I'm banking on that drone using motion detection. Don't anyone move a muscle."

We stood perfectly motionless and almost invisible to a species with no night vision. The vehicle powered away haphazardly, but the drone held its position above us. A few moments later, it silently slipped away in pursuit of the land vehicle.

"Don't move until it's out of sight," the general whispered. After the drone had vanished in the distance, he said, "Let's get the hell out of here before they catch on."

We picked up the soldiers' lightsticks and stuffed them into our packs.

"We only have another five miles before we reach the Depot.

It won't take long for the soldiers to realize their mistake, so I'm going to push hard," the lieutenant said.

He took us along a remote path and did indeed push our sore muscles to their limit.

CHAPTER 37

Hours later, we approached the fenced perimeter of the Seneca Army Depot. I noticed a group of pure white animals within the fencing. When the animals heard our advancing footsteps, they darted away like frightened ghosts. Whatever they were, they appeared more mythical than real.

"What were those?" I asked the lieutenant, hoping that more of them would magically appear.

"White deer. The largest herd of its kind in the world."

"And they live here? At the old Army Depot?" I said.

"Yes. The fenced area is over ten thousand acres. A few white deer began to reproduce back in the late forties. When the Depot shut down operations, the deer population grew unchecked."

The lieutenant smiled. "Now they provide us with a consistent food source."

I couldn't even recall the last time I ate fresh meat, but the thought of eating white deer took away any appetite I might have had. "Sorry I asked."

The lieutenant chuckled. "You'll learn to like it."

"Sounds good to me," Martin said.

We followed the fencing, which seemed to go on forever. The lieutenant stopped in a nondescript area, pulled back a section of chain link, and ushered us through the opening.

To the east, I noticed a red rim lining the sky.

"The sun's coming up. We need to get underground," the lieutenant said, without stopping.

We followed the lieutenant for another hundred yards and over to a well-hidden sewer pipe embedded in the side of a hill. He turned and motioned for us to follow him into the damp, stagnant passage. The pipe was only four feet high, so we had to hunch over to walk. I tried to use my hands to steady myself, but the walls of the pipe were slimy and my hands slipped with even the slightest pressure. This was not what I was expecting.

"I hope the greasy goo on this pipe isn't toxic," Martin said.

The lieutenant laughed. "No one's died from it yet."

We walked for several minutes and when I looked back, the opening of the pipe was beginning to show signs of a pink sunrise.

We soon came to a fork in the pipe and the lieutenant took us left into pitch-blackness. After we had slipped and struggled for another ten yards, he lit a candle, which made our progress slightly easier.

After another hundred yards, the water in the pipe was knee deep, ice cold and smelled rancid. No one said a word, but I was sure we were all wondering where the hell the lieutenant was taking us.

As we trudged through the thick sewage, we came to a heavy metal grate that stopped us from going any further. The lieutenant grabbed a lever overhead and pulled hard until it made a series of grinding sounds. Slowly, the barrier squeaked open. After we passed through, the lieutenant used another lever and the grate clunked shut.

We continued our journey through the pipe, passing yet another fork. My back had begun to ache from the constant crouched position. The lieutenant made a right turn and we came upon another metal grate. He opened this in the same way and we passed through into another tunnel.

My legs were ice cold and I couldn't stop my teeth from chattering. "How much f-further," I chattered.

"We're close now," the lieutenant reassured me.

Within minutes, he stopped below a hatch in the ceiling of the pipe. It had a round handle, which he spun eight times clockwise, four times counterclockwise, and two times clockwise. It reminded me of the combination locker I had at school in the old life.

We climbed up through the hatch, which led to another pipe that went straight down. A ladder bolted along the side disappeared into a black void.

"Don't look down. We have a long way to go. Stay focused on keeping a good grip and maintaining your footing." The lieutenant's voice echoed as he led the way down into the void.

The general climbed onto the ladder and followed directly

behind him, then me and then Martin. I guessed that we descended about seventy feet. At the bottom of the ladder, we found ourselves in a small space about eight feet by eight feet. The lieutenant felt along the wall until he found a switch, which turned on a dim light. The walls appeared to be made of metal sheets that had been securely bolted together.

On the opposite side of the room, the lieutenant had to dial another combination hatch. This one looked like the type of door you might see on a submarine. When the hatch groaned and swung open, we stepped through and entered the next room, which had roughly the same dimensions as the last one. I was beginning to feel like we were in some kind of insane labyrinth that would never end.

There was another, larger submarine hatch on the far wall, only this one didn't have a handle. Lieutenant McGregor walked over to the hatch and pushed a small gray button on the left.

"Is that a doorbell?" I asked, amused by the thought.

"Sort of," the lieutenant said with a half-smile. "Now we wait while they check us out. We affectionately call this the decompression room."

I looked around for cameras but saw nothing except metal walls with rows of bolts.

"How can they see us," I asked.

"A few of those bolts are actually wide-angle cameras. They've been watching us since we arrived."

I scanned the bolts, trying to locate the cameras, but they all looked the same to me. Several minutes passed before we heard clunking sounds coming from the other side of the door. When the door swung open, three guards were standing in a green metal tunnel pointing automatic weapons at us.

"Drop all your weapons," a deep voice demanded. "That includes clips, knives and explosives."

Martin and I looked to the general for direction. He nodded. We placed our rifles on the ground, and removed our knives, ammo and grenades. My handgun was still in my pack—I wasn't about to turn that over. I assumed, since the lieutenant was with us and we were all humans, they didn't feel the need to do body searches.

The guards led us down the green tunnel, which branched off in several directions. We followed them down the second left and then took a right into a small room furnished only with a table and six chairs. A large mirror, which I guessed was two-way, was built into the far wall.

"Please sit down," the man with the deep voice said.

The general, Martin and I set our backpacks on the floor and sat at the table. The lieutenant left with the men, and when the door closed the lock clicked into place.

Martin scowled. "I don't like being locked in."

"Do you suppose they're watching us?" I asked, looking at the mirror.

Martin flipped his middle finger toward the mirror. "I hope so."

"Hey, you two," the general said. "Don't forget we're on the same side."

After sitting for an impossibly long hour, the door finally clicked open. Lieutenant McGregor and two other men entered.

The lieutenant pointed to the gray-haired man with weathered skin on his right. "This is Colonel Stone. He's in charge of the operation here."

Colonel Stone took the time to shake each of our hands with a commanding grip and a head nod, but he didn't smile.

"And this is Major Anderson," the lieutenant continued. "This is General Henry Reynolds, Colonel Martin Connor, and Lieutenant Allie Spencer."

The major also shook our hands. He was younger than the colonel, and had dark hair and a stern, distrusting look in his eyes. I had the distinct feeling that he didn't like us.

"Let's get down to business," the colonel said as he sat down. "Lieutenant McGregor has told us a pretty amazing story and it's my job to separate fact from fiction."

CHAPTER 38

I could tell we were off to a bad start when Martin glared at the colonel.

"Well then," Martin said, "let me make it easy for you. It's all fact. Are we done now?"

"Slow down, Martin. I just have a few questions," the colonel said.

"What do you want to know?" the general asked.

"The lieutenant tells me you've developed a weapon that can penetrate the Draco body armor," the colonel said.

"Yes, and since you have our rifles in your possession, you can test them out," the general said.

"We did. The rifles fire, but the lasers only worked once and then stopped functioning," Major Anderson said.

Martin made a huffing sound. "Well, of course they don't work. You probably fired them down here."

"Colonel Stone," I said, "the lasers draw power from the

Draco wireless energy source. You'll need to test them above ground if you want them to work properly."

Colonel Stone hesitated and rubbed his chin. "So you're saying that you discovered the alien power source and then figured out how to draw energy from it?"

"Yes," I answered. "Nathan did."

Major Anderson rolled his eyes. "That's impossible."

"Look, Colonel, you can put this debate to rest by testing our equipment," the general said.

Colonel Stone nodded. "Fair enough. I also found your discovery of the oregano oil interesting. Our scientist's looking into it right now."

"Allie, why don't you hand over Nathan's journal to the colonel. That should clear up any remaining technology questions," the general said.

I hated the thought of turning over the information that took Nathan over two years to compile, but I obeyed the general's request. I opened my pack and pulled out the worn leather-bound book and handed it the colonel.

"Lieutenant McGregor also tells me that Nathan has done some preliminary research on a device which might reflect the death ray," the colonel said.

"Yes, he has some theories. You'll find them outlined in the book," I answered. "Colonel, I'm sure the lieutenant's told you that we believe Nathan's been taken hostage. Shouldn't our first priority be a rescue mission, especially considering how essential his work is?"

"We'll review Nathan's notes and learn more about what he's discovered, then we can talk about rescue missions," the colonel said as he looked at his watch. "You must be getting tired. Let's get you settled in so you can get some rest. We'll talk again tomorrow. Major Anderson will show you to your rooms."

"One more thing, Colonel," the general said. "We left the body of one of our own behind. It would mean a lot to us if we could retrieve him for a proper burial."

"Absolutely. My men will get the location from Lieutenant McGregor and bring your man back."

Relief washed over the general's face. "Thank you."

The colonel left and Major Anderson led us down a maze of tight passages until we came to an area with rows of doors on either side of the hall.

"Since we're currently under capacity, you'll each get your own rooms," the major stated.

"How many people can this facility take?" the general asked.

"Two hundred comfortably, but we could probably squeeze in three hundred if we had to," the major said. "Here are your rooms. The bathrooms are at the end of the hall, along with the caféteria. You can go there 24/7 to get something to eat. I'll pick you up at the caféteria tomorrow at eighteen hundred hours. Goodnight."

As I entered my room, I flipped the light switch and smiled when the lights came on. Using a light switch felt odd, but nice, and I wondered what the Depot used for a power source. The room was small and had two bunks, two desks and two closets. It reminded me of my brother's old college dormitory. I placed my pack in the closet and flopped down on the closest bunk.

I wasn't used to having my own room, nor was I used to the eerie quiet, so sleep was impossible. I tossed and turned for an hour and finally got up, went to the bathroom, then to the caféteria. I saw two other hallways past the caféteria that looked like more sleeping quarters. The lights in the hallway had dimmed to simulate nighttime and I wondered if everyone slept on the same shift. I helped myself to some water and headed back to my room.

As I passed by Martin's room, I noticed that the door was open a crack, so I knocked softly to see if he was still up.

"Come on in," he said.

I slipped quietly through the doorway.

"What's the matter?" he said. "Having trouble sleeping?"

"It's too quiet," I said. "I'm so used to your snoring that I can't sleep."

Martin shrugged and pointed across the room. "Feel free to take the other bunk."

I smiled. "Thanks, I think I will." I jumped between the crisp sheets and within minutes drifted off.

A bad dream jolted me awake. I'd been looking at Ed's burned body and he was pleading with us. "Don't leave me behind," he said over and over. I kept trying to reach for him but for some reason my legs and arms felt like cement, and I couldn't move. Nathan stood on a distant hill watching us. He was trying to tell me something, but I couldn't hear him. In my dream I felt like I'd failed everyone.

I sat up in bed and wiped a thin layer of sweat off my forehead.

"Bad dream?" Martin asked. He was sitting on the edge of his bunk, pulling on a pair of socks.

I just shrugged. I didn't want to talk about it.

"Come on, let's go get some breakfast. You'll feel better soon," he said.

Martin and I entered the caféteria and got in line for a bowl of gooey protein substance, fake orange juice, and a small cup of assorted vitamins. The women who served the goo told us this was what we could expect for breakfast and lunch, and for a snack we could pick up a protein bar anytime. They said they served "real food" at dinner. I thought of the white deer and cringed.

"By the way, my name's Margaret. Head cook and bottle washer around here," she said, extending her hand. "You can grab some coffee at the end of the line."

I shook her hand and smiled at the thought of a hot cup of coffee. "I'm Allie and this is Martin."

"You two look awful healthy to be newcomers," she commented, eyeing us up and down.

"Just lucky, I guess," Martin responded.

We sat by ourselves at a table in the corner. People came and went at a quick pace, but most were sullen and pale. A few nodded our way and said hello, but overall it felt like everyone was in a state of depression.

A short time later, the general joined us. After taking one bite of the goo, he put his spoon down. "I don't think I can eat this," he said, wrinkling his nose.

"You'll learn to tolerate it," Major Anderson said as he walked over. He had the same tough expression he wore the previous day. "The colonel wants to see you first thing. Come with me."

We gladly left our protein substance behind and followed the major through the network of hallways. We passed the conference room from yesterday and entered through an open doorway on the other side of the hall.

The colonel sat at a rectangular table with another man and a woman. The man had long stringy gray hair and a haphazard appearance, while the woman looked ultra-professional, with dark hair in a neat bun and a pair of heavy-rimmed glasses. Neither seemed like military types.

As we entered the room, everyone stood up for a formal greeting. For a moment there was an awkward silence, so I stuck out my hand.

"I'm Allie," I said to the woman as I shook her hand. "And this is General Henry Reynolds and Colonel Martin Connor."

"Nice to meet you," the woman said without a trace of expression on her face. "I am Dr. Jenkins, and this is Dr. Petrov. I believe you already know the colonel."

"Exactly what sort of doctors are you?" Martin asked.

Dr. Jenkins cleared her throat. "I'm a psychiatrist, and Dr. Petrov has PhDs in aerospace engineering and mechanical engineering. Please, have a seat."

We sat down, but sharing the table with a shrink who was probably evaluating us from the moment we walked in gave me a prickly feeling.

"We have a full day planned for all of you, so I'd like to review the schedule," Colonel Stone stated. "First, each of you will need to be evaluated by Dr. Jenkins."

Martin snorted. "Fat chance."

"It's standard procedure for everyone at this facility," Dr. Jenkins said, jotting down some notes. "We track the physical and mental wellbeing of every inhabitant."

The colonel continued as if Martin hadn't said anything. "Second, we'd like one of you to go to the surface with our team, for a demonstration of your rifles. Third, Dr. Petrov has some questions regarding Nathan's journal. And lastly, I would like to spend some time with Henry. I still have many questions regarding how you've managed to keep your group alive over the last two and half years."

Martin crossed his arms over his chest and leaned back in his chair, but remained silent.

The general nodded. "Agreed. Martin can go to the surface for the demonstration, and Allie should meet with Dr. Petrov, since she was the closest to Nathan's work."

"Thank you. I'd like to meet back here at the end of the day for debriefing," Colonel Stone said as he stood up.

"Dr. Jenkins mentioned that you checked everyone's physical state. When does that happen?" I asked.

"It doesn't. Unfortunately we lost our physician three weeks ago," Colonel Stone stated.

Martin and I were dropped off at the conference room with the two-way mirror, while Dr. Jenkins and the general continued down the hall for what we were told would be a short assessment.

"I'll be back to pick up Martin in exactly forty-five minutes," Dr. Jenkins said over her shoulder.

Martin sat in a conference chair, leaned back and put his

feet up on the table. "I don't want anyone judging my mental state."

"Just answer her questions and smile a lot," I said. "We need to get this over with so we can talk to the colonel about Nathan and the other kids."

"I think the colonel has his own agenda," Martin said curtly.

"Then we'll have to convince him that getting Nathan back is more important."

Martin stood up, walked over to the two-way mirror and straightened his hair. "They're probably watching us right now."

"Yeah, probably." I put my elbows on the table and rested my chin on my hands.

CHAPTER 39

Precisely forty-five minutes later, Dr. Jenkins came to the conference room and requested that Martin follow her. I was left sitting alone. Just me and the two-way mirror. For the sole purpose of annoying anyone who might be watching, I passed the time by having a staring match with the mirror.

Another forty-five minutes passed and Dr. Jenkins showed up again. She greeted me with a stiff smile. "Hello, Allie, are you ready?"

"Yes."

She took me to a small room several doors past the colonel's office. "Please have a seat," she said, pointing to a gray office chair in front of her desk.

I sat and felt awkward as she made herself comfortable in the oversized desk chair.

"Allie, tell me about your family before the invasion," she said in a clinical tone.

"Well, I had two parents, two brothers and a lot of friends." I couldn't help but think what a complete waste of time this was.

"Tell me about your brothers," she said.

She was starting to bug me. "Look, I don't want to talk about this stuff. We don't talk about this stuff, because it's a distraction. Everything we do right now has an impact on the future. Don't you think we should be talking about strategies involving the Draco?"

"I think your group has done a good job shutting out the past."

"Well, maybe that's why we've survived this long. Maybe that's how we've been able to develop weapons that actually work and you haven't." I didn't mean to sound as cynical as I did.

"Maybe," she said. Her voice was perfectly even, like a robot. "Tell me about Nathan."

Now we were getting somewhere. "Okay. He's responsible for all of our developments. He's brilliant." I went on to tell her the highlights of the past two and half years, up to Nathan's capture and Ed's death.

She nodded and took notes. "How do you feel about Nathan personally?"

"He's my best friend."

"How would you feel if Nathan never came back?" she asked, looking straight at me.

I didn't like where she was taking this and I stared back at her. "That's not an option. We're going to get him back."

Dr. Jenkins sighed and thought for a moment before

responding. "No one's ever been rescued from the Draco. Do you realize how difficult that would be?"

I looked at her like she had three heads. "Until yesterday you hadn't met anyone who had ever killed an enemy soldier. Well, I've killed dozens. Until yesterday, you didn't know the secret to repelling the stinkbugs. Until yesterday you had no hope whatsoever. So don't tell me what can or can't be done."

"Okay, I won't." Dr. Jenkins closed her notebook. "But just one last thing. Dr. Petrov tells me there are a few pages missing from Nathan's journal."

"Oh really?"

"Yes. Dr. Petrov tells me that critical information was contained on those pages." She looked at me over the top of her glasses.

"There might be." I formed the most innocent expression I could muster. "You know, it's also critical that we get Nathan back."

"Allie, you can't negotiate for something like that. Getting him back is not within our control."

I sat up straighter. "You're mistaken, Dr. Jenkins."

She stood up. "I think we're done here. I'll take you to Dr. Petrov's lab now."

As I followed the doctor down the long hallway, I noticed the lights were placed every fifty feet or so, and were very low wattage.

"Dr. Jenkins, what type of power do you use down here?" I asked.

"Geothermal energy," she answered as she opened the door to the lab. "I'm sure Dr. Petrov will be along shortly and will be happy to explain it to you. We'll speak again soon. Goodbye." She smiled and glided out of the room, smoothly and professionally.

I'll bet nothing ruffles her, I thought.

I found myself in a large white room with far better lighting than the rest of the Depot. Dr. Petrov's laboratory was full of tables and equipment, and had smaller adjoining rooms. Considering we were underground, the space was much bigger than I expected.

Dr. Petrov emerged from a small room off to the right. "Hello, Allie," he said with a thick Russian accent. It occurred to me now that Dr. Petrov hadn't spoken in the colonel's office, so this was the first time I had heard his accent.

"Hello," I replied.

His enthusiasm was obvious as he smiled widely and took fast energetic steps. "I have so many questions for you." He handed Nathan's journal to me. "We made copies, so you may have this back."

The doctor fired off questions in rapid succession and I answered as many as I could, but I had to repeatedly tell him that he really needed to speak with Nathan. Much of the material was too advanced for me, I told him. Dr. Petrov accepted my lack of knowledge, yet he still appeared interested in what I had to say and took pages of notes.

Then he brought up the inevitable. "Allie, the pages on how to tap into the power source are missing," he said slowly and with great concern. "Without that information we'll have to reverse engineer your existing rifles, and that will take a great deal of time."

"I realize that," I said, "but I'm sure you also understand how important it is to get Nathan back."

Dr. Petrov smiled and shook his head. "Wouldn't it be easier if you simply gave me the missing pages?"

"Yes, but those pages are the only leverage I have to convince the colonel to help us."

He nodded. "I understand the importance of both acquiring the pages *and* Nathan's return. I'd very much like to have him here with me in the lab. I'm sure we can reach some sort of agreement with the colonel."

I was starting to like Dr. Petrov.

CHAPTER 40

I spent over six hours with Petrov and then headed back to the conference room with the two-way mirror. The general and Martin were already seated, waiting for the debriefing. Martin had a smug look on his face.

A moment later, Colonel Stone entered with Major Anderson, Dr. Petrov and Lieutenant McGregor. Petrov was smiling and the group seemed more relaxed than at our previous meeting.

The colonel sat down and cleared his throat. "First off, I need to inform you that our men tried to locate your teammate, but the body was gone."

My heart sank. I looked over at the others and saw they were all shaken as well. We had let Ed down.

"Secondly, I'd like to thank Martin for his demonstration tonight." The colonel sat up straighter. "My men were impressed with your weaponry. Your developments could potentially change everything for the Resistance. We've already sent word to Langley, and as soon as we can get the specs sorted out, both facilities will ramp up for manufacturing."

"Langley?" Martin said.

"Yes. We have another underground facility in Langley, Virginia, as well as several other key locations around the country. Langley is the hub of the Resistance. They have tremendous manufacturing capabilities." The major took a deep breath. "This brings us to the focal point of the discussion. Apparently there are missing pages in Nathan's journal. Obviously, without that information production will be significantly delayed."

Here we go, I thought. I mentally prepared for a clash of wills.

"You need Nathan just as badly as you need those pages," I pointed out.

"Allie, this isn't the right timing for a rescue mission. We've lost so many of our people that we can't possibly risk more lives right now." Colonel Stone turned toward the general. "Henry, can't you talk to her?"

The general raised his eyebrows and looked at me questioningly. I hadn't told him about removing the key pages and I wasn't sure how he would react to the news. Within seconds he seemed to figure it out, because a small smile crept across his face. "Sorry, Colonel. I support Allie on this."

"I don't have the authority to put together an operation of that size, nor am I about to send what few men I have on a suicide mission," the colonel said in a clipped tone. "This situation is much bigger than one person; we're talking about the survival of the human race, for God's sake."

"Colonel—" I started.

"No! We don't have time for your games." The colonel's face took on a slight reddish color.

"Games?" I stood up, leaned forward and put my palms on the table. "We're not playing games, Colonel. We've survived because we don't abandon each other when things get rough. Why don't you take a hard look at your accomplishments and compare them to ours. Then tell me who's playing games."

The colonel took a deep breath and made a visible effort to compose himself. "All right, maybe we can compromise. If you turn over the pages, I'll speak to Langley for their input."

"That's not much of a compromise, Colonel. We need more than that," the general said.

"We can't sacrifice dozens of men to rescue one person."

I looked the colonel straight in the eyes. "Sometimes one person is that important."

"It's not that easy." The colonel slammed his hand on the table. "We simply don't have the resources."

The room became uncomfortably silent. I glanced over at Martin, who seemed to be the only person enjoying the disagreement.

Major Anderson's eyes narrowed and he leaned forward. "Of course, we have other ways to obtain the information we need."

"Do you really think threats of interrogation are going to scare me?" I raised my eyebrows and tried to appear unaffected by his warning, although deep down I was thoroughly intimidated.

The colonel let out an exasperated sigh. "Allie, no one's going to interrogate you."

The general leaned back and clasped his hands together. "If Allie gives you the missing information, you could ramp up production and be ready for combat in short order. At that point, would you feel comfortable attempting a rescue mission?"

The colonel hesitated. "Possibly. If you turn over the missing pages, we'll begin manufacturing as soon as possible. When we hit the production quota, which means all military personal have been outfitted with weapons, I'll help you pull a small rescue team together. But I absolutely cannot commit to a timeframe."

I didn't like the proposal one bit, but I looked over at the general for direction. He gave me a single nod. Reluctantly, I reached back and pulled the pages from my back pocket, then slid them across the table to Dr. Petrov.

Lieutenant McGregor chuckled and shook his head.

I looked the colonel square in the eye. "I'd appreciate it if you would keep your word, sir."

The colonel stiffened and appeared annoyed. "You can count on it."

That night, the general, Martin and I found a small room in the south wing that the Depot used as a chapel. The space was dimly lit, and a makeshift altar stood in front of about a dozen chairs. Together, we sat in the front row and the general said a few words in memory of Ed.

Later, back in my room, I checked my backpack and saw that it had been searched. I pulled out my handgun and verified it was still in working order. I was sure they were merely looking for the missing pages, yet I was surprised they didn't take the handgun as a bonus.

I grabbed Nathan's journal and went over to Martin's room to borrow his extra bunk again. Martin had become like a big brother to me and I felt safe with him. It was strange how much better I slept when I could hear his snoring in the background.

"Do you believe what the colonel said?" Martin asked as he leaned back in his bunk. "Because I sure don't."

"I don't know," I said, flipping through the pages of the worn journal. "But we have an agreement and I won't let him forget about his end of that."

A few minutes later, Martin's breathing slowed and transformed into the familiar rhythmic snoring. I stayed up for another hour, reading the worn journal page by page, determined to get to the end. Nathan's handwritten notes were all I had that proved he existed. It was unfair how someone could be erased from the world in an instant and so few people knew the difference.

Then I thought of Ed, and Josh, and Jackson, and all the others we had lost along the way. Who would know they existed?

I turned to the last page in Nathan's book. The cream paper was blank, with the exception of one line written in the middle of the page: *I love you, Allie.*

I don't know how I missed it before, but there it was in Nathan's slanted script. I read the words over and over. I missed him so much it hurt, and I wished I could tell him that I loved him back.

I cried for a long time, not for me, but for the horror that Nathan was facing alone. The colonel would have to keep his word; I made a solemn vow to make sure he did.

CHAPTER 41

Over the next few weeks, the general, Martin and I were assigned to multiple projects and the time flew by. We ran an occasional mission with Lieutenant McGregor to gather supplies, but most of the time we worked in the lab with Dr. Petrov and a dozen other folks, building an arsenal of laser weapons. Most of the personnel at the Depot had been recruited into the manufacturing process in one fashion or another. Multiple components had to be constructed separately and then fitted together to create the laser. Then the lasers had to be carefully fitted to the rifles. Six offices had been cleared out and converted into production units, and within a month we had an efficient assembly line running.

During this time Dr. Petrov was hard at work trying to adapt Nathan's discoveries to other devices. Using his newfound information, he developed a communication vehicle, codenamed "Ferret." Dr. Petrov's new system tapped into the wireless energy waves above ground and channeled the power via cable to the laboratory below. Then the Ferret system back-fed data in microbursts through the energy waves and transmitted the information to whoever had a receiver. While the system could only send and receive basic text, Dr. Petrov hoped that, given time, he could develop email and real-time audio transmissions.

Like most new technologies, there was a small catch. The microburst transmissions created a minuscule disturbance in the energy waves. Dr. Petrov believed he had overcome this by limiting the size and length of our transmissions, which in turn reduced the possibility of detection to .02 percent. He called it "almost zero." In my mind, almost zero wasn't even in the same ballpark as zero. Nevertheless, the Ferret System was another monumental breakthrough for the Resistance.

Shortly after the Ferret System had been successfully tested, Colonel Stone sent a team to Langley to set up the system within the Resistance command center. After the Langley installation was complete, the plan was to expand the Ferret System to Resistance facilities across the continent. Dr. Petrov repeatedly told everyone that Nathan's discoveries would change the course of history, and that although we had a long road ahead, our odds of survival had significantly improved.

During this time, the general had many conversations with Colonel Stone regarding the remainder of our sector still in the Bristol hills. The colonel was adamant that they should be brought to the Depot, where the children could be looked after and eventually relocated to the safe camp in Canada. After weeks of discussion, the general finally agreed.

It had been fifty-two days since our arrival at the Depot when the colonel called us together for a meeting to discuss a plan that he and the general had put together. Colonel Stone and Lieutenant McGregor were already seated at the table when the general, Martin and I arrived.

"Henry, Allie, Martin." The colonel nodded to each one of us as we took our seats.

It irked me that the colonel called us by our first names rather than recognizing our military status, although he wasn't the only one. Our military ranks hadn't been accepted by anyone at the Depot.

The colonel laid out a map on the table. "Henry and I have agreed to bring back the Bristol sector in small groups, one group per night. Henry and Lieutenant McGregor will depart for Bristol tomorrow night and retrieve the first group. They will follow this path around Finger Lakes." The colonel pointed to a route that led around the lakes and gave a wide berth to the areas occupied by soldiers. "You'll need to stay as far from the Draco traffic as possible. Dr. Petrov will set Henry up with a portable Ferret System so they can update us with their progress."

"What about us?" Martin asked.

"We need you and Allie to stay here and continue the work with weapons production," the colonel said.

The general looked at us. "I've already agreed to the plan."

I was disappointed, but I also knew from the general's tone that it was the end of the discussion.

"How long will the trip take?" I asked.

"We estimate five to six hours each way, depending on the

Draco activity," the general said. "We should be able to bring everyone back to the Depot with seven round trips, over seven nights."

"I'd like you to keep something else in mind," the colonel said, making eye contact with each of us, one at a time. "In the coming weeks we'll be sending small bands of civilians to the Canadian encampment. We hope to accomplish this while Draco traffic is low due to the cold weather. It would be wise for you to consider sending the younger children from your sector up there, where they can live in a safer community with other civilians."

"Understood. We'll discuss it after the entire team arrives," the general responded.

When the time came, I knew it would be a hard decision for the general to break up our sector, even if it was in the best interests of the children.

"I believe we're done here." Colonel Stone stood up.

I cleared my throat. "Before we go, when can we discuss a rescue mission for Nathan?"

"Allie, it's too soon," he said. "We're a long way from being ready for a mission like that. Let's stay focused on the task at hand. We'll talk again in a couple of months."

Months? I wasn't happy with his answer, but I also understood how important it was to focus our attention on bringing our sector safely to the Depot, so for now I dropped the subject.

The following night, the general and Lieutenant McGregor departed for the Bristol hills. I couldn't wait to hear how

Ivy and Alex were doing. Ivy's pregnancy was a clear victory against the soldiers' extermination plans, and I hoped having her around the Depot would breathe new life into this place. Most of the personnel at the Depot were either detached or depressed, and while the weapons production had given them a ray of hope, Dr. Jenkins certainly had her hands full.

After we finished our shift in weapons production, Dr. Petrov called Martin and me into the communications room. He had a big smile on his face as he quickly ushered us into chairs. A large flat-screen monitor sat on the counter in front of us, along with a keyboard and mouse.

"I've installed a speech-recognition program," he said proudly. "Just hit the control key, then the S key, and whatever you say will automatically be typed into the system. Then say 'End' when you're ready to send the completed message. I'll demonstrate."

Dr. Petrov hit control-S. "This is Dr. Petrov. Go ahead, Henry. They're here now. End." As the doctor spoke, his words automatically appeared on the screen. After he said "End," the words Transmission Sent appeared on the screen.

It took about two minutes for the response to appear on the screen: *Martin, Allie, I am happy to report that everyone in Bristol is safe. Also, Doc Hiro has done a great job keeping everyone healthy.*

I typed control-S. "How are Ivy and Alex? End." The system typed my words almost as quickly as I spoke them.

Again the response took about two minutes to appear: *Ivy still has morning sickness, but other than that they are fine. They are anxious to come to the Depot and see you both.*

Martin typed control-S. "When can we expect you to arrive? End."

As the text appeared on screen, I read it aloud. "We are leaving with the first group in about thirty minutes. We should be back in about six hours. See you soon."

Petrov pointed at his watch to let me know we were approaching the safety limits of the system. He hit control-S. "This is Dr. Petrov again. Looks like it's time to shut down, Henry. We're looking forward to the arrival of the first group. Godspeed. Over and out. End."

Dr. Petrov leaned over, flipped a switch and the Ferret System powered down.

CHAPTER 42

Five and a half hours later, Martin and I were waiting impatiently in the narrow hallway by the decompression room.

"Stop pacing," Martin said. "You're wearing a path in the floor."

"You can relax now," said an older man in the small control room to our left. "Looks like they've arrived. They'll have to sit tight until the colonel and Dr. Jenkins give the okay. Want to take a look?"

I stepped into the room and looked at a bank of monitors. One of the screens showed the decompression room, with seven people crowded together in the tight space. I strained to see who was with the general and the lieutenant.

"Ivy's in there. Squirt too," I shouted. I also saw Serena, Michael and Sam. It was so good to see some friendly faces.

Within a few minutes, the colonel and Dr. Jenkins had

arrived, along with two armed guards. Once it was determined the group was safe and no one had followed them, the door was opened.

We had a wonderful two-minute reunion, all hugging and laughing.

"Squirt, look how you've grown," I said, as I picked him up and spun him around.

Our celebration was cut short when the colonel and Dr. Jenkins whisked the group of five away. I had no doubt they would be analyzed and catalogued before being assigned rooms.

"How did the mission go?" Martin asked the general.

"Smooth as silk." The general gave a thumbs-up and smiled. "The cold's kept the aliens holed up. Just six more trips to go."

The pattern remained the same for the next five nights. The general made contact with us in the communications room, and then Martin and me, and now Ivy, waited impatiently outside the decompression room for their arrival.

Little by little the population at the Depot grew. Alex arrived in the second group, and Jon and Doc Hiro arrived in the third group. After speaking with Dr. Jenkins, Doc Hiro was immediately put to work in the infirmary and he quickly found himself swamped with patients. There seemed to be an immediate need for a medical doctor and it was clear that Doc Hiro would be expected to stay on at the Depot for as long as possible.

After five nights of hard travel, the general and Lieutenant McGregor were physically and mentally exhausted. Dr.

Jenkins, who had been analyzing and recording every second of the lengthy missions, insisted that replacements be found for the final trip.

The colonel assigned two other officers to handle the last trip and ordered the general and the lieutenant to get some rest. The general wasn't happy about being denied the last mission, but he had no choice. Orders were orders.

On the final night, the general waited with us outside the decompression room for everyone to arrive. It was evident how tired he was. He looked thinner and had dark circles under his eyes. I knew how hard it was for him not to have led this last mission. These were his people and he felt responsible for bringing them in. Not to mention that Laurie was part of the final group. I'd never forgotten the scene I'd witnessed between Laurie and the general; I knew his feelings for Laurie ran deep.

As the minutes ticked by, I could see him growing anxious. He repeatedly looked at his watch and raked his hand through his hair.

"They're only a few minutes late. I'm sure they'll be here soon," I said, trying to sound reassuring although I felt uneasy too. The previous groups had all been on time.

After another twenty minutes, the general looked at me and shook his head. "I don't like it, Allie. Something's not right."

I nodded in agreement.

After another hour had passed, the sun was up and we were all sick with worry. The general went to speak with Colonel Stone about sending out a search party. After a long discussion, the colonel agreed to his request, providing we waited until nightfall. Despite Dr. Jenkin's very vocal objections, the general was allowed to lead the search team. He chose three additional team members—Martin, Lieutenant McGregor and me.

We spent the daylight hours trying to get some rest, but could only manage a few hours of fitful sleep.

As soon as the sun had disappeared behind the horizon, we left the Depot and followed the same path to Bristol that the general and the lieutenant had previously traveled. The trail we followed was deserted. We saw no signs of our people, nor did we see soldiers.

When we arrived at the Bristol camp, everything appeared normal. It looked as though the last group had left on schedule.

Next, we retraced out route back to the Depot grounds. We ran across a few random clusters of stinkbugs, but they scurried away from us and we pushed on. We had been on foot for over ten hours, but regardless, we continued to search until sunrise. Still we found nothing. It was as if they had just vanished. Once the sun was up, we had no choice but to return to the underground protection of the Depot.

Colonel Stone was not pleased that we'd stayed out until dawn, but he was also sympathetic to our feelings for our missing teammates. He agreed to let us venture out one last time that night. But if we didn't find them, the colonel was adamant that we would have to give up the search.

We were silent as we hiked back to the Bristol camp for the final time. We each understood that this was our last chance, so we stayed intently focused on the task at hand. By the time we arrived in Bristol, the temperature had dropped and snow showers had moved in.

We began our search at Laurie's house, where we knew the group would have prepped for their departure. At first glance everything appeared normal, but minutes into the search I saw a small canvas pack lying on the floor under an end table in the basement. It was slightly crushed and had a broken strap. Somehow, in the darkness, we had missed it the night before.

Martin looked over at me as I picked it up and touched the broken strap. "Fuck," he whispered.

Tears pooled in my eyes as I handed the pack to the general for him look over. We all knew this meant we weren't going to find our teammates.

We decided to stay and look for other clues that might help us piece the story together. After finding nothing else inside the house we went back outside to search the surrounding land.

"Over here," Martin yelled from the far side of the house. Something was different about his voice. It sounded hollow.

The general and I looked at each other, both recognizing that whatever Martin had found would only add to the bad news.

Martin stood on the other side of a large tree, next to a dark lump on the ground. He had his hands jammed into his pockets and his head hung down. As we approached, it was plain to see that the lump was the charred remains of Max. The general stared glassy eyed at his faithful companion. Then he fell to his knees and, with a shaking hand, gently petted the charred fur.

Eventually Martin picked up Max's body and placed it on the frozen ground by the oregano garden. After we had buried him under a pile of rocks, the general knelt by the gravesite for a long time. I stood nearby, hugging the broken pack to my chest with silent tears streaming down my cheeks. Martin put an arm around my shoulders, but even he looked upset. The wind picked up and brought a biting chill, as we each in our own way tried to make our peace with the situation.

By the time we returned to the Depot, we were exhausted and thoroughly disheartened. I feared that Dr. Jenkins would be waiting to analyze us the minute we walked through the hatch, but after a brief greeting, she left us alone.

We went through the motions of submitting our official report to Colonel Stone and then retired quietly to our rooms. I went straight to bed, but despite my fatigue I couldn't sleep. After tossing and turning for two hours, I decided to take a walk.

I wandered down the network of hallways and found myself at the chapel. I entered the small room and saw the general sitting before the altar with his head bent. I walked over, sat next to him and said my prayers as well.

Sometime later, he looked over at me. His eyes were pools of pain. "I should've been there."

"It's not your fault," I whispered.

He looked back toward the altar. "I should've gone on the final mission. Maybe things would've been different."

"We'll find them," I said. "The soldiers are probably holding them with the other kids."

"The younger ones, maybe." The general's eyes welled with tears. "But not Laurie. She was twenty years old."

For the first time, I watched the general break down and cry. I felt helpless, but I put my arms around him and held him tightly as his shoulders shook with anguish.

CHAPTER 43

Aside from our weapons-manufacturing work, the Depot was quickly becoming an important way station for refugees, and a key stop in what was now known as the New Underground Railroad. The kids from our sector were housed in the same wing as the ever-increasing stream of newcomers coming up from the southern regions, who rested at the Depot while they awaited the next leg of their journey.

We enjoyed a few short weeks living with our former sector members. I read to the younger kids before bed and made sure they brushed their teeth. Squirt roomed with me and it almost seemed like old times, although I knew we still had tough decisions to make about his future.

The general pulled Martin, Ivy, Alex, Jon and me together for several long discussions to debate whether the Canadian camp was the best option for our kids. In the end we all agreed that the Depot was no place for kids to grow up and we unanimously voted in favor of the camp. It was obvious that a civilian camp, far from the threat of Draco activity, would provide a better life for our kids than a military hole in the ground. But still, we worried. The camp was five hundred miles northeast and the trip could take up to two weeks of dangerous travel.

The first group that departed for the camp carried an extra Ferret System so that when they arrived we would have ongoing communication.

As soon as word was received that the refugees had arrived safely, the next group was sent off. Each group was accompanied by two military personnel, who took them to a safe zone called La Tuque located one hundred and eighty miles northeast of the furthest known Draco outpost. With the exception of the heavily occupied Fort Drum area in Watertown, NY, and a small outpost in Montreal, most of the travel was through deserted snow-covered wilderness.

One by one, each group reached La Tuque exhausted and with minor injuries, but more importantly, they arrived alive. When it had come time for the last of our kids to depart, Jon spoke to the general and asked for permission to join them. The death of his brother still haunted Jon and he wanted a chance at a new life as far from the Draco as possible. Permission was immediately granted.

After two and a half months, all of our kids had been moved along the New Underground Railroad, and for a short time our lives at the Depot were quiet. The general and four others from our original sector, including myself, Martin, Ivy and Alex, remained behind to continue assisting with the resistance.

The general seemed despondent for the first few weeks after our kids had departed for La Tuque, but he soon wrapped himself up in the efforts of the resistance and regained his sense of purpose.

Colonel Stone and the general often sat together to discuss the Draco tactical approach and behavioral patterns, and they seemed to develop a solid relationship. It took time, but over the months it became obvious the colonel had changed his opinion about our team and had acquired a newfound respect for us.

Four months after the Bristol incident, Colonel Stone formally inducted us into his unit, giving us ranks and specific duties. The general became a major. Martin, Alex and Ivy were given the rank of lieutenant, and I was back to being a gunnery sergeant. I'd been spending so much time in the armory that this rank suited me just fine.

Now that the general was officially a major, he insisted that we refer to him by his first name, Henry. This was a difficult adjustment for us to make, but since we were now members of the Depot garrison, we had to adapt.

I worried about Henry; he had lost so much over the last few months. I also still sick with worry about Nathan. I said a prayer for him every night and begged God to protect him. It had been so many months since I'd last seen him, and I wondered how much he had changed. I knew I had changed over the months, so I was certain he had too.

Like most things on an aggressive timetable, the production of weapons ran behind schedule. Our biggest obstacle was acquiring the necessary components to build the precision laser units. Dr. Petrov informed us that other facilities were having similar production issues and no one had an easy answer. It wasn't like we could run to the store and buy what we needed; instead we had to go on dangerous operations to fill a never-ending shopping list.

We conducted multiple "shopping missions" to Syracuse to pick up needed components from an old Lockheed Martin plant. I went on many of these assignments due to my sharpshooting abilities, although I rarely had the opportunity to fire on the enemy. We were under strict orders not to fire unless it was a life or death situation. Langley was adamant about not starting a war, and more importantly, they did not want the soldiers to know how widespread the laser rifles had become.

We worked long hours and the weeks flew past. I worked as hard as I could, often putting in double shifts, so we could bring the weapons production up to quota and start talking about rescuing Nathan and the other kids.

By July we were almost caught up, but once again we ran low on supplies. Henry volunteered to lead a mission to locate and bring back additional rifles, preferably automatic weapons if they could find them.

We heard later that as his team had skirted around the town of Geneva, they spotted the Draco night patrol in the distance. The team was well out of lightstick range and assumed they were safe from an attack, but when the soldiers opened fire, our men found themselves being shot at with bullets rather than beams of light.

The team took cover and returned fire, and one man was shot through the heart and another was hit in the leg. Eventually our side won the skirmish, but it didn't feel like a win. This was the first death the Depot had experienced since we had arrived with the laser rifles eight months ago.

After that encounter, we focused on adapting to this new twist in combat. While we still had to deal with lightsticks, we found ourselves sporadically dealing with regular old gunfire as the enemy experimented with their new arsenal of human weapons.

In late August, Martin and Lieutenant McGregor went on a late-night search of a small group of refugees reported to be hiding down by Seneca Lake. It was a routine mission and I waited for their return near the decompression room, as I always did when I wasn't working my shift in the armory.

From the security monitor, I watched Martin and the lieutenant enter the decompression room and wait for clearance. There were no refugees with them and Martin's expression made me uneasy. Within five minutes, the security team gave the okay and the hatch opened.

"What happened," I asked Martin as he entered the hallway.

He shook his head. "You won't believe it."

"I didn't believe it at first either," Lieutenant McGregor said from behind him.

I scowled. "Did you run into soldiers?"

"Yeah, you could say that. The night patrol was right on schedule, but as we watched them through the scopes we saw one of us."

"What do you mean, one of us?" I felt sick.

Martin's eyes narrowed. "I mean a human. An adult human,

maybe forty years old. He was driving the goddamned land vehicle."

"Are you sure?"

"Yes, I'm fucking sure. One of us is working for them and training them to use our weapons."

CHAPTER 44

This information created a tremendous ripple effect throughout the Depot and also at Langley. Knowing that a human was working with the local soldiers explained a lot, and we had no idea how widespread the problem was. Was there only one traitor working with the Draco, or had the enemy recruited a small army?

Security was immediately stepped up, and each of us, along with every refugee that came into our fold, was put through a rigorous interrogation. Most of the analysis was done in the decompression room and involved several lie-detection steps. The lengthy process reduced the risk of a spy infiltrating our facility, yet it still allowed for the flow-through of refugees.

Eventually things settled down, and it wasn't long before new waves of refugees arrived, keeping us all busy. The colonel assured me that the focus on the New Underground Railroad would layer in perfectly with a rescue mission for the children at

Strong Memorial Hospital, but he also frequently reminded me to be patient. The correct timing would be critical to our success.

One of my roles was to set up each adult refugee with a weapon and teach them how to properly maintain it. Alex taught them how to use it. Others taught them survival techniques, and Dr. Jenkins nurtured their mental health. They generally stayed with us for about two weeks before we sent them on their way to La Tuque. Amazingly, we still continued to produce weapons on an aggressive schedule. The Depot had become a hub of activity, but no matter how much time passed by, Nathan was never far from my thoughts.

In mid-September, as Lieutenant McGregor and I returned from a simple mission to harvest oregano stems, we waited in the decompression room with overstuffed bundles of fragrant stems. When the door finally opened, Alex stood impatiently on the other side.

"What took you guys so long?" he asked with a big smile. "Ivy had the baby two hours ago."

I shrieked and threw my arms around Alex's neck. "Well, was it a boy or girl? How are they?"

"It's a boy and everyone's fine," Alex said, unable to contain his excitement. "Come on, Ivy and the baby are both with Doc Hiro."

As we entered the infirmary, Doc and Henry were standing near the bed. Ivy was sitting up and almost seemed to glow as she held her new little bundle. The arrival of a healthy baby boy was just the kind of good news everyone needed.

"Allie, you're back!" Ivy called out. "Come over here and hold the baby."

She carefully placed him in my arms and I felt as if I was all thumbs. He was so small and defenseless.

"Have you decided on a name?" I asked.

Ivy looked at Alex, then turned to me and smiled. "We've decided to name him Joshua, Josh for short."

"Good choice," Henry said with a grin.

Later that night I went to the caféteria, grabbed some venison stew and found a quiet spot where I could keep to myself and read through Nathan's journal for the hundredth time. Halfway through my meal Lieutenant McGregor appeared on the other side of my table.

"Is this seat taken?" he said.

"Hello, Lieutenant, have a seat."

He made a mock scowl. "I'd appreciate it if you'd start calling me Ian."

"All right. Ian."

He set his tray on the table and sat down. "Do you realize you're eating venison?"

"Yes." I stared at the chunk of meat hanging from the end of my fork. "It's not like I have a choice, so let's not talk about it."

Ian laughed. "You're one of the best sharpshooters I've seen, yet you struggle over eating a piece of deer meat."

I shrugged. "Killing the Draco soldiers is a lot different to killing those beautiful creatures. That's one assignment I couldn't handle."

Henry walked into the caféteria, helped himself to some dinner, and sat on the far side of the room. Lieutenant McGregor continued to chat, but I could feel Henry's eyes on us. I knew Henry well and I knew that look. He was evaluating something.

Later that night, before bed, I paid a visit to the chapel. I was glad to see it was deserted so I could be alone. This was always a good place for me to get some serious thinking and praying done, so I sat quietly in the front row and closed my eyes.

"You know, it was a year ago today that you found me under a pine tree in the cemetery."

Startled, I turned and saw Lieutenant McGregor leaning against the doorframe.

"I remember that. You were in pretty bad shape."

"Yeah, I was. In fact, I thought I was going to die, and then you came along and told me everything would be fine," he said as he moved across the room and took a seat. "And you were right."

"We knew what we were doing."

"You sure did. It's hard to believe a whole year's gone by."

"Lieutenant—"

"Please call me Ian," he interrupted. "I've been meaning to tell you something. I want you to know that when the time's right for the Strong Hospital rescue, I'll be the first one to sign up. I promise."

"Thanks, that means a lot to me."

Ian hesitated, as if he was deciding what to say. "Allie, I know you've held onto your feelings for Nathan, but don't forget that there are still other men in the world."

I wasn't sure what to say, so I just nodded.

He gave me a lopsided smile, reached over and planted a

light kiss on my cheek. "Let me know when you get approval for the mission." After that, he stood and left the chapel.

"Lieutenant." Henry nodded toward Ian as they passed in the doorway.

"Major." Ian nodded back and disappeared into the hallway.

"What's up, Allie?" Henry said. "It's not like you to be up this late."

"I was just thinking about Nathan," I said. "It's been almost a year."

He sat down next to me. "A year's a long time and a lot could've happened to Nathan in that time." He looked me in the eye. "Look, I still believe a rescue mission should be one of our priorities, but you need to accept the possibility that Nathan might not be there."

"I know that." I'd thought about the possible outcomes countless times over the past months. In fact, I held no naive notions that even if we were to find Nathan things would magically go back to the way they were a year ago. If we found Nathan at all, I knew things would be very, very different. "If Nathan didn't survive, I'll accept it, but either way we'll have the chance to rescue a lot of children. Maybe even some of our own."

I knew Henry would feel as strongly about that as I did.

"Agreed." Henry nodded. "The colonel's in Langley's good graces these days, so this might be the best time to approach him."

"Will you help me talk to him?"

"Of course I will. I'll try to set something up for tomorrow."

Henry touched my arm. "There's something else I wanted to talk to you about."

For a moment I was worried because he seemed so serious.

"Allie, you've recently turned seventeen and you're not a kid anymore."

"I know that too."

"Yes, but to other people you seem older than your age. What I'm trying to say is … there are forty-eight military men at this facility and only ten women." Henry seemed uncomfortable. "I just want you to be careful."

I smiled. "It's nice to know you care, but I'm fine, really. I can take care of myself. And if you're talking about Lieutenant McGregor, I have no interest in him other than friendship."

Henry nodded, but his expression remained serious. "Allie, I care about you and I don't want to see anyone take advantage of you."

I had to stifle a laugh. We'd been in countless life-and-death situations together and here he was worried about some guy flirting with me. But I supposed Henry would always feel responsible for "his" people.

He stood up. "Get some sleep. You'll need it if we're going to convince Colonel Stone to get this mission underway."

I stood and gave Henry one of my bear hugs. "Thank you."

CHAPTER 45

The next day, Henry and I met with Colonel Stone at 2300 hours.

"Please sit down," the colonel said as we entered his office. "Somehow, I think I can guess why you're both here."

"We came to discuss the rescue mission for Strong Hospital," Henry said.

"I thought so." The colonel absently looked at his watch. "I've already had preliminary discussions with Langley, but I still can't promise you anything."

"That's all we can ask for. Maybe a recon mission would be in order to learn more about what's currently happening at the hospital," Henry said.

"We've already done that."

"What?" Henry stiffened.

The colonel hesitated as if he was debating how much to tell us. "I sent up two men for a small recon mission last month.

They estimated that anywhere from two to four hundred children were being held captive at the hospital. They also saw at least a dozen human adults. I didn't want to tell you earlier because I know some of your kids might be there and I didn't want you to get your hopes up prematurely. We absolutely cannot make a move until Langley gives us the okay."

"Understood," Henry said. "I want to assure you that you can trust us."

"Henry, I trust you and your team more than you know. As soon as I learn more, we'll meet again." Colonel Stone stood up.

Henry and I thanked the colonel and exited the office calmly, but as soon as we rounded the corner I squealed and threw myself at Henry for another bear hug. "Progress! We're making real progress!"

Henry hugged me back tightly. "Finally, I think we are."

I had no concept of how long approval from Langley could take, but apparently it can take a very long time. For four weeks we continually asked the colonel for an update, but each time his response was to simply "sit tight."

In the meantime, Langley began to send up large shipments of materials, which significantly cut down our need to run dangerous shopping missions. In short order, we were able to return equally large shipments of completed weapons back to Virginia. This made everyone happy, especially Colonel Stone, who was quickly becoming Langley's golden child.

Baby Josh also contributed to the sense of optimism at the base. I guess nothing symbolized hope for the future like a newborn. For the first time, things seemed to be headed in a positive direction for the resistance.

. . .

In early January, Dr. Jenkins met with me for a routine psychological evaluation. She still made me uneasy when we met, but I had seen how gifted she was at treating the refugees and had grown to respect her.

"Please sit down," she said when I entered her office.

I took a seat in the chair directly across from hers.

"Do you know why you're here?" she asked.

"I'm hoping this is the final step before the rescue mission's approved."

"It is." Dr. Jenkins nodded. "Allie, what do you hope to achieve with this mission?"

"I hope to rescue a number of children from enemy captivity."

"And what if you find there are no children to rescue?"

"Then we'll gather what intelligence we can and return."

"And what if Nathan isn't there?"

"I know full well that the odds are against that."

She nodded again. "According to my records, he would be eighteen now."

"If he's still alive, yes."

"And how would you feel if he is alive, but he now supports the Draco? We know some humans are working with the enemy. What if Nathan's turned as well?"

"Nathan can't be turned. You don't know him."

"Everyone has a breaking point," Dr. Jenkins stated.

I leaned forward. "Nathan was beaten by his drunken father for the first fourteen years of his life. He knows exactly what it's like to be in constant fear of dying. As long as he's still alive, Nathan will endure anything."

"I hope you're right."

Dr. Jenkins jotted notes on her pad and we continued to talk for another twenty minutes. At the conclusion of our visit, she stood. "Allie, I wish you the best of luck. I mean it." Then Dr. Jenkins actually gave me a smile.

The next morning the colonel requested that Henry and I meet with him first thing. As we entered the office, he motioned for us to sit at the table.

"I just received communication from Langley approving the Strong Memorial Hospital mission."

I had waited a long time to hear those words and nearly jumped out of my chair.

"That's good news, Colonel," Henry said, as he looked over at me. He didn't smile but I could see the spark in his eyes.

"As you know, leadership at Langley feels strongly that our primary focus should be finding and relocating as many refugees as possible, making this mission a great opportunity for us. Now we have communications and weaponry in place, we're ready to proceed. This will be the first assignment of its kind and it'll send a clear message to the Draco that the resistance has organized. There's no room to screw up this assignment." The colonel cleared his throat. "Let me be perfectly clear. You cannot fail."

"That's never been an option for us, Colonel," Henry said.

"I don't need to tell you how dangerous this will be. We'll need soldiers who are experienced in Draco combat. Dr. Jenkins has cleared your team, Henry. We'll need as many of your people as possible."

Henry nodded. "No problem."

Planning for the upcoming rescue mission took almost a full week. This type of operation required an elaborate strategy that took into consideration multiple outcomes. As we made our final preparations, we attended endless meetings, reviewed maps, and memorized maneuvers. By the end of the week we were more than ready—and itching—to go.

At the last minute Dr. Petrov surprised us with a special invention. He had created three small motorbikes that ran off of the Draco power source. At full throttle they could only reach twenty-five miles per hour, but they would save us from pedaling bikes or traveling on foot. More importantly, the motorbikes couldn't be picked up by the soldiers' electromagnetic detectors. Instead, they would blend in with the vast amounts of alien energy already streaming through the air, in much the same way as our laser rifles.

Departure time came quickly. I was a bundle of nerves. Outside the decompression room, as Henry and I triple-checked our weapons and supplies, I reviewed the strategy in my head several more times.

Since we had received reports of heavy Draco activity, Henry and I would leave first, sharing one motorbike. Once we had established a safe path through the hot zone, we would stop in the town of Mendon and give the rest of our team the go-ahead to follow.

At that point, Alex, Martin and Ian would join us and we would set up a command center in our old cavern. Next, we would proceed with a brief recon at the hospital, where we hoped to learn the optimal timing for our penetration. Then we would execute the actual rescue.

Another team, consisting of Major Anderson and a dozen of his men, would come up from the south and serve as the armed escort for groups of children as they were freed. It was critical that the two teams traveled different paths in case either was followed or captured.

Once I was satisfied that my gear was ready, I looked across the hallway at Ivy. She gave me a weak smile as she stood beside Alex with Josh in her arms. At Alex's request, she was staying behind.

Colonel Stone approached us just before it was time to go. "Dr. Petrov is waiting for you topside. Henry, he packed a Ferret System on the back of your motorbike and he'll give you instructions." The colonel shook our hands. "Make this work."

Ivy gave Henry a hug, and then she turned to me and whispered in my ear, "Allie, please stay alive, and please make sure Alex comes back."

"We're *all* coming back," I answered. And I meant it.

CHAPTER 46

The trip from the Depot to Mendon was effortless, and the few night patrols we spotted were easy to avoid. The motorbike made little noise other than a light hum, and since it was snowing the Draco activity was greatly reduced. Our biggest concern was the obvious imprint the motorbike left behind in the snow, although nature seemed to be working in our favor by covering the path with new puffy white flakes.

As we rode into Mendon, I held on tightly to Henry's waist.

He pointed to an old red building. "Let's set up in there," he said. He pulled the bike around to the back lot and parked.

Our first task was to familiarize ourselves with the exits and escape routes. So after entering the building, Henry lit a candle and we quickly learned the layout. We decided to set up our equipment in a small room by the back door, where we would have easy access to the bike.

I wiped a thick layer of dust from a small table and Henry set down the Ferret System. It was amazing how dirty a place could become when there were no inhabitants. After a few moments he had the system up and running, and typed in a message laying out the safest travel route for the rest of our recon team.

All we could do now was wait. I looked out a small window laced with spider webs and watched the wind swirl snowflakes into a frenzy. The air was as icy inside as it was outside and I rubbed my hands together in an effort to stay warm.

"Are you cold?" Henry asked, stepping over to the window.

"A little."

Henry took my hands in his and rubbed them. His fingers were warm and gentle. It was an intimate gesture that I wasn't expecting. In Henry's eyes I saw something I hadn't noticed before: his expression was a haunting mix of sadness and loneliness.

For a moment we just looked at each other, then Henry let go of my hands and reached for my face. His hands were barely touching my skin as he leaned forward and pressed his lips to mine.

I was caught off guard, yet at the same time completely caught up in this new twist of events. His kiss was firm, but warm and gentle, like his hands. I felt safe and protected, and couldn't stop myself from responding. My lips parted and Henry's tongue touched mine. He pressed closer and I could sense a hidden need in his kiss.

I couldn't think about anything other than how good it felt.

Abruptly, Henry pulled away and stepped back. He was breathing heavily. "I'm sorry," he whispered.

I didn't know how to respond. It was as much my fault.

"I shouldn't have done that." He looked out the window, his face now unreadable. "Allie, I'm sorry."

"It's okay," I said, feeling a little embarrassed that he appeared to regret his actions. "It's just something that happened. Let's forget about it."

We were good at forgetting, although deep down I knew that kiss would be hard to forget.

A short time later, Alex, Ian and Martin arrived. They came on two motorbikes and we met them in the back parking lot. After exchanging information, Henry led the seven-mile trip north to the village of Pittsford.

Snowflakes continued to fall, and the wind twisted and carried them on an erratic path.

As we entered the village, I noticed how everything looked the same as when we had left. The memories I had from our time in the yellow house, and then in the caverns, were still fresh in my mind, despite being gone for a year. After we had hidden the motorbikes inside the St. Louis Church and began walking the rest of the way, I had a strange feeling that I couldn't identify.

"I don't like this," I said. "It's too quiet."

"It's January. The Draco are probably holed up at the outpost," Alex said.

"Allie has good instincts," Henry said. "Stay alert, weapons ready."

We approached the house on Lincoln Avenue and Alex

immediately pointed to the back door, which had been left open about an inch.

"It could've been left that way from a previous search," he offered.

I didn't feel reassured and tightened my grip on the rifle.

We entered the house and went straight down to the basement. As we wound our way over to the bricked-up entryway, Martin stopped short.

"Wait," he said. "Look at the bricks."

The loose bricks had been replaced haphazardly in the wall. In the past, we had always replaced each brick meticulously so that the wall appeared to be solid. We would never have done such a sloppy job.

"I know I'm stating the obvious, but someone's been in there since we left," I said.

"We need to be cautious." Henry looked closely at the bricks. "They could still be down there."

"I suggest we divide up," Ian said.

"You're right," Henry said. "Whoever came in here might not know about the other passageway. Ian, you and I will go in through the yellow house. Allie, Alex and Martin, stay here"— he looked at his watch—"and at exactly twenty-three fifteen, begin your descent. That'll give us time to get into position down there before you enter. And remember, everyone, once you're underground you won't have access to the Draco's energy source. You'll only have enough reserved power for one shot with your rifle."

We all nodded in unison.

While we waited, Alex quietly removed the bricks to create

an opening just big enough for us to carefully slide through. When my watch read 2315, I looked at Martin and Alex and nodded.

I stepped through the small opening first and held my rifle in the firing position. Martin and Alex came in behind me. The stairway was pitch black, so I took each step slowly, silently and with the utmost care. After about twenty steps, I picked up the familiar scent of fresh water and damp limestone. As we descended past the ceiling of the cavern, I saw a small amount of light emanating from below.

Martin grabbed my arm and motioned for me to stop. He took the lead and cautiously bent down to look into the cavern.

He quickly stepped back and scowled. "I think it's a trap. Take a look," he whispered. "And Allie, I know you want to believe Nathan's down there, so don't do anything stupid."

I couldn't blame Martin for his comment; I'd done my share of stupid things in the past. I took two steps and bent my head down so I could see below the ceiling. In the distance, within our old living space, was the dim glow of a lantern. I didn't have a clear sight line due to the stalactites and rock formations, but there didn't appear to be any sign of movement. Other than the sound of flowing water, and an occasional drip, the cavern was silent.

I stepped back and let Alex take a look.

"I can't get a good sight line. What should we do?" I said.

"Keep going very carefully and hope Henry's in position," Martin said. "Are you ready?"

Alex and I both nodded.

Martin took the lead and resumed the descent.

When we reached the bottom of the steps, we were still too far away to get a clear view of our old living space.

"It's pitch black over here. If we stay in the dark areas along the perimeter, whoever's over there won't be able to see us," Martin whispered. "Follow me."

We slowly made our way from rock formation to rock formation, always staying obscured by the shadows. When we slipped behind the last column of stone that would keep us hidden, Martin stopped. Going any further would put us in full view of anyone who might be out there.

"Cover me while I take a look," Martin said.

"Let me do it," I whispered, grabbing his arm.

Martin hesitated.

"Please," I said. "I want to do it and I'm faster with the rifle than you are. You and Alex can cover me."

He thought for a moment and nodded.

With my weapon ready and my palms sweating, I took one small step away from the edge of the rock. It took a moment for my eyes to adjust to the soft lantern light. I looked around and saw nothing out of the ordinary. My eyes settled on our old table. Seated quietly, staring back at me, was a sole figure. There was no expression on his face; he simply stared at me.

I immediately backed up several steps and bumped into Martin. My heart was suddenly pounding and my breath was coming hard.

"Oh my God, you're going to think I'm crazy," I said with a shaky voice.

"What is it?" Alex asked.

I thought for a moment and pictured the scene in my mind, making sure I hadn't hallucinated.

"Nathan is sitting over there, and he looked right at me."

CHAPTER 47

Martin scowled. "Like I said before, it's a trap."

"He saw me and didn't say anything," I whispered. "He just stared at me. But there's no way anyone could've known we were coming, not even Nathan. What should we do?"

I was suddenly confused and my legs felt weak. I was thrilled to see Nathan, but also scared because the circumstances were wrong. Really wrong.

"Stay here and cover me. I'll go and talk to Nathan," Martin said.

"No, I should do it."

Martin shook his head. "I can't let you. It could be suicide."

"He's already seen me, but he doesn't know that you and Alex are here. We need that advantage."

Martin thought for a moment. "No, I don't like it."

"Think about it. It makes the most sense. Nathan's already seen me," I repeated.

"Fuck." I saw sweat forming on Martin's brow. "Okay. Keep your rifle on him and just talk to him. And don't do anything …"

"I won't do anything stupid."

I took a deep breath, lifted my rifle back into the firing position and stepped back into the dim light. Nathan was in the same position at the table, still staring at me intently. This time I noticed that his hands were behind his back and his expression was odd. I knew that if everything were all right he would be happy to see me.

I took a couple of steps closer. He looked different. He wore a thin T-shirt, which made it easy to see that his body had filled out with muscles. His face appeared years older and his eyes were tired and filled with regret.

As I took a few more cautious steps, he slowly moved his head back and forth as if to say "No." I took another step and stopped. Nathan was silently pleading with me. He didn't want me to be here. Something was very wrong.

"So," a strange voice said, "this must be the girl."

A balding man with a protruding stomach stepped out from the darkness and stood behind Nathan. He was human and he was arrogant, but the long knife in his hand was what captured my attention. "Well, Nathan, is that her?"

The muscles in Nathan's jaw flexed with tension, but he remained silent.

"Maybe she'd enjoy seeing you die," the man said, as he put the gleaming blade of the knife against Nathan's throat.

Nathan didn't flinch, and nor did he break eye contact with me.

I held fast to my rifle, already pointed at the man's head. "I wouldn't do that if I were you."

"Put the gun down, little girl, or I'll slice his throat wide open." The man had a glint in his eye that told me he meant what he said. "You can trust me when I say this is something I've done many times before."

Giving up my weapon wasn't an option. I held my ground stubbornly.

The man's eyes narrowed. "Apparently you think I'm bluffing. Well, I can assure you that I'm not." He took his blade and sliced across Nathan's muscular arm, just below the shoulder. Blood oozed through his thin shirt and dripped down to his elbow.

Nathan swallowed hard, but didn't move, his eyes on mine unwavering.

"Now put your gun down or next time it'll be his throat." The man placed the blade back against Nathan's neck.

I knew that some humans had been turned, but to see it with my own eyes was terrible. I couldn't understand how any human would do this. It didn't make any sense. But it was clear that he was serious about killing Nathan and I was out of options.

"Okay," I said. "You win." Slowly I set my rifle on the floor.

"I always win." The man raised his eyebrows. "Now, put your handgun on the floor."

Carefully I pulled the SIG Sauer from my belt and set it down.

"That's better. Now, what's your name?"

"Allie," I replied. My voice sounded small and weak.

"Allie. See, that wasn't so hard. My name is Tompson, Eric Tompson." The man flashed a toothy grin. "I've been trying to get your name out of Nathan for weeks, but he can be quite inflexible when he wants to be."

Tompson waved his free arm through the air and three Draco soldiers stepped out of the shadows. They had lightsticks pointed in my direction, and I was well within range.

"Nathan, I think we may have to kill your friend Allie, just to make a point. What do you think?"

Nathan's tired eyes welled with tears. "No, please don't."

The man sighed. "Well, Nathan? Are you ready to start talking or are you going to force me to make my point?"

Nathan closed his eyes. "All right, Tompson, you win. Just don't touch her."

"Like I said, I always win."

I knew Nathan would gladly give up his own life before turning over information, but he would never hand over my life. I couldn't be sure if Henry and Ian were in position, but if they had made it into the cavern I knew they would be well hidden, silent and ready to attack. If they hadn't made it, Martin and Alex wouldn't have enough firepower to save my life. My only option was to play the odds.

"Nobody always wins," I said.

"Allie, don't," Nathan said. "Do what he says, please. Tompson's a mercenary and he'll kill you without a second thought."

I looked directly at Nathan and the depth of pain I saw on

his face frightened me. Nathan didn't scare easily, so he must have been through the pits of hell.

"And I'll enjoy it," Tompson said, as he applied more pressure to the knife. A small trickle of blood oozed across the blade. "Tell her, Nathan. Tell her how much I enjoy watching the non-compliant ones die."

I needed to communicate with Nathan. I wasn't sure what to do, so I did the only thing I could think of. I winked.

"I'm losing patience," Tompson said. "I want the information *now*." He swiftly moved his knife and sliced the zip tie that held Nathan's hands behind his back. Then he slammed a pen and paper down on the table. "You know what I'm looking for. Start writing."

Nathan picked up the pen, scribbled something and set the pen down.

Tompson leaned over and read the paper. His face turned red and the vein in his neck expanded. "Why, you little shit," he hissed as he lifted his arm and backhanded Nathan hard across the face.

CHAPTER 48

Tompson turned to the soldiers. "Kill her," he said in the alien language.

My knees started to shake.

"No!" Nathan's shout echoed loudly in all directions.

I relied on my training and hit the ground. I saw a light flash out of the corner of my eye, just as consecutive shots exploded in the cavern. The sound was deafening. It was impossible to tell where the shots came from, but the target was clear. The three Draco soldiers were pushed back by the intense force of the bullets and fell to the ground. Their helmets made sickening cracks against the limestone and thick red blood pooled rapidly into the indentations on the rock floor.

In an instant, Ian appeared behind Tompson and pressed the barrel of his handgun against the man's bald head. "I suggest you drop the knife and raise your hands slowly," Ian said.

"You can't win. In the long run, you'll all be destroyed. The only way to survive is to work with them." Tompson dropped the knife on the table and put his hands behind his head.

"Allie, are you okay?" Henry shouted.

Martin helped me up.

"Yeah, I'm good," I said.

Henry turned toward the balding man and picked up the knife. "You're in some serious trouble, Mr. Tompson. Put your hands behind your back."

Ian roughly tied Tompson's wrists.

"You better not touch me," Tompson said. "They know I'm here and they won't take kindly to you if anything happens to me."

"I know some people who won't take kindly to this either," Ian replied, his voice laced with sarcasm. "Hmm, let's see, treason against humanity. I wonder what kind of punishment befits the worst crime in the history of mankind."

Henry approached Nathan. "It's good to see you, Nathan. We should wrap your arm up."

"It's good to see you too," Nathan said, standing up, "but I'm fine."

Nathan turned toward me and took a step, but then stopped short. He stood frozen, as if he was afraid to come any closer. "I didn't think I would ever see you again," he whispered.

I closed the distance between us and touched his arm. "Nathan, I'm sorry we didn't come for you sooner." My voice choked up and it was hard to speak. "I missed you."

His eyes were older, but they were still the same soft blue I remembered. I sensed that my best friend had changed so much, yet in some ways he was still the same.

Slowly, almost as if he was afraid, he reached out and wrapped his strong arms around me. "Allie, there are no words for how much I missed you," he whispered in my ear.

Henry and Ian went back to the surface to set up the Ferret System and report our current situation to the colonel. Alex and Martin tied Tompson to a chair and began to question him.

I worked on Nathan's arm, carefully applying butterfly bandages to close the gash. "I'm not sure these will hold. You might need stitches." I noticed burn marks on this forearms and hands, but didn't mention them.

"It's nothing," Nathan said. "I'll be fine."

As I pushed the sleeve of his shirt up higher to wrap his arm with gauze, I noticed a long scar extending down from his shoulder. "How did you get this?" I said, running my finger along the raised white tissue.

He didn't answer.

I couldn't see where the scar ended, so I pulled up the back of Nathan's shirt. I gasped when I saw a dozen additional long scars. A couple of the marks were bright red and still healing.

"Oh, Nathan," I said, as I placed my hand on his exposed back.

His muscles flinched when my fingers touched his skin.

"What happened?" I asked.

"Disobedience wasn't tolerated."

"But this looks like you were whipped ..." I put his shirt back down and sat in front of him. "That doesn't seem like something the Draco would do."

"It isn't." Nathan looked over at Tompson with sheer hatred

on his face. "But it is something humans would do. And they're capable of far worse than an occasional whipping."

"Are there many others like Tompson?"

"Yes. The Draco are much too sterile and civilized for torture, especially when it comes to torturing kids. They're not good at guerrilla warfare either, so when they need a certain kind of cruelty they find the proper personality type for the job."

"But why would humans do this to their own kind?"

"To stay alive. And the Draco military rewards them heavily for their efforts," Nathan said acidly. "The Draco tested and recruited men from Attica State Prison to do their dirty work. These men are great at being brutal and they do it without a conscience."

"And Tompson was one of these men?"

The muscle along Nathan's jaw flexed. "He's a heartless murderer who'll kill anyone or do anything for a price. He's been my own personal nightmare for months."

I'd never heard Nathan speak with so much hatred before. His face had a rougher, harder quality about it now. I put my hand on his cheek and leaned over and kissed the other cheek. "Everything's okay now," I said.

He closed his eyes. "Allie, don't. It's not okay. You don't know anything about what's happened or what I've done."

"Whatever it was, it doesn't matter. That's in the past. What matters is what we do now."

Nathan shook his head and whispered, "Not this time."

After finishing with Tompson, Alex and Martin walked over.

"He seems willing to talk," Martin said, "but I wouldn't trust him for a minute."

Nathan scowled. "Good, because the second you do, you're dead. He has no allegiances."

Moments later, Henry and Ian returned with the Ferret System.

"The colonel wants us to proceed as planned," Henry told us. "We leave here at twenty-three hundred hours. That gives us two hours to debrief with Nathan. I'm hoping your knowledge will cut our recon time in half," Henry said to Nathan.

Nathan spent a few minutes removing a small gray component from each of the Draco helmets. He said that these were access keys, specifically programmed for the hospital area. We spent the next hour listening to him go over the layout and inner workings of the facility where the children were kept. He confirmed that they were holding over three hundred kids, with more arriving weekly. The Draco used approximately thirty convicts—hardened souls who didn't think twice about the harshest activities—to run their operations and serve as guards.

The main hospital was a highly secretive genetic-engineering operation, while most of the surrounding buildings were focused on botany. The children were kept in a large dormitory on the hospital grounds. They slept in the basement and performed manual labor on the upper floors in shifts. The labor crews worked around the clock raising alien plant species and preparing them to be introduced to Earth's environment.

"Several species are dangerous to humans," Nathan said, "and a few are even toxic."

Next, Nathan drew maps while we memorized escape routes and learned the shift changes. The children worked fourteen-hour shifts, with ten hours off for eating and sleeping. Shifts overlapped, with a rotation taking place every eight hours. The older children were given aptitude tests, and the strongest and most intelligent were assigned as team leaders in charge of the production units.

Nathan stared at the table as he talked. He seemed to be forcing himself not to make eye contact with us.

"I was in charge of the blue team for almost ten months. But when human resistance became an irritant for the Draco and small skirmishes began to pose a threat to their upcoming colonization plans, I was pulled out and interrogated. I'd been seen with other humans who'd escaped capture, and the soldiers wanted to know where you were. Of course the soldiers didn't want to deal with the messy task of information extraction, so this was assigned to the mercenaries."

Nathan took a deep breath and the pain on his face was plain to see. I knew how strong Nathan could be, so it frightened me to think about what might have been done to get him to talk.

"I'm sorry." Nathan put his head in his hands. "I never should've brought them here. I would've died before I gave away our location, but Tompson and his men have ways of keeping you alive while they inflict various punishments and drugs."

"It's not your fault, Nathan," Ian said. "Look how much information you've given us. Our mission will be stronger now because of your help."

"Nathan, how did you happen to be here on the exact same

night we came back to the cavern?" Henry asked. It was a question we were all curious about.

"I've been here for over a month," Nathan said, as he gazed off at nothing. "Tompson felt if we waited long enough, someone would show up. I didn't think anyone would come, but obviously he was right."

Nathan didn't tell us how much information Tompson and the other mercenaries had extracted from him, and we didn't ask, but it was an easy guess that he'd told them about the Bristol camp. Nathan's remorse was obvious and even Henry didn't want to dwell on the subject. For us, it was always more important to look forward, not back.

Just before departure we took a short break. We triple-checked our weapons and supplies, and made sure Tompson was tied securely to the chair. While we all wanted to see him put to death in a less-than-humane manner, we knew he would be far more valuable after a thorough interrogation. We couldn't take him with us, and we couldn't leave him topside due to the freezing temperatures, so we decided to leave him in the cavern and deal with him later. We had to hope that he was bluffing about the soldiers' knowledge of his location.

"Allie, could I talk to you for a minute?" Nathan asked.

"Sure." I took Nathan's hand and led him over to the steps, where we could sit in private. For a long moment he stared off into the shadows.

"Tell me what happened in Bristol," he finally said.

"It's not your fault, Nathan. We can talk about this later."

"After Tompson injected me with a cocktail of drugs, three of the younger kids from Bristol showed up at Strong Hospital.

That could only mean that I gave away the location and that the soldiers found our sector." Nathan took a deep breath. "Please tell me what happened."

"I don't think that's a good idea," I said, shaking my head.

Nathan turned and grabbed my arm. "Allie, please. I need to know."

As soon as I saw the pain in his eyes, I gave in.

"Okay. When the Draco found the camp, we'd already relocated everyone except Laurie, three kids and Max. Two officers from the Depot went to retrieve them, but the group never returned. We searched everywhere for them, but the only thing we found was a backpack with a broken strap and the remains of Max."

Nathan held his head in his hands. "I can't believe I did this."

"No one will hold you responsible."

"You don't understand—I *am* responsible. And they aren't the only deaths I'm responsible for. There were others." He looked at me with such anguish that I wanted to cry. "I lost eight kids on my team due to the toxic plants. It was my fault. The process of taking care of the growth pods was extremely complex. I knew that kids wouldn't be able to safely handle the toxic plants without making deadly mistakes. I tried to manage the care of the pods myself, but I couldn't keep up with the twenty-four-hour workload. I was punished for that and forced to readjust the schedule, which ultimately caused injuries and deaths on my team."

"Is that how you got the scars on your back?" I asked quietly.

Nathan nodded. "Some of them."

I couldn't imagine how cruel Nathan's life had been while we were apart. "I'm so sorry, Nathan."

He looked at the ground. "I'm pretty screwed up right now."

"Things will get better now that you're back with us."

I tried to sound reassuring, but I was worried about Nathan's mental state. Physically he was stronger than ever, but emotionally he seemed fragile. I was thankful that Dr. Jenkins would be waiting for us back at the Depot.

"Allie ... I need to know something else ... are you and I ... " His voice broke off and he couldn't seem to finish his question.

I reached out and turned his face toward mine. His eyes were so tired and sad. I leaned forward and kissed him gently. At first he didn't respond, so I applied more pressure and parted his lips. Nathan let out a small groan, then slipped his arms around my back and pulled me closer. Many things about Nathan had changed, but not the way he tasted—sweet and hot.

As the team signaled our departure, Nathan held me and whispered in my ear, "I love you, Allie. I never stopped. And I wish you weren't going anywhere near that place."

CHAPTER 49

We rode the motorbikes as far as East Henrietta Road, then parked them in a clump of trees at Brighton Park and continued the rest of the way on foot. The closer we traveled to the hospital, the more land vehicles we saw, as well as excessive numbers of stinkbugs. Nathan told us that the stinkbugs roamed freely in this area to discourage the children from trying to escape.

We were extremely cautious as we approached the old dormitory where the children were kept. Stinkbugs were poking around everywhere, but fortunately, after taking one whiff of us, they moved on. We quietly positioned ourselves behind an old rusted dumpster, where we could observe the shift changes and set up the Ferret System.

We watched for two hours and, just as Nathan had predicted, everything seemed to take place like clockwork. A group of land vehicles arrived, dropping off the new crew and picking up the old shift workers right on time. Each vehicle was operated by two Draco soldiers and transported four ex-convicts. One soldier waited in the vehicle, while the other went up to the main entrance, escorting the passengers.

While we made our observations, Henry transmitted our location, along with frequent updates, back to the Depot. As expected, we didn't see any sign of the children. Nathan had said they never left the building, sleeping, eating and working all within the same structure. Not much of a life.

A short time later we received a communication stating that Major Anderson's team had arrived and was in position to the south. As planned, they were nearby, holed up in a white house on Crittenden Boulevard, waiting for the handoffs.

We watched the group of vehicles pull away. If events took place on schedule, we wouldn't see another shift change for four more hours. We knew that when the next crew arrived, it would only take the convicts a matter of seconds to realize a number of children were missing, but as long as everything went according to plan we'd be long gone by then.

As the last vehicle departed from the drop-off point, Nathan, Henry and Ian ran to a side entrance along the north end. Nathan held up one of the components he'd removed from the Draco helmets, and after a couple of seconds, the flashing on the unit synchronized with the flashing on the control panel embedded in the door. The panel blipped a few times and the door unlocked.

I held my breath as the three dark figures disappeared inside the building. I wondered how Nathan felt, having just escaped from hell and to be now returning by choice. Martin, Alex and

I kept our weapons trained on the doors, waiting for the next step to our plan. If something went wrong and our team didn't return within an hour, we were under strict orders to abandon the mission and leave the premises. Nathan had assured us that the moment the guards suspected anything, the building would be securely locked down and there would be nothing any of us could do about it.

After twenty minutes, Martin shifted uncomfortably. "It shouldn't be taking this long," he whispered.

I pointed to the door as it partially opened and Ian slipped out, holding the hands of two small children wrapped in tattered blankets. Then Nathan and Henry came out, each with two children. They ran to us quietly and we executed the next steps as planned.

Henry and I took the six kids, staying under dark shadowy trees, and made our way to the white house on Crittenden Boulevard. Alex followed closely behind as a rear guard and monitored our distance from any potential detection. Martin stood guard by the dumpster while Nathan and Ian re-entered the building to retrieve another group of kids.

Major Anderson met us at the back door of the white house and ushered us in. One of his men came over, sat the kids down, and began giving them specific instructions. Another man handed out warm coats. The temperature outside was bitter cold and I was glad to see the major's men had a supply of warm clothing for the kids. Within minutes the kids would be making the long journey south to a safe house, where they would rest and then make the remainder of the trip to the Depot.

Henry turned to the major. "You can expect Nathan, Ian and Martin with the next group in fifteen to twenty minutes. Allie and I should be back with another group twenty minutes after that."

Major Anderson nodded. "My men also have you covered from the roof of the house."

Since Nathan's group was working on the north end, Henry and I ran back to the south side of the dormitory. Alex positioned himself under a pine tree to give us cover, while we ran to the side door. Just as Nathan had done earlier, Henry carefully adjusted one of the gray helmet components, which caused the lights to synchronize and unlock the door.

Within moments I was following him into the dark building. According to Nathan, the layout was an exact mirror of the north end. Henry maneuvered easily down the stairs and made a left turn into a long hallway, which had rows of heavy metal doors along both sides. We walked up to the first door on the right and again Henry used the component to open the lock.

The room was tiny and dark. Six children, cramped together, slept on the floor in a bundle of torn blankets and quilts. Two at a time, heads popped up and looked at us curiously. We quickly gave them instructions to be quiet and wrap themselves in blankets. Then we gave each child a dose of oregano oil.

The children were young, six to eight years old, and frightened to a level I hadn't expected. One little girl started crying, so Henry picked her up and carried her. As we left the room, he gently closed the door and re-engaged the lock.

We were back outside within minutes. Alex continued to cover us as we traveled to the white house and handed over the kids. Major Anderson confirmed that this was the third group to arrive and that the mission was ahead of schedule.

We worked with speed and care, and when we made our sixth delivery to the house on Crittenden Boulevard, we ran into Nathan, Ian and Martin.

"We are running short on time," Nathan said. "The next trip will have to be our last."

"Got it," Henry replied.

Nathan reached out and touched my arm. "See you back here in a few minutes," he said as he winked at me.

For a moment he seemed like his old self.

For the seventh time, Henry and I headed down the stairs and into the long hallway. Henry unlocked another door and we entered another small room. This group was a little older and sharper, and listened eagerly as we gave them instructions and issued their doses of oregano oil.

"I'm Tommy and I'm thirteen," said the tallest boy. "We knew you'd come for us someday. We were part of Nathan's blue team. Are you his friends?"

"Yeah," I replied. "But you need to be very quiet now. We'll talk later." I noticed burn marks on Tommy's arm, similar to those I saw on Nathan.

As we wrapped the children in blankets and prepared to leave the room, an ear-piercing alarm went off and bright lights flickered on. I jerked my head around and looked at Henry.

"We need to move fast," he said, reaching for the door.

Tommy grabbed Henry's arm. "No," he whispered. "They always seal off all the exits before sounding the alarm. You'll run right into the guards and you'll be trapped."

The sound of a door slamming made me jump. Men shouted in the hallway, as several more doors creaked and then slammed.

"They'll be here for a head count any second," one of the girls whispered. "You have to hide."

The kids held up their worn quilts and pushed us into a cocoon of dirty fabric. They seemed to know what they were doing as they jumped on top of us and moved the pillows around.

Seconds later, the door flew open.

CHAPTER 50

"Heads up," a deep voice commanded.

Six heads popped up.

"Two, four, six, all here. Mark this room counted."

The door slammed shut. Tommy sprang up and ran to the door, pressing his ear against the metal.

"They're saying thirty-six kids are missing from the north side," Tommy said. "And thirty are missing from our side."

If thirty-six were missing from the other side, it meant Nathan and Ian got out with their final group. If any of us had to be stuck in this hellhole, I didn't want it to be Nathan.

Henry climbed out of the pile of fabric. "Tommy, is there a way out of the building when all the exits are sealed?"

Tommy made a face. "Just one and it's pretty gross. You'll have to climb down into the sewer."

"Can you take us there?" Henry asked.

"Our shift starts in a couple of minutes. If we're not lined up at the door at exactly six o'clock, there'll be hell to pay. But I can draw you a map."

"I don't understand. If you have a way out of here, how come you haven't used it?" I asked.

Tommy shook his head gravely. "Sam tried it. They brought him back the next day and put his burned body in the caféteria for two solid days so we could see what happens to the kids who rebel against them. No one ever tried to escape again and I don't think the guards ever found out about the sewer."

Tommy quickly drew lines in the dust on the floor, showing us how to get to the maintenance room, where we could gain access to the sewer system. "Be extra careful near the stairs. There'll be a guard posted at the top," he said.

"Shift change," a deep voice bellowed from the hallway.

The kids immediately jumped up and assembled in a line at the door.

"We'll be back to get you, I promise," I said, as we ducked back under the rumpled quilts, blankets and pillows.

The door opened and the kids silently marched out with Tommy leading the group. Within second the lights went out.

We waited another twenty minutes until the area was quiet before moving or speaking.

Henry took a deep breath and looked at me. "Are you ready to do this?"

"Yes." I didn't feel as confident as I sounded.

"Remember what Nathan said about the convicts. If we get caught, do whatever they say."

I nodded. Nathan had warned us about the type of weapons the convicts carried. They were allowed to use the human weapons of their choice. Since guns, knives and whips were no threat to the soldiers, the convicts had free use of them to control their charges.

Henry unlocked the door and took his time assessing the hallway. The basement was dark and deathly quiet. When he determined the coast was clear, he motioned for me to follow.

We approached the stairs and saw a well-armed guard pacing restlessly at the top, just as Tommy had mentioned. Echoing through the stairwell were the shouts of the guards as they counted heads and slammed doors. We stayed against the far wall and quickly made our way to the end of the hall, and then down another corridor. The maintenance room was just around the next corner.

Henry rounded the corner and reached the door first. He pulled the handle, and it opened with a creak.

I was just a few feet behind him. As I began to round the corner, a powerful hand clamped down on my shoulder and spun me around. An enormous dark-haired man shoved me against the wall, knocking the air from my lungs. A knife instantly appeared and was pressed against my throat.

"Drop the gun, little girl," he said. He had a grisly appearance and his breath smelled rancid.

I let go of my rifle and it clattered to the floor.

"Who the fuck are you?" he demanded.

I could feel his hot breath on my face as I struggled to suck air back into my chest.

He pulled the knife away from my throat, and with little effort, stabbed it into my right shoulder. I gasped with pain. My knees buckled, but he easily held me up with his large arm.

He smiled. "Maybe this will motivate you into talking," he said, as he twisted the knife deeper into my shoulder.

A scream left my lips that sounded distant and far away. Then I fell to my knees and the knife slipped from my shoulder, skidding across the floor. As I regained my senses, I saw the huge man lying on the floor in front of me, clutching at his neck. Blood flowed freely through his fingers and gurgling noises bubbled from his mouth as he tried to draw a breath. The expression on his face twisted from rage to fear as he began to drown in his own blood.

I looked up and saw Henry put his own bloody knife back into his belt. He reached for my good arm and pulled me up, and with his other arm he grabbed my gun and threw it over his shoulder.

"Allie, move fast," he said, pushing me forward into the maintenance room.

He quickly shifted a table, pried up the cover to the sewer and helped me into the hole.

"Grab onto the ladder," Henry whispered.

My shoulder was killing me and the pain was traveling all the way down my arm, but somehow I managed to hold the rungs and move downward into complete blackness. I was thankful that my arm still worked well enough to get me down into the pipes below.

When we reached the bottom, Henry lit a candle and pointed southward. We traveled in a crouched position for about fifteen minutes until we came to a manhole, which Henry hoped was Lattimore Road, four streets over.

When we crawled out onto the street, the area was still dark, but a slight pink haze was beginning to form in the eastern sky. Henry pointed to the street sign, which read Shelbourne Road. We had overshot our mark. He grabbed my left hand and we zigzagged our way through the snow. When we heard the distant search parties move closer, Henry picked up the pace and pulled me along. With every step I felt warm sticky blood ooze from my shoulder.

We found our motorbike within the clump of trees where we had left it. The other bikes were gone and we knew our teammates had followed orders and left the area. They had had no choice.

Henry turned and looked me. "Are you all right?" he asked breathlessly.

"I think so," I said. "Just a little light-headed."

Henry pulled my coat back to look at my shoulder. "You've lost a lot of blood. That asshole tore your shoulder up pretty good." He pulled a wad of gaze and some tape from his supply belt. He patched up my shoulder as best as he could, but I could tell by his expression that he was worried.

"I'm fine, my arm still works so I don't think he did any real damage. Let's go."

We climbed onto the back of the motorbike and I wrapped my left arm around Henry's waist. My right arm was throbbing badly, so I let it hang by my side. In the distance the electronic rumble of multiple land vehicles sounded like an army of death heading toward the hospital.

We pulled away with a soft hum. Henry carefully maneuvered the bike out of the park and through back lots, trying to stay as far from the main roads as possible. Several times we were forced to stop and remain motionless as brigades of soldiers and stinkbugs passed by in search of the missing children. Each time we stopped I prayed for Tommy and the other children we had left behind.

It took us over two hours, but eventually we wound our way out of the city and into the sprawling suburbs. The glaring sunlight made both of us uneasy, but at least it wasn't snowing so we wouldn't be leaving easy-to-follow tracks.

When we finally reached Mendon, Henry stopped at the old red building to rest and check on my shoulder. I sat down in the small back room, and Henry pulled back my coat to check the bandage.

"The gauze is soaked, but it looks like the bleeding's stopped." He sat down and looked at me. "It would be safer if we stayed here until dark."

"I'm really cold and tired. I'd like to rest for a while." I leaned back and closed my eyes.

"Allie! Don't close your eyes, it's too cold." Henry's breath came out in big puffs of white steam.

I was unusually tired. "I just need a little sleep," I said.

"Come on, get up," Henry ordered.

He sounded upset so I opened my eyes.

He grabbed my arm and made me stand. "We can't stay here. I won't be able to keep you awake all day and if you fall asleep you'll freeze to death."

Reluctantly, I followed Henry out of the building and we got back on the motorbike. Where our bodies touched, they radiated warmth and I started to feel better. Henry stopped often, both to avoid the Draco traffic and to make me stand

and move around. It took us another four hours to get to the outskirts of the Depot. The sun was high in the sky as Henry parked the motorbike in the old shed where we had been instructed to leave it.

I was in pain, beyond exhausted and my feet were so cold that I could barely feel them. Henry gently held onto my good arm and helped me through the fence and over to the mouth of the pipe.

Just inside the pipe I sat down and thought about how I couldn't wait to get into my warm bunk. "Henry, please, I need to rest for a minute."

He knelt down and looked at me. "Allie, I know you're tired, but we have to keep moving."

"But I'm so sleepy."

Henry looked at me again and touched my cheek. Then he checked my shoulder. He looked scared. I'd never seen Henry look scared before. "You're too cold." He took off his coat and wrapped it around me. "Come on, Allie, you have to get up."

"No, I can't." I closed my eyes and tried to shut him out. I felt myself drifting off and it felt so good that I almost thought I felt warmer.

"Allie, wake up!" Henry shouted.

"No, leave me alone," I said, but my words sounded funny even to me. I kept my eyes tightly closed.

Henry grabbed my left arm roughly. "Allie, you're going to get up and start moving. That's an order. Move!"

I forced my eyes open, although my brain couldn't process why he was so upset.

He pulled me up, but my legs felt rubbery. "Start moving," he said, as he guided me down the tunnel.

Every muscle hurt as I tried to maneuver through the frozen pipes. Each time I started to fall, Henry caught me and pushed me along. When we finally reached the long pipe that went straight down for seventy feet, Henry hesitated.

"Okay, Allie, this is the hard part. I need you to focus and really work at this."

I nodded, although I didn't feel very strong.

Henry stood behind me and tied our waists together with a length of rope. We went down in unison, with Henry directly behind me, one step at a time. It took much longer this way, but I was able to make it to the bottom without falling.

"Just hang in there, Allie, we're almost home," he said into my ear.

He put his arms around my waist and guided me into the decompression room. As we waited for security to open the hatch, I put my good arm around him and rested my head on his shoulder. He was warm and strong, and it felt so good to lean on him.

"Henry, don't let me go," I whispered.

"I won't," he whispered back.

Doc Hiro and Martin were there to meet us when the hatch finally swung open.

"Injuries?" Doc asked as he rushed to our sides.

"Allie's right shoulder," Henry said. "She's lost some blood and her body temperature's dropped."

Doc Hiro pulled the blood soaked gauze back and checked my shoulder. "Get her to the infirmary, quick."

Martin picked me up and carried me to the infirmary, where he placed me on the first of six beds.

"Where's Nathan?" I asked.

"He's in a meeting with Colonel Stone and Dr. Petrov. He's really worried about you. Once he finds out you're arrived, he'll be here before you can blink your eyes," Martin said.

I couldn't understand why I felt so exhausted. Doc Hiro placed some warm blankets on me, made me drink a warm sugary beverage, and checked my temperature every few minutes.

I reached for Henry's hand with my good arm and gave him a weak smile. "Can I sleep now?"

Henry looked over at Doc Hiro. "Doc?"

Doc nodded his approval and Henry squeezed my hand. "Yeah, you can sleep now."

CHAPTER 51

Iwoke up as Doc Hiro was checking my shoulder. I blinked several times to focus. "How long was I asleep?" I asked.

"About ten hours. Your friend here's been by your side almost the whole time." Doc smiled. "You might want to wake him up and tell him the colonel wants to see you both at oh-two-hundred hours."

I looked past Doc and was expecting to see Nathan, but it was Henry who was asleep in the chair next to my bed. He was in an uncomfortable position with his head bent to the side.

Doc Hiro closed up the dressing on my shoulder.

"Well, you have a hell of a hole in your shoulder," he said, "but it'll be fine. You won't have any permanent damage other than a small scar. You also suffered from hypothermia, but again, you'll be fine. You can leave anytime you feel up to it, but try not to use your right arm, and I need to check your wound once a day for a while."

"Thanks, Doc. Have you seen Nathan?" We had an entire year to catch up on and I was concerned about him.

"He arrived just after you fell asleep and was worried sick about you. After that, he had a long talk with Henry and then met with Dr. Jenkins. I'm sorry, Allie, but I have to go. The kids started arriving hours ago and I have my hands full." Doc turned and hurried off to the next bed.

I looked around and saw that the kids from the hospital now occupied the other beds in the room. They all looked extremely thin and had tubes pumping liquids into their arms.

I sat up and touched Henry on the arm.

He opened his eyes and slowly straightened up. "How are you feeling?" he asked as he rubbed his neck.

"Good, thanks to you." I smiled at him. "Henry, I appreciate everything you did to get me back here in one piece."

He looked embarrassed. "You would've done the same."

Henry and I arrived at the colonel's office on time for the meeting at 0200 hours. Nathan and Ian were already seated at the conference table.

As soon as I entered the room Nathan jumped to his feet. "Allie, are you all right?"

I smiled. "Yes. My shoulder's just a little sore, but I'm fine."

We took our seats just as Colonel Stone and Major Anderson walked in to join us.

"It's good to see you up and around, Allie," the colonel said.

"It's good to be up and around."

He took his seat. "First of all, congratulations to everyone on a successful mission. So far, twenty-six children have arrived and we're expecting forty-four more throughout the next twelve hours. Doc Hiro's currently treating five of them in the infirmary for malnutrition and severe depression. The rest will be staying in the east wing, and starting next week we'll begin moving the healthiest children to the Canadian camp."

I looked over at Henry. "Did we find any of the kids from Bristol?"

Henry shook his head. "Not this time."

"We have to go back," I said.

The colonel held up his hand. "Slow down, Allie. Major Anderson, please give the team your update."

"We were expecting a reaction from this incident and now we've got it. The two recon teams we currently have positioned to observe the city have reported that airships and land vehicles have been moving into the area in large numbers. It also seems that higher-ranking, more-qualified personnel are being transferred to our region. We've spoken to Langley and they've given us approval to continue moving forward with the rescue missions, although we fully expect our operations to become more difficult. Next time it won't be as simple as walking in and opening doors."

Colonel Stone laid a map of the world on the table. "I'd like you all to be aware that Langley has received intelligence which indicates the Draco have been landing large transport ships in Nazca, Peru, approximately four thousand miles due south of here. We believe this is the beginning of the colonization efforts."

He pointed to Nazca, on the west side of South America. "On the positive side, our scientists at Langley have been experimenting with Nathan's work and believe they've developed a theory which could enable us to go to war. They've requested that Nathan be sent down immediately to help with development." Colonel Stone looked at Nathan. "I'm sure I don't have to tell you how anxious they are to speak with him."

I knew Nathan would be asked to go to Langley at some point, but I'd hoped it wouldn't be so soon. I looked over at Nathan and again noticed how much older he appeared.

"When are you going?" I asked.

Nathan met my gaze and then looked away. "Tomorrow, as soon as the sun goes down."

"We'll be sending Nathan with two escorts," Ian said. "He'll be in good hands."

The colonel folded the map. "In the meantime, I need Major Reynolds and Major Anderson to pull together a comprehensive plan to get the rest of those kids. I'd also like you all to seriously consider the complexities of new Draco leadership in the area."

"Yes, sir." Henry nodded. "We'll begin working on it right away."

"What about Tompson?" I asked. "He should be a good resource."

"When we went back to retrieve him, he was gone," Ian explained. "We should've killed him when we had the chance."

The intercom beeped and Dr. Petrov's voice crackled across

the room. "Excuse me. Colonel, could you send Nathan down to the lab as soon as possible?"

"We were just wrapping up. He's on his way," the colonel responded. He dismissed us, but asked Henry to stay behind for further discussion.

Nathan and I walked down the hall together. I noticed his brow was wrinkled. "Is something wrong?" I asked.

"Allie, we need to talk. Can I come and see you after I finish up with Petrov?"

"Sure, I'd like that."

He nodded and turned down the hall that would take him to the lab.

I was starving so I decided to go to the cafeteria. As I entered, the smell of venison lasagna made my stomach growl. I filled my tray with rolls, lasagna, and spinach salad, and sat down.

Within seconds Dr. Jenkins had sat down next to me with a cup of coffee. "Allie, do you have a minute?"

"Yes." Inwardly I cringed. I really wasn't up to talking about my feelings.

"It's about Nathan," she started. "I'm sure you know he's been through a lot this past year."

I nodded. Now she had my full attention.

"Nathan's going to be in therapy for a long time. I know you realize how brilliant he is and how important he is to Langley, but from a mental health perspective, he's on very shaky ground right now. I want you to understand that he's going to the best possible place. He'll get good care in Langley."

I wasn't sure how to respond. Over the years Nathan and I had been through a lot together, but we'd always managed to get through it. I tried to wrap my mind around the fact that Nathan needed more help than Dr. Jenkins or I could give him.

"Allie!" Ivy shrieked as she ran to my side and leaned over to give me a big hug.

Dr. Jenkins stood. "I'll let you two catch up. Allie, if you'd like to talk further, please come see me anytime."

As soon as Dr. Jenkins left the caféteria, Ivy began pelting me with questions about the mission and Nathan.

By the time I'd eaten half of a roll, Ivy had asked me a least a dozen questions.

"Have you had much time to talk with Nathan? I can't get over how much older he looks," she said.

"We're going to catch up after he finishes up with Dr. Petrov."

"You might want to ask him what he and Henry got so heated up about."

"What are you talking about?"

"Well, I came to see you while you were in the infirmary and I happened to overhear Henry and Nathan getting into it just outside the door." Ivy scowled. "As soon as they saw me they clammed up, so I have no idea what it was all about."

That news didn't make sense to me. I couldn't understand why anyone would be anything other than happy right now.

After Ivy and I had finished our conversation, I went to take a long hot shower. Then I returned to my room, put on clean clothes and waited for Nathan.

Two hours later I became impatient, so I took a walk. I stopped by Petrov's lab, only to find out that Nathan had left over an hour before. I spent several minutes trying to locate Nathan's temporary bunkroom, but when I finally found it I hesitated outside his door. After Dr. Jenkins' update, I wasn't sure what to expect.

As I stood trying to decide whether or not to knock, the door opened.

"I'm sorry, Allie. I was just going to come see you. Come on in." Nathan's expression was more serious than I liked.

"Is everything all right?" I knew full well that everything wasn't all right, but I was hoping we could talk about it like we always had in the past.

He closed the door behind me and didn't answer.

"Nathan, what is it? Is it your trip to Langley?"

He shook his head. "That's not it. I know they need me down there. This is critical timing for the resistance." Anguish flashed through his eyes. "I'm sorry, Allie, but I have to go."

"I understand." I smiled and took his hand, trying to reassure him. "Just do me a favor and invent something that helps us win the war."

"I'll do my best." He searched my eyes with a strange, lost expression on his face.

"Nathan, what's wrong?"

He reached out and touched my face. "I love you, you know that. Don't ever forget it. I love you more than anything."

I took a step toward him and gave him a soft kiss. When he didn't respond, I pressed my body against his and kissed him harder. Nathan made a sound of defeat. His arms encircled me and he returned the kiss with heat and passion. Our tongues intertwined as we held each other tight. I began to feel the old familiar connection with Nathan.

"Allie, I don't deserve you," Nathan whispered as he trailed kisses down my neck.

The intercom beeped and the colonel's voice crackled. "Nathan, pick up."

Nathan slowly pulled away and closed his eyes. "Yes, sir," he said.

"We've had a change of plan. You leave in an hour. I need to brief you in my office in fifteen minutes."

"Yes, sir, I'll be there."

CHAPTER 52

Nathan sat on his bunk and put his head in his hands. "Allie, I'm not sure how to put this, but ... it would be best if there wasn't any commitment between us."

"What?" My stomach tightened. "I don't understand."

Nathan looked up, his face now an emotionless mask. "Things are going to be different for us now. We'll be in a full-blown war soon, and I have a lot of work ahead of me at Langley. I've decided to stay there indefinitely." He looked away. "I don't want you to spend any more time waiting for me."

"Nathan, that's not fair. I spent the last year waiting for you. I *want* to wait for you." I fought back the tears that threatened. "Maybe I could come down to Langley."

"No, Allie, this is where we end it."

"End it? Nathan, we've been best friends for as long as either of us can remember. We can't just end it," I choked out.

"It's for the best. You haven't seen me for a long time and you have no idea how I've changed. I'm not good for you anymore … and I don't want to talk about it." Nathan stood and walked over to the door.

"That's total bullshit, Nathan. I might not know what you've been through, but I know you."

"No. You don't. Not anymore."

Tears spilled onto my cheeks. "But you said you loved me."

I tried to read his face, but saw only a cool detached expression as he considered my statement. "I shouldn't have said that. Our relationship needs to end here. Goodbye, Allie."

He turned and left the room. I followed him out and stared dumbfounded as he walked away, away from me, down the long hallway.

"Why?" I whispered, even though there was no one to answer me.

Ivy, Alex, Martin and Henry gathered outside the decompression room to say goodbye to Nathan. With red-rimmed eyes, I quietly joined the group. Ivy looked at me questioningly.

As Nathan's escorts executed a final gear check in the decompression room, Nathan stiffly shook everyone's hand, including mine.

"This is for you," I said, handing his journal over.

He nodded once and took it, his expression unreadable.

When it was time to go, Nathan stood stoically in the decompression room, with his back to us, waiting for the door to close. He didn't even turn around for one last look.

I angrily wiped away new tears and decided to head back to my room, where I could sort out my feelings. My teammates stood along the wall and watched me pass. I saw sympathy on their faces, but I didn't want sympathy. I wanted to understand why, after so many years of loyalty toward each other, Nathan had deserted me.

For hours, I sat on the floor beside my bunk thinking through the situation, but it didn't help. I couldn't understand why Nathan didn't want any ties to me, yet he had said he loved me "more than anything." Maybe he felt he had committed too many sins, or maybe he just wanted his freedom; it really didn't matter because it didn't change the fact that he was done with our friendship.

A short time later, I heard a soft knock on my door. "Come in," I said.

Henry entered and sat on the floor next to me. "How're you doing?"

"I'm hanging in there, considering Nathan permanently ended our relationship."

"I'm sorry." Henry gave me a kiss on the top of my head. "It gets better with time. I promise."

"I hope so, because I feel like someone who won the lottery and then was told it was all a big mistake." I leaned my head on Henry's shoulder. "His behavior was so strange."

"He's been through a lot. We all have."

"What did you and Nathan talk about while I was in the infirmary?"

"We talked about what had happened to him at the hospital. He also asked a lot of questions about what happened at the

Bristol camp. I think he was looking for redemption and forgiveness."

"Did you give it to him?"

Henry took a deep breath. "Yeah, I did," he whispered.

After Henry left, I thought about the three years that had passed since the invasion.

The world had changed and I had changed. I had grown up fast, I was tough and I was survivor. Losing Nathan was heartbreaking, but with so much important work ahead of us I knew I needed to stay focused.

We had demonstrated our resistance against the Draco through our actions at the hospital, with Tompson, and in a hundred other small ways. Soon we would find big ways to send the message of our defiance.

There was a war coming and I clearly saw what my future held.

My place was with the military, helping to drive the resistance. And Nathan's place was with the scientists at Langley.

ACKNOWLEDGEMENTS

Writing this book has been a personal journey and a wonderful learning experience. I would like to thank the generous people who helped me transform this story from a mixed-up plot in my head to a published novel. First, thank you to my beta readers who gave me incredibly helpful feedback: Matt Seton, Kim Kawecki, Shelley Schleich, Tricia Corwin and Charlotte Wallace. Then there was my dad, Warren Wallace, to whom I have dedicated this book. He patiently read through at least five drafts, each time giving me valuable pointers and advice, and always encouraging me to finish. Lastly, I'd like to thank my talented editor, Penny Springthorpe, whose genius abilities helped bring this book to life.